Books by Seymour Epstein

PILLAR OF SALT

THE SUCCESSOR

LEAH

A PENNY FOR CHARITY

A Penny for Charity

A Penny for Charity

Short Stories

by Seymour Epstein

LITTLE, BROWN AND COMPANY · BOSTON · TORONTO

LIBRARY OF CONGRESS CATALOG CARD NO. 65-18135

FIRST EDITION

"Wheat Closed Higher and Cotton Was Mixed" first appeared in *Redbook* under the title "Shed One Honest Tear"; reprinted in *Best American Short Stories 1962.* "Toy Village" first appeared in *Redbook* under the title "The Girl with the Golden Hair." "The Ride Back from Lenox" first appeared in *Redbook* under the title "Sunrise." "Each Man in His Time" first appeared in *Redbook.*

"The Wreckers," "Come to the Fair," "Summer Place," "Mr. Isaacs" and "My Brother's Keeper" first appeared in *The Antioch Review.*

"Playgrounds, Parties, and the Primordial Molecule" first appeared in *Esquire.*

Published simultaneously in Canada
by Little, Brown & Company (Canada) Limited

PRINTED IN THE UNITED STATES OF AMERICA

for Joan Levy

Contents

A Penny for Charity

In the Deep Sea

EARLY September was a bad time. Hot, unclouded days — perversely missing from August — lined up in close formation, sweatily eager to be marked present for the season. Wellfleet's dunes and herded gray clouds were memory. School was a persistent rumor. The neighborhood playground to which Ralph Delman had returned with such elaborately prepared scenes of reunion was a wasteland. It was as though the maladjusted summer had flooded through, leaving a worthless silt of mothers and infants. As for Ralph's own friends, some were out of the city, some still being carted off to their accursed day camps and Bath and Tennis Clubs. Rotten timing. Miserable boredom.

"There's nothing to do," he said, putting the fact before his mother with what he thought was flat, simple honesty.

"Get that tone out of your voice," cautioned Mrs. Delman.

"What tone?"

"That tone of quivering injury," she said. "I don't want to hear it." This soul-crushing ennui had been anticipated, dreaded, and her determination to deal with it calmly agitated the edge of her voice. She said, "The world —" and Ralph's attention formed a skin, like a cup of coffee that's been left to stand; lectures that began with "The world —" ended nowhere, not at a pool, or a zoo, or an air-conditioned movie "— doesn't exist solely for the pleasure of Ralph Delman." Ralph turned his head, "Are you listening to me?" demanded his mother. *"Yeh*-ess," said Ralph, who couldn't bear the field of his vision, filled as it was with Laura, his fanatically engrossed younger sister, and COLOR ME, her lunatic coloring book. (The jaws of the crayon box were agape; sixty-four different colors; it made Ralph feel giddy.) ". . . millions of children who have never had and probably never will have *one,* not to mention *six* weeks of vacation at Cape Cod. I can't feel sorry for you. I can't in the least feel sorry for you. Have you looked at a book yet? You were supposed to review last term's spelling . . ."

"I got a headache," Ralph said.

He did.

"Lie down for a while. It's cool in your room. Lie down and close your eyes."

Ralph went to his room. Sometime during the day, he would find the opportunity to slam Laura one. She would take something of his, and he would slam her one.

It *was* comparatively cool in his room. Ralph took off his shoes and fell on his bed. He closed his eyes and listened to the raucous snore of Mr. Krieger's power lawn mower. He rubbed the palms of his hands against the tufted chenille, gradually becoming aware of the secret message in braille: *enemy-attack-tonight-have-machine-guns-and* . . . Suddenly Ralph remembered Kevin, the boy at the Cape whose father owned the little supermarket. Crazy. A real nut. Ate cold baked beans and mayonnaise. Opened up cans of beans with the electric can opener in that house of theirs behind the store, dumped the beans on a plate, then plopped the mayonnaise on top . . . *"Hey, it's great! Y'oughta try it."* . . . A little sea swell of nausea started up.

Fortunately another memory intervened. In that same house was the strange room where everything was dirty, broken, torn or stained. It smelled of sour milk. Their big black dog, Ginger, lay on the old red sofa and slapped his tail against the seat whenever they came in, raising a cloud of dust. There was an armchair whose seat sank so low you could put your hand in the crevices and feel the collected crud. A big chunk of marble was broken from the shelf over the fireplace, but *in* the fireplace was piled Kevin's personal library.

Ralph had never seen anything like it. Comic books. *Hundreds* — and one more gruesome than the next. Green monsters. Bare brains. The remarkable thing was that Kevin didn't have to hide them. He was allowed to read them as if they were *Hans Brinker* or something. Why then, Ralph wondered, did his parents make such a fuss over something as tame as *Superman*. It was a good thing they didn't know about those hours spent in Kevin's place. They would have had him to a doctor, summoned the police. After all the warnings of mental disaster, he would have loved to tell them that he had read and read, and nothing bad had happened to him — if you didn't count the dreams.

Ralph's thoughts left Kevin's house, slid down an embankment and proceeded to the bay, where on a day rare for its bright sun and clear water he had cruised with mask and snorkel two inches from the dappled bottom. Funny, that. Nice. Quiet. Personal. Like a toy he had once wished for, very large, with living things in it, baby crabs, a toy too large to keep anywhere except maybe under his bed, and even there it was a problem because the leg of the bed got in the way no matter how he tried, and even finally caused the ringing of a bell that announced the impossibility of the enterprise, and waked Ralph from his doze.

He heard his mother answer the telephone.

"Hello . . . oh, Mother, how are you? . . ." It was his grandmother. Ralph paid scant attention, until he heard his mother say, "Well, I'm sure they'd both love to, but please, Mother, you know that having both is just too tiring —" and then he knew that either he or Laura would be spending a weekend at his grandparents'. Laura, probably, because she went practically out of her mind with joy at the thought of it, and he could no longer conceal that he was finding those once-adventurous visits rather lifeless and unending.

Later his mother pronounced the ritual words, and in them Ralph thought he could detect an undercurrent of irritation at everybody — him, Laura, Grandma and Grandpa, even herself for having to say them: "They would like to have *both* of you for the weekend, of course, but you know they're getting older and it's a little too strenuous for them . . . Ralph, you were there just before we left for vacation. It's Laura's turn. Is that all right?"

"It's always her turn," he felt obliged to say. "What am *I* going to do?"

"I don't know," his mother replied. "I haven't given it any thought. I refuse to worry about it. You'll be eleven in December. You should be able to entertain yourself once in a while."

Ralph examined his mother's face. It would have been too complicated to challenge her last statement, but that it was an untrue and unthinking accusation played between them with the swiftness of an electrical current; a kinetic situation that usually resulted in softening and some sort of amends. Rather than softening, Ralph observed a hardening against the accustomed impulse. She would let it stand. She would let the falsity stand. Things were in a bad way. They were all like that fat man who had gotten himself snared in a hammock. Sunk in the middle, the hammock had folded round him like a giant leaf, and he had writhed and struggled in the most undignified manner.

What was it? What was the matter? Something to do with the house, the heat, the drooping curve of time between vacation's end and school's beginning. He knew his mother wanted to "get started on the house" — whatever that meant — buying things, fixing things, probably — but that she couldn't because of the heat, the dead weight of two children always seeking something "to do." Yes. That. But something else besides. The tidal mystery of good days and bad days; the deep ocean bed of concerns that pulled the corners of his mother's mouth down and tucked the middle of his father's eyebrows up. It had to do with growing. Grandma and Grandpa were growing old; he and Laura were growing up; and all this growing one way and the other was somehow a fret. Wasn't this the way it was supposed to be? Had they miscalculated? Was there a flaw in the plan they had always advanced as being quite wonderful, full of promise, shot with colorful and worthwhile illuminations?

"What's the matter?" Ralph asked.

"With whom?" asked his mother.

"You."

"Me? Nothing. Why?"

"You look mad."

"I'm not mad. Look at the time. Aren't you hungry? Wash your hands, both of you, and we'll have lunch."

Soon after dinner that evening, they drove through the warm blue twilight to deliver Laura to her grandparents. The trip took them across an articulation of highways and bridges so complex that Ralph knew for a dead certainty that he would never master the divining art of direction. It was something, he felt sure, that men of his father's age had acquired out of the extraordinary necessities of their time, but that would not transmit itself to *his* generation.

The moment he stepped into his grandparents' home, Ralph understood the special nature of the occasion. They all hadn't seen each other since the beginning of vacation, and his grandparents (who looked exactly the same to him) expanded with wonder at the way he and Laura looked.

"Grown!" . . . *"Inches!"* . . . *"Wonderful!"*

"Well, now, Ralph, did you have a good time this summer?" asked his grandfather, after they had all gone to the screened-in porch with a pitcher of iced tea and a plate of home-baked cake. "What did you do?"

"I went swimming," Ralph said.

His father snorted. "Is *that* all you did?"

"I played," Ralph enlarged, feeling vaguely troubled and put upon. It was a nuisance, like having to run back to the house for a clean handkerchief; but since both father and grandfather looked to him for an adequate response, Ralph put himself to the wholly profitless task of rummaging through memory. "Dad and I went fishing a couple of times. I caught six flounders. Didn't I?"

"You sure did," Mr. Delman confirmed. "I don't know who was more surprised, you or the fish."

"— and I met a kid by the name of Kevin —"

"Did you?" said his grandfather. "Well, that's fine. I can see you had a good time." Then, turning his head from grandson to son-in-law, the old man said, "George, do you remember me telling you about that piece of property over by the filling station? Well, they've finally made me an offer. Heard from them about a week ago."

"Go on!" exclaimed Mr. Delman. "A good offer?"

Ralph watched his grandfather put his hand to his face, pinching his big nose between thumb and forefinger, then performing a downward wipe that left a grimace too peculiar to be called a smile on his face. He finished the little charade by rubbing the side of his chin. A rasping sound. "I would say so," he said at last. "Yes, I think so. I'd like to get your opinion. . . . How does seven thousand sound to you?"

Ralph saw his father shake his head slowly, wondrously. His grandfather had depressed his mouth in an almost sour expression, but his narrowed eyes concentrated the diffuse yellow porch-light into brilliant points of jubilation. Then Ralph heard his father say in a low voice, "You old —" but he couldn't catch the last word, and his grandfather responded to that with a strangled grunt and one jiggle of his overhanging belly.

This is what his grandfather had been longing to tell, Ralph surmised. Pleasure swelled his jowls. The hackle of cropped white hair at the back of his neck bristled in triumph. Now the old man grinned, and Ralph's father grinned too, and Ralph succumbed to the contagion and grinned at he knew not what. But despite the grin, Ralph felt the familiar, big-bodied affront of being shunted aside. This latest occasion added its portion to the residue of countless other such affronts, and Ralph could at last make out the form of what had been so long in shaping and would never again go unrecognized.

His grandfather, his grandmother, sometimes his father, even at times his mother, didn't really *care*. Oh, yes, they cared about *him,* but for all their intense focus and persistent questioning they didn't really care to know about his fun, his friends, the *important* things. For reasons of their own, they felt obliged to ask, and they were never content with answers no more serious than their questions, yet when they finally forced him to *think,* to *tell,* that glaze would quickly appear in their eyes, and the nods of their attention would invariably become the quickening tempo of their impatience. This knowledge didn't anger or disillusion Ralph; it left him, rather, in the bemused and fortified condition of one who has gained a useful piece of information.

"Alice, there's no reason in the world why Ralph couldn't stay too," said his grandmother, when they were preparing to leave. "Wouldn't you like to stay, Ralph?"

"Oh, I think they can use the separation," Mr. Delman said. "They've been getting a little edgy. Wouldn't you say, Ralph?"

"Me?"

"Tell you the truth," Mr. Delman continued, "I'm all for shortening the summer vacation. It's too long. They'll tell you they're happy with it, but the fact is they're not. Idleness mortifies the spirit."

"The last two weeks are the worst," Mrs. Delman joined in. "They don't know what to do with themselves any longer, and frankly I don't know what to do with them either. George is right. They're dying for school, but they won't admit it."

"Oh yeah!" said Ralph.

"I want to go back to school," Laura said.

"You would," said Ralph.

"See what I mean?" said Mr. Delman. "Laura, how about a perishing kiss for your father?"

After much kissing all around, they left. It was dark. Ralph always experienced a shivery thrill at the prospect of nighttime trips. They had a forbidden and beckoning quality, a premonitory taste of his life to come. It made him at once drowsy and nervous.

"Honey, you curl up on the back seat," his mother said, knowing of his tendency to fall asleep on the homeward trip. Her voice was soft, as it always became when Laura remained with their grandparents. It was as if she imagined him suffering bereavement at the separation, when in fact he felt absolutely fine; freer, somehow.

They drove in silence for a while. Then his mother and father began to speak in low tones. There was nothing in the content of their talk to alert him to wakefulness. They spoke of the way Grandma and Grandpa looked, of the sale of property, and of clothes to be bought. Everything they said merged and flowed along the downward slope of sleep. Yet he did not sleep. He heard his father say, "I'll bet *he's* conked out," and the rustle of his mother turning around, whispering, "Ralphie?" — to which he didn't bother to respond.

"Out," she said.

A little later the car slowed, then stopped, and Ralph knew they had come to a toll booth. *Clink* went a coin. They continued on, and after some minutes his father spoke:

"I'll take him off your hands tomorrow. You want to get started on the house, don't you?"

"That isn't necessary," his mother said.

"I think I'd like to," his father said. "Seems like I never get the chance to talk to him any more. You know, alone . . . Truthfully, it's this — and I've been feeling it more and more of late — it seems that as the years go by I know him less instead of more. I don't think he's the secretive type, and I know I'm not indifferent, but it's happening just the same. I don't think it should. I'd like to prevent it, if I can."

"I know," said his mother. "Wasn't it ever thus? And Laura?"

"Laura I still know. Clear bold type on sweet pink pages."

"That's what you think."

"Please. One at a time."

"Well — *what,* exactly? Man to man talk? Facts of life?"

"Don't be ridiculous. He couldn't be less interested. No, I just think there ought to be more open area between us."

"All right. I think it's a good idea."

"Mind you, I'm not trying to start a men's club in the family."

"Of course. Where were you thinking of going?"

"Oh, I don't know. I'll see."

. . . Words that merged and flowed along the downward slope of sleep.

The next day, Ralph and his father drove across different highways. Ralph had never been this way before. Tunnels were not new, but the Brooklyn shipyards were; and so was the bay with its tankers and liners lying at anchor.

"That's a new bridge," Mr. Delman pointed out. "It's not finished yet. On the other side over there is Staten Island."

"Is that going to be the biggest bridge in the world?" Ralph asked.

"No, I don't think so," his father replied. "Perhaps the largest single span, or something like that. I'm not sure. But it's a beauty, isn't it?"

Ralph nodded. The question of beauty was a problematical one. It had been brought to his attention that flowers were beautiful, days were beautiful, people were beautiful, and now bridges were beautiful. The word stuck up opaquely in language, like a tall person's head in a movie house, obstructing his view. As for the bridge they had just passed, it was certainly big, but the only other feature about it that Ralph could determine for himself was that it looked rusty.

They were on their way to the aquarium, which was exciting, although Ralph had little to do with the decision to go there. He knew that he was going to be taken *somewhere*. He had awakened that morning with the certainty firmly implanted in his mind, but he couldn't remember how or when the certainty had come to him. Over breakfast, they began to speak of it. His father had said, "Ralph, let's you and me take off somewhere today. Just the two of us. We'll leave your mother to do a little soul communing."

Agreed. Wonderful. But where? A big discussion ensued. Movies were out, his father swore — o-u-t! Damned if he'd sit through a feature-length imbecility and six pastel-colored cartoons, the usual Saturday fare at the local movie house. Museum? Dinosaur bones? Now Ralph groaned. He'd been there *thousands* of times. His mother supported him. The museums would be roasting on a day like this . . . "I know," she said. "Do you remember last spring when we were supposed to go to the aquarium with the pack and you came down with the virus? George, why don't you take him to the aquarium? I think that would be instructive and interesting."

"Where the devil is the place?" his father asked. "It's not at the Battery any more, is it?"

"Good heavens! It hasn't been there in years. It's at Coney Island somewhere."

"Coney Island!"

"It's really quite direct. I remember going over the route with Ann Nathan. We were supposed to den-mother the trip."

There was much map consultation, and the aquarium was decided upon.

His father was being unusually informative. He told him how they had to dig underneath the river to make the tunnel, and how air pressure kept the river from falling in on the workers. He told him that big boats from all over the world came through this body of water to reach New York harbor. He told him about the bridge. It occurred to Ralph that his father might be feeling just as he did — about Laura — not having her around — the liberating effects of it. They could talk.

"You'll be going into — let's see — the fifth grade?" Mr. Delman asked. "Or is it the sixth?"

"The *sixth,*" Ralph said, shocked. "Gosh, you don't know that?"

"Now just a minute," his father said. "The setup is different from when I went to grade school. It used to be 1A, 1B, 2A, 2B . . . I'll never get used to this system. That's not the important thing, Ralph. The important thing is to know where you are in the educational sense, and that I do know. After all, I *have* helped you with your homework, haven't I? Remember that 'Power of the Atom' project we worked on together?"

"Sure. That was great."

"Of course, I don't believe in doing your homework *for* you. You wouldn't get much benefit out of that. But once in a while, if you'd like me to work on a project with you, I'd be glad to."

"O.K.," said Ralph.

He kept his gaze on the bay, where a fusillade of golden lights shot from the surface of the water. It was a compelling sight, the kind that induced a pleasant blankness of mind. Ralph struggled against yielding to it completely, conscious as he was of the respect owed to his father's mood — which was also compelling and curiously reminiscent. Ralph would have liked to respond to it more openly (because indeed he welcomed and treasured it), but for some reason he couldn't overcome the awkwardness that beset him. It was not that his father's solicitude was so rare in coming, but that this time it seemed to have proceeded from nothing.

"I haven't seen Jimmy Baker since we got back from the Cape," his father said.

"They went out to California this summer," Ralph reminded him. "He's not back yet. I haven't seen him."

"Oh, yes, I forgot . . . Is Jimmy still your best friend?"

"Uh-huh."

"I remember you went through that blood brother ceremony at one time. That makes you pretty close. I guess you and Jimmy have lots of secrets."

"Blood brothers are supposed to have secrets," Ralph said, looking a little askance at his father. Mention of Jimmy reminded him that his father hadn't been as understanding as he might have been about the episode. He didn't have to *smile* so much. That sort of ruined it. But Ralph observed that his father wasn't smiling now. "Why?" he asked.

"Just asking," said his father. "I was wondering if you would tell Jimmy things that you wouldn't tell me."

"What things?"

"Oh, I don't know. Anything. Well, for instance, if something was bothering you, would you tell Jimmy about it, or would you tell me?"

"Like what? Like what bothering me?"

Mr. Delman pursed his lips. He gripped the steering wheel and pressed away from it, as if to ease a kink in his back. "Let me put it this way," he said. "Have you ever told Jimmy anything that you haven't told me?"

"Sure. Lots of things."

"Is that so? Well. That's nice to know. And how come Jimmy is more in your confidence than I am?"

"Oh, they're just kid things," Ralph declared. "You wouldn't be interested."

"Try me."

"Huh?"

"What was one of the things you told Jimmy that you never told me?"

Ralph looked at his father's profile to judge the seriousness of his question. Apparently he was serious. But surely he couldn't be asking that he betray Jimmy. "We swore not to tell anybody," he protested.

"O.K.," his father said. "I wouldn't want to tempt your honor. But on the other hand I'd like to think I'm as much your buddy as Jimmy Baker is."

"Sure you are. It's not that. They're only — you know — *kid* things."

"Right," his father said tersely.

Ralph turned his gaze back to the sparkling bay. Uneasily he wondered if some forgotten misdeed had come to light, something he and Jimmy had done, something that in honor required confession before accusation. But he couldn't think of a thing. No. It couldn't be that. It was something else. Ralph wished that he had betrayed one of the blood brother secrets to his father. Maybe if he told him one now, but didn't tell him that it *was* a secret, then that in some way would satisfy both loyalties. Yes. That was a good idea. One of the secrets.

Ralph set about to extricate a single nugget from the rich lode of secretive hours, but as he turned back to locate the place where it might be found he could espy only the more recent landscape of dune grass and horror comics and Kevin, the eater of cold baked beans and mayonnaise. The mine was caved in, grown over, the secrets lost. Had there ever been any secrets? He didn't know. He couldn't remember. But if he were to tell his father this truth, he would only deepen and perpetuate a disloyalty he had never intended and could never define. Ralph was silent. He was beginning to feel a little carsick.

They arrived at the aquarium parking lot not a moment too soon.

Unbelievable! To stand eye-level to two white cavorting whales was to materialize fantasy into huge, sight-doubting being! Yet there they were — two — swimming upside down as gracefully as right side up; white to luminosity in pale green water netted with sunlight; nosing each other in unmistakable good humor; curving to the surface to release a jet of vapor, then curving down with blowhole closing like a rubber valve. Why, he had never fully accepted the *existence* of whales, assigning their doubtful reality to the fabulous realm of dragons and winged horses, and now here they were! It was almost too much to take in. The egregious marvel of it was in his eyes as he turned to his father, and Mr. Delman, who felt a bit of it himself, smiled more in mutuality than condescension.

"How about that?" he said. "Something, eh?"

"Gee!" Ralph breathed. "Lookit 'em go!"

" 'Beluga — The White Whale,' " read Mr. Delman. " 'Northern North America, Spitsbergen and Siberia. Males may reach a length of seventeen feet and a weight of more than four thousand pounds.' "

"They're *playing!*" Ralph said incredulously, scarcely able to credit that familiar activity to such other-worldly creatures.

"Like puppies," his father agreed. "You know, Ralph, as whales go these fellows are sardines. They wouldn't even be noticed by really big whales."

"How big are big whales?"

"Well, I don't know for sure, but some must be at least twenty times as big as these."

"Twenty!"

"Maybe more."

"What do they eat?"

"Fish, I guess. They just open their mouths and swim through schools of fish, swallowing them by the thousands."

"Where do they live?"

"In the ocean. From the North Pole to the South Pole."

"The same ocean we bathe in?"

Mr. Delman laughed. "Same ocean, but not the same part. It's a big ocean, Ralph. It's hard to imagine how big. Some day we may take a boat to Europe, and then you'll get an idea."

Ralph was reluctant to move away from the whale tank. Mr. Delman had to promise they'd come back for a second look before leaving the aquarium. Ralph felt sure there would be nothing worthwhile to see after the whales, and indeed the electric eel was disappointing to look at, lying like an inert limb at the bottom of a dim tank, but when the man ran a metal hook under its belly and lights flashed and voltage crackled, Ralph began to feel a corresponding tingle of horror at the living strangeness that shared his world. What was one to make of all of this?

"Enough voltage to kill a man," said his father, shaking his head in kindred awe. "Good Lord! . . . Just think, Ralph, if we had one of those at home we'd just have to tickle him a few times and he'd run all the appliances in the house. The vacuum cleaner, the toaster . . ."

Ralph let out a shrill burst of laughter. That was funny! That was very funny! He must remember that. He would tell the kids about the electric eel and how his father said that if they had one they'd tickle him and run the vacuum cleaner. . . . But even as they moved away from the tank the humor dissipated, because the electric eel with its tiny eyes lay like a brown piece of wood at the bottom of the tank, harboring in its dull, dense, mysterious body the power to kill a man.

They went on to view seals and walruses, zebra fish and the deadly piranha. There were tiny chocolate-colored fish with phosphorescent dots, and a lumpish sort of fish with a face like a pig. They came at last to the tank wherein swam the sharks — other weird creatures, too — but above all the sharks. These had Ralph's complete credulity. He had seen movies, TV shows. The terrible fin slicing the water. There they were. One, not so big; then another, further back in the tank, much bigger; then, looming out of the murk, a third!

Ralph recoiled with a little gasp. Head on it came, like a slow projectile, its underslung mouth partly open, revealing an arsenal of teeth for which no amount of legend could have prepared the senses. As it approached the plate glass front of the tank, it turned with monstrous languor, and all the gray, sleek symmetry slid past Ralph's eyes. Small, oblivious, milky-blue eyes, row upon row of inward curving teeth, palpitant gills, fins and flank nicked with the scars of unimaginable battles, and a tail as intricately fashioned as a jet plane's assembly.

"Wow!" exclaimed Mr. Delman, in a thoroughly respectful voice. "There's a killer for you!" Instinctively he put his arm around Ralph, as if to support him in the revelation that such savages lived in the sea. Stunned, Ralph heard only in snatches his father's comments ". . . almost blind . . . one of the oldest species . . . millions of years . . ."

They waited for the big one to make his second tour, and when he moved past, propelled, it seemed, by the sheer power of murderous intent, something of the creature's millennial past registered on Ralph. *Dumb*, he thought. *Dumb, dumb, dumb!* Not a flicker of intelligence in the beast's clouded eye. The millions of years had left it stupefied, blinded, with only the instinct and machinery to tear and eat. An eating machine! A dumb, gray, hideous eating machine! Ralph loathed the shark. He loathed it from the tip of its stupid snout to the tip of its assassin's tail.

"He looks so *dumb!*" Ralph dared to say in a half-whisper, almost fearful of the consequences of his insult. But his hatred was more powerful than his fear, and he hurled his contempt into the shark's awesome teeth. "I bet he's the dumbest thing in the world!"

Mr. Delman gave a short laugh. "I don't know about that," he said, "but I have to admit he's a very unappealing specimen."

They left the shark tank shortly after and began to stroll back toward the exit of the aquarium. On their way, they paused at the exhibit of the bathysphere. They examined the ponderous steel ball, and then turned to the fanciful sketches on the wall. There was a legend there. It was lengthy and discouraging for Ralph to read, so his father read it aloud.

It told about the strange world below the last ray of the sun's light. In that everlasting darkness there were creatures with no eyes and with long slender fins to feel their way. Others had enormous eyes and tentacles and barbels of blazing, cold light which may be blue or green, yellow, red or white. Still others had huge, toothless mouths as large as their whole bodies; and others, distensible, rubber-like stomachs that could swallow creatures three times their size. And this collection of gargoyles lived less than one hundred miles from where they were standing!

When he had finished reading, Mr. Delman turned to Ralph. He made no comment. For the space of several seconds, man and boy stood spellbound within the same circle. All the differences of years and wisdom and sophistication dropped away, and they shared in simple humanness the terror and wonder of the world. Barbels of blazing light and the shark's teeth. Frolicking whales and electric eels. There was no combination of words subtle and inclusive enough to formulate the hovering question; and if the question couldn't be formulated, the answer couldn't be forthcoming. Ralph and his father held this perfect understanding between them for another instant, and then their glance wavered and broke, each knowing, as they had always known, that there is nothing to do with the inexpressible but bear it separately away.

They stopped for sandwiches and soda at the aquarium's restaurant. Then they viewed once more the white whales' tireless turns and pirouettes, this time from the upper platform, looking down. From that platform they could also see the beach, where crowds had gathered to enjoy the climactic outpouring of a late summer sun. A sea breeze blew. Off to the right, the roller coaster plunged down, and frightened, delighted screams flew raggedly behind.

"Well," said Mr. Delman. "Had enough?"

Ralph nodded. They walked to their car and drove away. On the highway, Mr. Delman noticed Ralph's glassy expression.

"Tired?" he asked.

"A little."

"Why don't you stretch out," his father suggested. "Put your head on my lap."

A favorite position, when there were just the two of them. Ralph felt comfortable and drowsy.

"Did you enjoy today?" Mr. Delman asked.

"Boy!" said Ralph.

Mr. Delman smiled. It had been a good day. They *had* enjoyed themselves. The strange creatures were going back to their depths, the waters closing over. Mr. Delman put his arm over the boy, patting his thigh.

This contact, the outer touch and semblance, was forever incomplete, forever imperfect — and perhaps the great appeal of love's gesture was that it constantly asked forgiveness for this mortal failing.

Wheat Closed Higher and Cotton Was Mixed

BERNIE HALPERN met and married Sue several years after the war ended. They were both taking part in an amateur production of *The Seagull.* Bernie directed. Sue played the role of Masha. A newspaper theatre critic was present at the performance, and he shed a few lines of grace over the efforts of the group. He wrote that some professionals heavy-laden with success might spend a profitable hour watching the enthusiasm and intelligence of these young people.

That same evening the whole cast, extras, helpers, all met at someone's apartment and picked over those few words like augurs over the entrails of a chicken. Visions of triumph mingled with the cigarette smoke, and each one made out the shape of his own destiny.

"I still say the important word is 'intelligence,'" Bernie declared at one o'clock in the morning. "There are any number of dopes with the gift of talent, but an actor without brains is like a plant without water. He just won't grow."

Since all present were still too young to admit of any

shortcoming, Bernie's remark was found acceptable as a parting shot. About fifteen people filed out of a room that would take two days to ventilate. In the street, they deployed singly and in pairs towards the various subways that would take them to slumbering boroughs. It was no accident that Bernie fell in with Sue.

Throughout rehearsals he had managed to avoid so much as a single glance of partiality. This despite her gray eyes and short nose and hair as dark and ample as a moonless sea. There was an amplitude in her figure as well which filled every hollow of Bernie's desire. Nor was that desire made up of loneliness and inexperience. Bernie had known women, being himself handsome in the way of physical virility and generous features. He wasn't tall, but he was large. Big head, heavy shoulders, large mouth, and prominent nose. His neck could have used another inch, and he had a way of hunching forward when he walked. A football coach would have singled him out in any group of freshmen.

Bernie and Sue walked toward the Seventh Avenue subway, where the New Lots train would take Sue to her home in Brooklyn. Even Manhattan can be quiet along its side streets at one in the morning, and their footsteps sounded brash and intrusive. A young man for whom words came easily and adeptly, Bernie found himself stricken with silence. It was Sue who spoke.

"I'd like to ask you a question," she said. "Would you tell me the truth?"

Bernie smiled. "If I know the truth," he replied.

"Do you think I have intelligence?" Sue asked.

This was as he had expected. The appeal to his honesty missed its target, deflected by self-interest.

"Only people who have intelligence question it," he

answered, feeling that he did not so much lie as bedeck his love with silks and spangles.

For Bernie Halpern was in love, right there on Forty-eighth Street between Fifth and Sixth at one in the morning. He walked on as if nothing had happened, but he felt as if he had been dealt a blow which passed through his flesh, broke no bones, and landed smack on the core of his being. He could have doubled over with the pain of his joy.

"I wish you would tell me the truth," Sue repeated.

"You are intelligent," Bernie flatly stated. "And lovely," he added.

"Sometimes I wonder if I can act at all," she said, exacting gentle usury.

Bernie lifted his face to the neon-obscured sky. In his mind was an image of Sue as she stepped out of the wings in her long dress and tiara of braided hair. She held her hands as he had shown her (precisely; a blueprint; no variation of her own) and spoke her lines in the same way. If Truth was Beauty, then Sue was Truth. And can Truth be anything but intelligent? That she could not act was a matter of some regret and questionable significance. A deception for her sake was already coloring his love with poignance.

"You can act," Bernie said, ready to sign checks of any amount. "You can act beautifully. Why do you ask? I know. It's like being in love. You can't hear the words often enough. Are you in love, Sue?"

She turned and looked at him with her remarkable gray eyes.

"Now, do you mean?"

"Ever?"

"Yes."

"Are you in love with someone now?"

"No."

"Good. Will you see me tomorrow? Will you go with me to a movie? a play? dinner? anything?"

"All right," Sue said.

Two months later, Bernie asked Sue to marry him. Sue said yes, but made it clear that she intended to go on with her acting career.

"What do you take me for!" Bernie cried. "I know a little something about ambition myself. Why should I deny it to you? . . . Listen, darling, will you do me a favor? I ask it only because I'll shrivel up and die if I don't hear you say it soon. Say you love me. I must have said it to you no less than six million times."

"Of course I love you," Sue said, taking his face between her hands. "Bernie . . ."

"Please don't say anything else," he pleaded.

"Tell me the truth . . ."

Bernie swore that she had a rare, rich, and beautiful talent, and that the world would know it some day.

They married in August and almost perished from the heat in their wonderful room-and-a-half on East Twentieth. With slight exertion, Bernie could sweat in December. In August, with two small windows facing a brick wall three feet away, his adoring face dripped continuously into the scrambled eggs, the fried chops, the very act of love. They took long walks in the city, since they could afford little else, and Bernie made every view and quaintness his personal gift to Sue. He gave her the Village, Chinatown, Riverside Drive, and all the magnificent bridges of New York. About the Queensboro Bridge, he said:

"I was driving over it once before the war. It was just about twilight. Maybe a little later. Anyway I was coming from the Queens side into the city, and I saw Manhattan lit up like the Arabian Nights. I felt like climbing to the top of the bridge and taking a flying swan right into the city. I thought: what else do you want? If you can't make it here, you can't make it anywhere."

"Make what?" Sue asked.

"Anything! Golden apples! My private fairy tale! Turn thrice, Bernie Halpern, Lord Mayor of Third Avenue!"

"Why not Fifth?"

"Fifth it is!"

"How much money *do* we have, Lord Mayor?" Sue wanted to know.

Bernie took out a handkerchief and wiped his face. "There's a couple of hundred in the bank and about eight hundred in bonds. We're on easy street. Don't worry. I'm a provider."

It was Bernie who did the worrying. He had been promised a showcase production around the end of September, but there was no money in that. The immediate future was resplendent with moneyless doings. Sue was already cast in the Synge play Bernie planned to do. That, too, would contribute a big, fat zero to their income. In addition, Sue was continuing her classes at the Academy. She miserably suggested that she quit and take a job. Bernie burst into laughter at the look on her face.

"Honeybunch, slash my wrists and see what you can get at the blood bank!" he mocked.

"I didn't say it that way at all," Sue protested.

"Please remember that expression," Bernie said. "It was great!"

But the question of money yipped at his heels like a Pekingese, too insignificant to be menacing yet embarrassing in its persistence. He had held a variety of jobs after finishing school on the GI bill. He had worked in a department store as a salesman. His father had thrown some sub rosa house painting jobs his way. For a few months, he crouched next to the driver and pointed out the splendors of New York in a plastic-domed bus. And just before taking on the production in which he had met Sue, Bernie had discovered a latent talent. He became a worker in leather.

It happened that a friend of his with a real ability for the craft had set up shop in the Village as a custom maker of leather handbags and sandals. Very arty and bizarre stuff, but requiring innate skill if a lot of expensive leather was not to go to waste. The friend did quite well in the marginal way of such businesses. Bernie dropped in often at the shop and began toying with the knife and awl. It became immediately apparent to both Bernie and his friend that he had the touch. He was able to pick up a few bucks helping out on occasional afternoons.

When Bernie cashed in the second hundred-dollar bond, he paid a visit to his friend in the Village. The friend said yes, sure, he could damn well use some help.

The Playboy of the Western World scourged Bernie. He gripped his skull between his hands as though he wanted to crush it. He asked himself in hoarse supplications why he had to pick such a play. To take innocent children from the Bronx, Brooklyn, Jersey, God knows where, and make lilting Irishers out of them! Madness! He had counseled himself a thousand times never to make the sinful error of going on with a thing merely because he had begun, and here he was treading quicksand up to the navel. All right, the lead part was good. That boy would be an actor. But everyone else! . . . including Sue! It was a goulash! A parody!

He had his first bad fight with Sue.

"Ear," he said to her, pulling on the lobe of his own. "You listen, and then you reproduce the accent, the inflection. An actor who doesn't have that is a tone-deaf singer."

"I hate you!" Sue screamed. "You louse!"

The thing rolled downhill like a vehicle without brakes. When certain death stared him in the face, Bernie's nervous system reacted with a charge of adrenalin. He took the leading man aside and asked him if he could play it straight, no accent. The answer was yes. Then Bernie assembled the cast and informed them that they could stop torturing themselves. No brogues. He challenged them all to capture the spirit of the lines without the music. It would fail, he assured them, but it would fail interestingly rather than ludicrously. That's the best he could offer them at that late date.

The effect was somewhat like the baseball player, who swings three or four bats so that the one he wields at plate will seem light. Just playing the roles without having to worry about the treachery of their tongues broke the tension and gave them an art and ease above their normal level.

The performance annoyed some, puzzled many, and persuaded an all-important few. There is an attractive legend that great discoveries have been made through the inadvertence of somebody's maid leaving something where it shouldn't have been. Bernie's "experiment," as it was called, fell into such a category of fruitful accident. The same reviewer who had found *The Seagull* an enthusiastic and intelligent production found *Playboy* ". . . a worthwhile experiment with a play which normally has to wait upon a miraculous pooling of accents and talents. It is to Mr. Halpern's credit that he persevered in the face of what he must have known would seem high treason to lovers of the Irish theatre. Certainly we missed the melodies of Synge, but we did enjoy a good play, well acted."

In their room, Bernie improvised a wild Irish dance while whistling a jig through his teeth. Sue held onto his hands like the tail of a kite on a windy day. Then Bernie went down to the German delicatessen and bought two pounds of roast beef, a rye bread with caraway seeds, four bottles of beer, and a container of Russian dressing. They made sandwiches, just the two of them, and ate and drank until their ears rang.

As a result of that one good review and several complimentary mentions, the production wound up having an unprecedented, if profitless, run of three months. More important, Bernie received an invitation from a producer to "read" a play. The producer wanted Bernie to submit his judgment on an original play, and, if he found it good, to offer some suggestions about casting and direction. There were no contract, no promises; just a chance, if Bernie Halpern wished to take it. Bernie Halpern wished, in all modesty and trembling, to take the chance.

There followed days of perfect wholeness, into which hope and activity flowed in ideal amounts. Sue was acting, receiving a nightly potion of applause, which her thirsting heart drank greedily. She would come back to the room a stimulated drunk, a courtesan.

Bernie was spending his days at home. He read the play the producer had given him. It was not, to his mind, a good play, but he also knew that a producer doesn't go around asking people their opinion of what he considers a bad play. And it was not a *bad* play. It was just not a good one. With proper direction, it could be made into something.

Bernie paced endless miles from the sink, to the windows, to the bathroom — an isosceles triangle at the apex of which he finally had his revelation. One character played as a self-perceiving opportunist instead of a Chekhovian failure not only made that character's lines wink with humor but added a wonderful ingredient of exasperation to all the other parts. It only remained to get his ideas on paper and see the producer.

There was no hurry about this. The producer had said he would like to see something in about a month, and Bernie had had the play in his possession for only a week. He checked his impulse to run with both hands full of bright ideas. There might have been some gain in doing this, but he succumbed to a more subtle pleasure.

It seemed now to Bernie that he had never doubted his eventual success. His personal contract with fate permitted much latitude, and at a guess Bernie would have put the date of delivery much beyond his twenty-ninth birthday. His twenty-ninth birthday was only four months away, and fate appeared to be frantically busy with gift wrapping and silver bows. Bernie wanted to pause. He wanted to savor. He wanted time to walk around like a long-barren woman confirmed in her first pregnancy, patronizing the world out of the overflow of her secret wealth.

Sue left their place at ten in the morning. She had her classes at the Academy, which were over by five. She then came home for an early dinner with Bernie before leaving for the theatre. This left the whole afternoon free to Bernie.

He spent those afternoons roaming around in the city. Even the thought that there was less than three hundred dollars between the Halperns and starvation couldn't put him off his tour of euphoria. The days were cloudy and cold, and this, for some reason, was in perfect keeping with his mood of ordainment. He strolled around the Village and looked into stores where he and Sue had mentally tagged items against their day of affluence. He walked into little coffee shops at an off hour, delighting in the atmosphere of detachment generated by empty stools and apathetic counter girls. The city was busy, busy, but Bernie Halpern opened a book, sat sideways and crossed his legs (since there was no one on either side of him), and took a criminally long time over his Dutch apple pie and coffee.

His wanderings took him as far north as the Cloisters and as far south as the Battery. In all his life, he had never enjoyed the city as much as he did in those few weeks. It spoke to him of creation and joy, of his name on billboards, of rights he could claim because he was a gifted young man beloved of the gods. Now was the time when he could have clambered up the Queensboro Bridge and taken his magnificent swan dive into all that awaited him.

At four o'clock, wherever he was, he would start back home. He would stop at the market on Third Avenue and buy things for their dinner.

"I won't have you cooking," Sue said.

"How are you going to stop me?" Bernie asked.

"But you *shouldn't!*" Sue protested. "You have your own work. How are you doing on the play?"

He had given her no inkling of the beautiful silk purse he had fashioned out of a sow's ear. He didn't know exactly when he would reveal it to her, but it would probably be about the time he had exhausted his little affair with Bernie Halpern.

"It's a stinker," he told her, "but I've got ideas. I don't know why it is, but my finest inspirations come to me over the stove. My boiling point is about the same as water."

After Sue left, Bernie cleaned up the dishes. He really didn't mind kitchen chores. He performed them with a background of music provided by the tinny little radio Sue brought with her from Brooklyn. At that hour only the soppiest kind of music was to be heard. Neither good jazz, nor good swing, nor good classical. Tea-room tunes, overtures, the kind of stuff that could start a forest fire out of a spark of melancholy. But Bernie enjoyed it. It edged his thoughts with a pleasing blankness, like the margins of a printed page. It also created a time stasis for what followed.

Bernie always managed to finish the last of the dishes just as the seven o'clock news broadcast was concluding. He even regulated his tempo to synchronize the two. At the end of the news broadcast, there was a summary of the stock market activity for the day. Bernie wasn't interested in stocks. He wouldn't have been interested if he had thousands of fallow dollars lying around begging for a safe investment. But during these days of solitary and delicious communion with his life — present and future — he had discovered a phrase which was a perfect distillation of all he felt. Perfect because it meant nothing and evoked everything:

". . . wheat closed higher and cotton was mixed . . ."

Wheat didn't always close higher, nor was cotton eternally mixed — whatever the devil either meant. There were variations to the formula, but for the sake of keeping his symbol pure Bernie translated every stock-market report into that precise phrase. And when it fell upon his ears, Bernie Halpern contracted his whole being into one transcendent discharge of love and hope. The million artifacts in the city that had assumed the shape of his dreams, his love for Sue, the long lifetime of good and happy work which lay before him — all these streamed into Bernie from every direction. These and the one ineffable thing no man can describe when he is young, stammers about in his middle years, and replaces with sleep when he has grown old. Perhaps it is a secret suspicion of immortality; a narcissism so profound that it finds its reflection in every facet of life.

Bernie didn't get to direct that original play. In fact, he never even had the satisfaction of having his ideas discussed. The producer simply vanished. Well, he didn't exactly vanish, but he might as well have. He left for California. This was the information Bernie received when he called the number the producer had given him.

"Any idea when he'll be back?" Bernie asked.

"Dunno," was the answer. "Couple of months. Maybe more."

"Is this his home?" Bernie asked.

"No. This is the Consolidated Syndicate."

"The *what?*"

"Con . . . It's a buying office."

Bernie ultimately discovered people who knew the producer. He talked to them. They told him that his man was known for his erratic behavior. Yes, he had produced several plays on Broadway, but he was essentially a businessman. His Muse was money, and he followed his Muse wherever it yelled the loudest. Forget it, they told him.

Bernie, naturally, didn't forget it. He didn't mind his own loss of time and effort or the man's defection as much as he did the feeling of foolishness he was left with. The warm flow of felicity suddenly froze and everything was caught in a posture of mockery.

"The city is full of nuts," Sue said, by way of consolation.

But Sue failed to console. She said all the things a man might expect to hear from his wife under the circumstances, but she said them as one who understands rather than feels. The disappointment was not as much hers as his, and this crack of distinction marred the surface of his love.

"Don't take on so," Bernie said to her. "You'll get over it."

"What do you mean by that?" she asked.

"Nothing."

"Well, it's not the end of the world," Sue said, aware of her failure of feeling. "You said yourself it would be idiotic to pin any hopes on a thing like this."

"So I did. So it was. Amen."

"I don't know what you expected me to do."

"Shed one honest tear," Bernie snapped. "Just one of the many you would have shed if something of the sort happened to you. As *I* would have shed, God damn it!"

Then Sue did cry, but her tears were not for the right thing.

Bernie went job hunting. He had no negotiable skill outside the theatre, and the salaries offered were ridiculous. He took a job selling a food freezer plan to housewives and closed three deals the first day. That evening he figured out what the housewife was getting for her money, and he didn't show up the next day. Bernie went to see his friend in the Village.

"Look," said his friend, "I can use you, but I can't have you hopping in for a couple of hours a week. Can you give me three or four eight-hour days?"

"Sure," said Bernie.

Things settled down to what is normal for young people who hope to earn their bread in the arts. The bread was earned elsewhere, and the arts glittered like stars. Several million light-years away, but in the dark, clear night of longing, it seemed as though you had only to reach out your hand to pluck one.

Sue continued with her classes during the day, finding occasional work as an usher in the Broadway theatres in the evening. Bernie became more proficient in leather craft, and his friend allowed him to design some bags on his own, for which he received a percentage when they were sold. Their combined incomes, however, added up to the kind of financial hole acceptable only to those whose eyes are fixed on the heavens.

If they couldn't have heaven (the particular heaven they sought), they could at least gather together with other apprentice angels and imitate the noises of Paradise. Their friends were people like themselves: young; predatorily ambitious; and chronically separated from their rightful status by a hairbreadth of prejudice. They gathered at each other's cubicles in the city and drank wine or beer while flagellating this senile actress or that cretinous actor. If someone of their acquaintance made it in a Broadway show, they were loud in their acclamation — so loud that it stifled the cries of pain rasping in each throat.

And after these prayer meetings, Bernie and Sue would return to their apartment so confirmed in their belief, so absolute in their hunger, that it seemed as if fate could not much longer withstand the pressure. It would succumb merely to get the Halperns off its neck.

One such night, Bernie and Sue lay unspeaking in their totally dark room, their thoughts privately prating in the silence.

"Bernie . . ." Sue whispered.

"Yeah?"

"I didn't know if you were asleep."

"Not even close. What did you want?"

"I'm not a good actress," Sue said.

"You are."

"I'm not. I know I'm not. I've always known it. What am I going to do? I thought maybe I'd get over it, but it gets worse all the time. There's nothing else I want . . . Bernie, do you want very much to succeed as a director?"

"I can taste it."

"What would you do for it?"

"I don't get you."

"I mean," said Sue, "supposing you could make a pact with God. You could have success but at a sacrifice. Like five years of your life, or someone who meant very much to you . . . you know, something important . . . would you do it?"

"I wouldn't sacrifice you, if that's what you mean?" Bernie said. "Would you me?"

"No."

"Meaning yes."

"I said no."

"I know you did," said Bernie, "but you were thinking something else. I'll tell you what you were thinking. You were thinking that sleeping with the right guy would be such a small thing compared to what you might get that you wonder how I could possibly make a fuss about it."

Her own unguardedness and Bernie's terrible accuracy left Sue bereft of words.

"Bernie . . ."

Bernie moved his arm and touched Sue, not in a caress, but adjuringly, as one might put his hand on a child to forestall its panic penitence.

"There's a good likelihood neither one of us will amount to a damn in the theatre," he said, in a voice dry and lifeless enough to be prophetic. "Why ruin everything?"

When Sue became pregnant, she was in rehearsals for her first Broadway production. It was a musical.

"You did it on purpose!" she raged and sobbed at Bernie. "You couldn't stand to see me get ahead!"

Bernie caught the fists she tried to use against him between his big hands and held them captive.

"Think a minute!" he said, beseechingly. "For God's sake, Sue, think a minute! It's no one's fault. You always took the precautions. I mean . . . look, no one has to know. For *months!* There's not a chance of endangering yourself. It's just a walk-on part . . ."

A walk-on part, and a miracle of percentages. A thousand-to-one shot. The director at that point was simply looking at faces, and Sue's was one of the faces he chose. There were exactly three speaking lines — forty-two words — and these were spoken in a chorus with six other girls.

"You can certainly be in rehearsals until the show opens, and even if you have to quit afterwards you'll still have the show to your credit," Bernie soothed.

"And what happens after?"

"Didn't you expect you'd ever have children?" Bernie asked her.

Sue didn't answer. There was nothing to say. The question wasn't fair or honest. Neither of them had thought of the possibility. There was no more room in their lives for a child than there was for a grand piano in their room. Sue didn't allow herself to dwell on the future. Bernie did. He went to see his father.

The elder Halpern scratched the bristles on his cheeks with nails as tough as bears' claws. Three decades of house painting had changed the composition of his flesh. It had the dry, grainy look of sun-baked wood.

"How much you'll need?" Mr. Halpern asked.

"I figure I can set up shop for a thousand," Bernie said.

His father nodded. "A thousand I got," he said.

"This is a loan," Bernie emphasized. "I want it made out in a regular form. A note."

Mr. Halpern nodded again without smiling. "Tomorrow I'll see a lawyer," he said.

With the thousand dollars, Bernie went searching for a store in the Village, as far away from his friend's shop as possible. When he found one, he signed a year's lease and then set about to purchase the materials of his trade. He knew where to look. He had found out while working for his friend.

The show in which Sue appeared closed after one week. The reviews were awful and the backers pulled out. Sue cried half the night, and lay silently awake the other half while Bernie slept. She woke up Bernie at six in the morning to tell him they would have to go to the doctor.

Sue stayed in the hospital for several days after her miscarriage. Bernie came every day with a fresh bunch of flowers. He tried to console her for everything: for the show that closed; for the child she didn't want; for the child she didn't have. She listened to him, her remarkable gray eyes ringed with a tired bewilderment.

"Sue, I've started in business for myself," he finally told her.

"What business?"

"A leather shop. I borrowed some money from my father."

"Why did you do that?"

"We were going to have a child!"

"What are you going to do with it now?"

"Keep it," said Bernie. "We've got to have something to fall back on."

The jobs Sue would find were transient, as though there existed a mutuality of understanding between those who employed her and her own state of being. She was a receptionist, a salesgirl, a poll taker, and, of course, intermittently, an usher. There were amateur acting groups all over the city, and Sue was always among them. Sometimes she had a part. Sometimes she sat on a folding chair in a church basement or social hall and listened to other voices resound loudly in the emptiness.

Bernie's workday began at noon. He kept the shop open until ten in the evening on weekdays and eleven on Saturday. At times he wondered whether he had given a single thought to the hours this business would entail.

Half of the thousand was gone the first month in business, and Bernie saw that he wouldn't make it with the output of his own hands. So he rearranged the store, putting his workshop in the rear and taking in other merchandise he could turn over more quickly. He now sold ceramics and silver jewelry in addition to his leather things. It was just another store in the Village, but Bernie was saved from the worst implications by thinking of it as temporary.

At times rebellion seethed in his heart, and he would put out the lights and close the door of the shop. He would walk around the streets for an aimless hour, biting seeds of bitterness, telling himself it was impossible, *absolutely impossible,* to go back and face that desultory customer who fingered a dozen items and walked out with empty hands and a vague smile. But he would finally go back, because not to go back would commit him to something of which he had grown afraid.

"This is ridiculous," he said to Sue. "I must have some time to myself. I see no one. I'm a slave to that goddam store."

"Get rid of it," Sue replied.

He looked at her. Her style as a woman had come to full flower. She had put on some flesh, just enough to bring to perfection her gray-eyed voluptuousness. . . . *My Russian Princess,* Bernie groaned to himself, limp with helplessness and dread.

"I'm closing the store at seven two nights a week," he said. "The hell with it. Let's see some people."

So they began to invite people to their apartment again. Since they had more money now, they served liquor and elaborate spreads of food. The people who came were something like themselves, but not exactly. They were a little younger, a great deal more certain of their future. But the excitement generated by these evenings was almost the same.

Bernie would watch Sue at those parties. He saw with a sick heart the encroachment of mannerisms he knew too well.

The extravagant gesture, the elocutionary speech, the whole synthetic bag of tricks of the would-be actress who hadn't made it and never would. He watched these things as a man might watch prescribed symptoms of a fatal disease, and he felt a scouring pity for his pretty afflicted darling.

When one such evening had come to an end, and they had cleaned the mess, mounted the fan on a windowsill to exhaust the fumes, Bernie turned to see Sue standing in the center of the room, her beautiful arms lifted as she slowly removed the pins from her hair. Her eyes met his, and in that instant before she spoke Bernie made out his life.

He saw this room, and all the rooms they would eventually occupy. He saw the store, every item in it, and the small segment of sky vouchsafed from the window. He could hear the eternal seven o'clock news broadcast telling of trouble and the fact that wheat closed higher and cotton was mixed. But the words evoked nothing, because Bernie had pinched off the nerve which fed illusion.

"Bernie . . ." Sue said.

"Yes."

"Tell me the truth . . ."

Then Bernie went to Sue, kissed her, and carefully chose the words he would have to go on saying.

The Wreckers

On fine mornings, Mr. Kaplan got off the Fifth Avenue bus several blocks before his stop and walked the rest of the way. He did this in order to stroll past shop windows and appraise merchandise which was as familiar to him as his own. His approval or disapproval of the latest display registered plainly on his face. Some few of the older merchants or employees had come to recognize him, and although they knew more about him than his habit of looking critically into their windows at a specific hour, it eased the terror of their years to know that one such as themselves still continued active.

This particular morning, Mr. Kaplan's review of the shop windows was, at best, perfunctory. His real interest was up ahead, opposite his own building, where a wrecking crew was in the last stages of demolition. All that remained now was a wooden scaffolding around what had once been a fixture of the landscape. The huge gap gouged out of the avenue's solidity affected him in the manner of a recently pulled tooth. There was something unnatural and heartless about it, and a point of his consciousness reached for it as the tip of his tongue might have for the missing tooth. The empty space was hard to believe.

Arriving at his own building, Mr. Kaplan paused for a moment before entering and stood gazing at the activity across the street. A crew of men on the scaffolding were engaged in heaving crusted palings of old lumber onto a truck. The hollow, rattling noise sounded out of place in the concrete density of Fifth. Over to one side the ponderous rear of a crane was just backing out on the sidewalk, its tall, delicate-looking tower swaying and bouncing, and Mr. Kaplan experienced a little shiver of revulsion at the strength and ingenuity of the thing. He had seen it pick apart a building with such fine deftness that the human being inside the cab didn't sufficiently account for its cunning. Mr. Kaplan half-feared that it possessed a prehistoric intelligence of its own. Shaking his head, he entered his building and said good morning to the unresponsive elevator man.

Alighting at the twelfth floor, Mr. Kaplan gazed down the hallway to the transom of his door. It was open, of course. In the past five years the transom had been open at an hour and with a regularity that were a remarkable tribute to Miss Jaffe. That she was the best girl he ever had he stated tirelessly to friends and relatives, but never to Miss Jaffe. There were many times when he was tempted to do so, but instinct warned him that such a compliment would sit uneasily on so maritally doomed a person.

Miss Jaffe looked up and nodded to Mr. Kaplan as he entered. She was a thin, flat-chested, red-haired woman against whom nature had worked a vicious spite. The touch of redemption one looks for in the blighted was shockingly missing in Miss Jaffe. If her skin was bad, her teeth were more so, and teeth, skin, hair, figure, all contributed toward a hopeless unity. It was not surprising, then, that she plunged into her work like an avenging blade, and that her manner was formal to the point of surliness.

"Mr. Gavin called," she announced to Mr. Kaplan. "He said he would be here sometime between two-thirty and three."

"Aha," said Mr. Kaplan, nodding his head. He pursed his lips and continued to nod meditatively. "Aha," he said again.

He walked past Miss Jaffe's desk into the room where the merchandise was displayed. The office was divided into three sections. There was the small room where Miss Jaffe greeted customers and turned out faultless correspondence; then a fair-sized sample-room; and then, toward the front of the building, facing the avenue, the office where Mr. Kaplan had conducted his business for thirty-three years.

Each of these rooms partook of the order and cleanliness which was Mr. Kaplan's business credo. Not that he was an inordinately fussy man, far from it, but an old boss of his, a man of considerable rectitude and cruelty, had once given him a cutting lecture on these virtues before firing him. The event made its impression, and many years later, when he went into business for himself, Mr. Kaplan made the practice a strict rule of his own. He was never quite sure in just what way the maintenance of order and cleanliness would insure success, but he clung to it as to a talisman which had proved its worth.

Taking his customary look at the gleaming display of toasters, irons, table radios, cocktail sets, and other items coming under the general heading of gifts and appliances, Mr. Kaplan proceeded into his own office and removed his topcoat. He sat down at his desk, looked at the pictures of his wife, his daughter, his grandchildren, pulled at the lobe of his ear, and began to hum a tune under his breath. In the street, a pneumatic drill barked once experimentally and then went to work in earnest. Mr. Kaplan leaned back to catch a look at Miss Jaffe, and seeing that she was busy at her typewriter he got up and went to the window.

Twelve stories below, men in brown helmets moved within the rutted square of rocks and earth. Their presence was part of the ceremony that had gone on for nine months. Since that first wrecker had appeared on the roof of the building opposite and had begun to pry at the cornice with his crowbar, Mr. Kaplan had followed the demolition stone by stone, beam by beam. The fascination was all the more irresistible for the element of horror provided by his own fancy. Solid, ugly, enduring, the building seemed to catch its breath at the purpose of these man-bugs. It seemed to draw in upon itself, set its teeth, and decide to do battle for every brick which was its flesh, every girder which was its bones. From the outset, Mr. Kaplan was on the side of the building, and when the thick walls resisted the efforts of the men with crowbars, he suffered vicariously the injustice and impact of the murderous steel ball swung from the end of the crane. To the building he credited all dignity. To the wreckers nothing but a mean ferocity.

Two short rings of the phone on his desk made Mr. Kaplan turn and look toward Miss Jaffe. She made a motion with her head and raised her eyebrows, a gesture which had come to signify his wife. Mr. Kaplan cleared his throat and picked up the phone.

"Yes?" he said.

"Ben?" said Mrs. Kaplan.

"Yes."

There was an astringent pause after this identification. Mr. Kaplan could literally see his wife twist agitatedly on the chair next to the phone. Her voice was flat and ominous.

"What do you want from my life?" she asked.

Mr. Kaplan closed his eyes and squeezed the bridge of his nose between his thumb and forefinger. Suddenly he looked his sixty-five years. The flesh of his face was loose and deeply lined. A puffy blue vein throbbed beneath the white hairline.

"What's the matter?"

"Why didn't you take breakfast?"

"I wasn't hungry."

"Since when aren't you hungry in the morning?"

Mr. Kaplan leaned back in his swivel crair and looked at the ceiling. He had been expecting this — these precise words in this precise manner.

"Everything happens once," he said. "This morning I didn't feel hungry, so I didn't take breakfast."

Mr. Kaplan now saw his wife nod with lifetime grievance and insight. The words she spoke were perfect accompaniment to the gesture.

"You wanted to make me feel bad?" she said. "Believe me, you didn't. If you want to starve, starve. I'd like to know what kind of man you are anyway. A baby wouldn't carry on . . ."

"Anna," said Mr. Kaplan.

"For weeks . . . !"

"Anna."

"What?"

"Do you want to have dinner downtown tonight? We'll go to a restaurant."

Anna Kaplan could never cope with the unexpected.

"Are you crazy?"

"What's crazy about that? We'll celebrate. If you like, we'll go to a movie after."

Mrs. Kaplan recognized nonsense when she heard it. Her voice came down like an axe. "I'm going over to Mildred's house. Mildred and Sid are going out tonight, and we're going to take care of the children. Come straight over here after work. I'm preparing dinner here."

Mr. Kaplan then did a curious thing. With his free hand, he lifted the desk blotter, as if remembering an important note he had slipped under there. There was nothing, but the momentum of urgency continued, and Mr. Kaplan's eyes reflected a critical state of alarm. Rarely in his life did rebellion against outrage reach such proportions, and each time it did he always ducked under some distraction to give himself time.

"Mildred?" he said, still holding the blotter ridiculously aloft. "All right. After work." Quickly he hung up.

Now Mr. Kaplan let fall the thing he had seized in his anger. He shook his head slowly. He had waited for a sign . . . but not this. Certainly not this! That his daughter and her husband should choose this night to go out, and that his wife should see no corruption of the heart in this action, made him a man bereft of family.

Swiveling around toward the window, Mr. Kaplan experienced that lurch of vacancy which viewing the empty space across the way gave him. He was not used to it. To have an accustomed sight before one's eyes for over thirty years and then have it suddenly removed was more like a trick than a serious undertaking. The senses demanded some restitution.

Particularly he missed the gray stone coping of the roof, that catwalk of aimless pigeons, that receiver of spring rains, winter snows, summer heat. But more than a backdrop of the seasons, the coping had become an inextricable part of the years he had spent in this place of business.

Mr. Kaplan's memory roved over those years, and the picture was one of almost unrelieved anxiety. The truth of the matter — a truth he had faced many times before without effect — was that he was not a businessman, was never a businessman, was never meant to be a businessman. Others he had known had become wealthy men, using no more lever to success than he had always held in his hands. His wife and daughter recognized this and treated him at best with indulgence, at worst with scorn.

Still, for a man who had no talent for the thing life had thrust upon him, he had not done too badly. He had married off a daughter in acceptable style, and had given his wife each of those things her suffering pride could not do without. He had done this like a stranger to his own involvement, making business deals with businessmen, buying, selling, creating solid contacts, gaining a reputation for reliability, and throughout knowing that the whole thing was not real.

It was with this secret of unreality that he had lived most closely, confiding in no one but Mr. Nicoletti, and even with him he had never been explicit. Nicoletti, the thin, dried-up tailor two floors below, was a man of much head-nodding and little speech, and whatever he might have guessed about Mr. Kaplan's life he kept behind his metal-framed eyeglasses, letting it peek over the rim occasionally in a blue-eyed, sorrowful stare.

They had become friends that first time, many years ago,

when Mr. Nicoletti came up to Mr. Kaplan's place of business wishing to buy a toaster for his wife.

"I'm Nicoletti, the tailor, two floors down," he announced, standing stoop-shouldered and myopic, several needles and pins threaded through his ratty-looking vest. "Can you sell me a toaster?"

Mr. Kaplan sold him a toaster, a reasonably good toaster but not the best. When it was all wrapped, the man smiled and said, "For my wife. Her birthday." Mr. Kaplan was wrenched with pity and guilt.

"Birthday?" he said. "You should say so. For birthdays we got something a little special." He exchanged the one he had given Mr. Nicoletti for a better model.

Thereafter, when his suits needed altering, he brought them to Mr. Nicoletti. It was something of a mystery how the man made a living, getting so few orders, but for those few he did get he charged a good price — more than Mr. Kaplan could afford. His shop was a clutter of sample swatch books and tailor's paraphernalia; an airless, dusty place, but one which contained something Mr. Kaplan had never found in the chrome showrooms where he went to buy his merchandise. It contained satisfaction and the work of hands.

Their talk never ventured beyond politics or family matters, and even here they told only what was pleasant and harmless to tell. Sitting on a stool next to the scarred workbench, Mr. Kaplan would sip the tea that Mr. Nicoletti had prepared on his electric burner and watch the bony hands of the tailor as they laid a pattern, as they chalked, as they handled the shears, as they sewed lining into a coat, as they fashioned a garment out of a few yards of cloth.

Wonderful, thought Mr. Kaplan. He saw beauty and purpose in Mr. Nicoletti's shop. This, to him, was real. And because he admired and envied the man's craft for its own sake, the skinny tailor one day presented him with a suit. A bravura gesture, like an artist, done without a fitting, for his own pride and Mr. Kaplan's appreciation. Mr. Kaplan offered to pay for it, but Nicoletti waved him away impatiently. He had the suit still. The best he owned.

And what had he to offer after thirty years of business? A roomful of assembly-line samples. The latest models. That — and fear. One unvarying model. "Who will buy from Ben Kaplan tomorrow? next month? next year?" Not even to Nicoletti but to the stone coping which was no longer there had he confided that recurrent fear. Sitting in his chair, staring out across the way, he had, from time to time, examined the threads which held his business together, and always he found them dangerously weak. If this or that one dies, or if I in some unknown way offend him, it will be my ruin. The large orders, the ones he depended on, came from companies which made gifts or premiums part of their operation. From habit or trust they bought from him, but he never had faith in it. A lower price, and he was out. An imagined slight, and he was out. Periodically he would thumb through these anxieties, and the stone coping across the way would look on, mutely implicated.

It was implicated, too, that one Christmas when a couple of drinks and a profitable season had melted the shell of his pessimism. That year was the high point of his career, the time when he almost believed he would be a success. He had four people working for him then — two girls in the office, an extra salesman on the floor, a delivery boy — and he had given them bonuses and a party. It was a very nice party, no one had gotten drunk, at least not objectionably drunk, and after they had all gone he had come into the office to sit for a moment before putting on his overcoat and galoshes.

Satisfaction did not come easily to him, having lived so long on the brink of insolvency. If he felt it at that moment, it was not without some superstitious fear. Like all people who cannot imagine themselves recipients of a generous fate, Mr. Kaplan felt almost burdened with his luck. He sought for someone with whom to share it. He thought of Anna, but Anna was no person for sentiment, and besides she was too firmly convinced of his eventual futility. Nicoletti he did not as yet know. The city below him was wrapped in its own vast mood of gaiety. There was no one, really, and so he sat and watched the snow drift and sweep around the coping. It shared with him an ease and elation he never enjoyed again.

"Do you want to sign these now?"

Miss Jaffe stood at the door with letters in her hand.

Mr. Kaplan turned in his chair. "Yah," he said, and watched her as she crossed the room to put the letters on his desk. He studied her profile, trying to read something from her overlong nose, her thin lips. Impossible. Miss Jaffe's thoughts were stern secrets. It occurred to Mr. Kaplan that he must do something for her. But what? What he could do she already expected and despised.

"I hope you made the usual corrections," he said.

She nodded.

"What do you think?" he asked, coaxingly. "Disgraceful, eh? A man so many years in business can't write a decent letter?"

Miss Jaffe permitted herself the ghost of a smile. She looked down at the corner of the desk and moved her hand across it as if to remove some dust.

"You mentioned something yesterday about getting up an inventory," she said.

Mr. Kaplan sighed and pulled at the lobe of his ear. "Yes," he said.

"How many copies?"

"Two. Two should be enough. Don't you think so?"

Miss Jaffe nodded. At that moment, the telephone rang. Mr. Kaplan answered it. He said: "Yes . . . Oh, Mildred . . ." He looked at Miss Jaffe and saw the name pull at the corner of her mouth, leave a smudge of distaste in the hard opaqueness of her eyes. She walked back to the office.

"Yes, Mildred?" said Mr. Kaplan.

"Are you coming over tonight?" his daughter asked.

"Why not? You invited me. How are the children?"

Her tone brushed the inquiry aside, "Fine," she said. "Mom just called me . . ."

"Yes?"

"She told me that you didn't take your breakfast. What's that supposed to be — spitework? Look, Pa, I've got two children and a husband to take care of. I've got my hands full as it is. I'm not going to put up with nonsense on top of everything else. Don't misunderstand me. I don't mean to be disrespectful, but under the circumstances I think you can understand that I simply must have the maximum of cooperation. I mean, after all, it *is* something of a burden on Sid and myself. What happened, I mean. Not that anyone is blaming you. Don't misunderstand me . . ."

"I don't misunderstand you, Mildred," Mr. Kaplan interrupted.

"Then, *please,* Pa, let's try to make life easier for everyone. . . . Now, listen, Sid and I have to go out tonight. Mom is preparing dinner for you here. You're perfectly welcome to spend the night. There's plenty of room."

"Thank you," said Mr. Kaplan. "Let Mama decide. How are the children?"

"Fine."

"Give them a kiss from their grandpa."

"O.K., Pa. I'll say good-bye now."

"Good-bye."

Mr. Kaplan put the phone on the cradle. He got up and went to the window, looking down at the brown-helmeted man who sent up a little spray of gray rock-dust with his pneumatic drill. He felt bruised, pelted by words. *"Maximum of cooperation . . ."* That sounded fine, full of tenderness, like a business contract. That she learned from her husband who was a first-rate businessman, one who knew how to get the maximum out of everything. Mr. Kaplan allowed himself a quick glimpse of the future, and then he shut his eyes. Other words came to him.

"Surely goodness and mercy shall follow me all the days of my life and I will dwell in the house of the Lord for ever."

He turned and walked into Miss Jaffe's office.

"I'm going down for a minute to Mr. Nicoletti," he said.

Mr. Gavin arrived precisely at three. He came in followed by two boys who carried folded up corrugated cartons, newspapers and cord.

"Well, Ben," greeted Mr. Gavin, shaking his hand.

"Everything is ready," said Mr. Kaplan.

Mr. Gavin looked around the sample room with a practiced eye. He was a stout, tired-looking man with a brown wart on his upper lip. From his appearance one would never guess that he was a rich man, but it was well known that his discount house in the downtown area spouted gold. He reached into his vest and brought out a cigar, slipping off the cellophane jacket. He bit off the end, prepared to spit it on the floor, but then remembered himself and picked the tip from his tongue with his fingers, depositing it in an ash-tray.

"All right, pack it up," he said to the boys. "Wrap each piece in paper first, and stuff plenty in between. I don't want any scratches." Then he turned to Mr. Kaplan. "Did you take an inventory?" he asked.

Miss Jaffe handed the sheet to him. His eye ran down the list swiftly. He handed it to Mr. Kaplan.

"Did you check it?" he asked.

"I made it up," said Mr. Kaplan.

Mr. Gavin took the sheet, folded it, and put it in his pocket. He looked at Mr. Kaplan and nodded his head, his heavy face ironic and compassionate.

"There's not another man in the city I would buy such a lot from and not check over each piece," he said. "You've got a good reputation, my friend."

"How much will you give me for it?" Mr. Kaplan asked.

Mr. Gavin snorted. "Five cents," he said. "You're right. What's it worth. Tell me, what are you going to do?"

"Retire."

"Got any money?"

"At least a million."

"Children?"

Mr. Kaplan couldn't keep his gaze off Gavin's boys as they wrapped the pieces in newspaper and packed them into cartons.

"Children?" he said. "I have a daughter. My son-in-law

is a wholesaler in electrical supplies. I'm going to help him for a while."

Mr. Gavin's eyes showed comprehension. They dwelt on the other man's fate for a moment, and then withdrew, turning to supervise the packing.

The whole lot took about an hour to pack. There were four medium-sized cartons in all. When it was finished, Mr. Gavin took out his checkbook and wrote out a check for the agreed price.

"On the barrelhead," he said, waving it a few times and passing it to Mr. Kaplan. "Take a look and make sure it's right."

Mr. Kaplan looked at the check and put it in his pocket.

"Well," said Mr. Gavin, extending his hand again, "I wish you good luck, Ben. If you want my advice, you'll take yourself a nice vacation in Florida. Couple of months. You deserve it."

"Thanks," said Mr. Kaplan. "I'll think about it."

The two boys and Mr. Gavin lugged the cartons out of the showroom and down the hall toward the freight elevators.

Miss Jaffe stared at the door with hatred. "The crook!" she said in a bitter voice. "The dirty crook! 'A nice vacation in Florida.' He should talk after practically stealing the whole showroom!"

"He gave me the best price," said Mr. Kaplan.

"He's a crook in his heart!"

They both stood in the center of the showroom and looked at the empty, blue-lined shelves. There was a hollow resonance in the room. In an hour, a business had become an empty office.

"Well," said Mr. Kaplan, "when do you want to start work for Morris and Sons?"

Miss Jaffe began walking back to her desk. "There's no hurry," she said. "Two, three weeks. They said I could come whenever I'm ready."

Mr. Kaplan was fishing in his pocket for the check he had made out. "I want you to take this," he said, holding it out between two fingers.

Miss Jaffe looked with hostility at the check, at Mr. Kaplan. "What's that for? You gave me two weeks' pay."

"Be a good girl and don't argue," Mr. Kaplan pleaded, suddenly overcome with weariness. "If you didn't deserve it, I wouldn't give it to you."

Miss Jaffe took the check and put it on her desk. Then she stood before Mr. Kaplan, looking down at her own thin, unfeminine body. She gave her perfectly straight skirt a twist of adjustment.

"I'll be a secretary my whole life," she said, as if she were pronouncing sentence on someone she despised. "I'll die a secretary. I wish I could have died here."

She looked up then, and allowed Mr. Kaplan to see her face made even uglier by tears.

After Miss Jaffe left, Mr. Kaplan went into his own office. Only a few things remained. He had to clear his desk. He had to remember to leave the key with the people on the fourth floor, the ones who had bought his office equipment. That was all. He looked at his watch. It was four-thirty. Time enough for a little stroll on Fifth Avenue before taking the subway to his daughter's home in Queens.

Mr. Kaplan stood before the window and stared down. The certainty that he would never look out this window again caused him a sudden flurry of panic. He felt like a man who has forgotten the important symbol of a solemn event

— a ring, a medal, some token of commemoration. Worriedly he touched his memory, as if there were pockets there to be felt, a corner where the thing might be hiding. But there was nothing, and because this knowledge troubled him deeply he put it out of his mind — as one puts out of his mind the recollection of a troubling dream.

Toy Village

MEMORY is a complicated and stubborn mechanism. It's easy enough to recall something if all you want is a black-and-white photograph of personal history; but when you're after the true essence of the past, you've got to depend on chance and memory's own laws. My coming back to that particular street was in itself chance. I happened to be in the neighborhood on a matter of business; and although impulse drew me those extra half dozen blocks, I wasn't at all sure that I would recognize the apartment house when I came to it.

I did, of course. It was on the corner of a street I had once rolled down on skates, gathering dangerous momentum, and more often than not coming to a crash landing instead of executing the smooth eagle turn that identified the adept and eluded the clumsy. But this was not the special fear I had come to find. That fear — *the* fear — and also the love would be down the stone steps, through the sinister corridor and into the eternally sunless and rusting back yard of an old apartment house. Here is where Elsie ran, scattering her mocking laughter. Here her father, the terrible Mr. Froelich, trod like an ash-gray giant, symbol of all the terrors that stalk the young.

Naturally I found none of it. The dimensions of the place had shrunk to pathetic proportions. The corridor was a damp and dark little tunnel. The back yard was every bit as sunless and rusting as in my memory, but the effect was now one of overwhelming drabness rather than exquisite menace. Quickly I decided to pursue the thing no further. I knew that if I went so far as to invade the fateful cellar, I would find nothing more than walls of ancient cement from whose surface the hieroglyphs of the past had been effaced. I turned around and began to climb the stairs.

In doing so I gripped the scaly metal railing that lined the staircase. Perhaps I needed this last contact to make the current of memory flow. I'm not sure. In any event I recalled a bit of it; and having a bit of it, I had it all.

Elsie . . . But let me speak first of her father, the monolith in overalls, the fierce Mr. Froelich. He was the janitor of the building in which I lived. I use the word "janitor" now because that is the word I used then. "Super" is no doubt a more respectful word, but for me "janitor" is alive with awesome meaning.

Like all janitors of that time and in such buildings, Mr. Froelich carried on his private war against chalk scribblings, rubber balls, and scrawny whelps who hung by their knees from fire-escape ladders. Mr. Froelich was true to type, but with a difference. He inflicted punishment — real, painful punishment. Directly across the street, between two other apartment houses, was a sorry-looking lot too small to attract real estate interest but ideal for shrill afternoon wars. The lot was full of rocks and refuse, but off in one corner was a dust-covered privet bush. This was Mr. Froelich's chopping block, gas chamber, rack and thumbscrew.

The role of the privet bush was made known to me shortly after my family moved to the Froelich apartment house. The other kids were quick to tell me of the local ogre and his unique method of punishment. I had some time to wait before I witnessed my first scourging; but when I finally did witness it, I stood off in wide-eyed horror, resolved to scream myself to death if ever I fell into Mr. Froelich's clutches. For what the grim-faced janitor did when he caught some unfortunate who had chalked the sidewalk or shattered a window was to grab him by the seat of the pants and carry him across the street to the privet bush. There, like an executioner, with no visible sign of pleasure or regret, Mr. Froelich would dump his victim into the spiny tentacles. As far as I can recall, no father had ever dared take revenge, and the legend of Froelich grew like Jack's beanstalk.

A Froelich performance was usually witnessed by some dozen of the victim's cronies, who from a safe distance bayed and howled, half in defiance of the enemy, half in relief that we ourselves had escaped his grasp. Remorselessly Mr. Froelich would complete the execution, and on his way back to his lair in the cellar would halt and level a huge, knotty finger at the rest of us.

"The next one I catch, it's down the cellar," he would rumble.

A terrible shiver passed through us. "Whatcha got down there, Mr. Froelich — rats?" someone would scream, and then imagination ran rampant. "Snakes!"... "Tigers!"... "Elephants!"... "Crocodiles!" Neither denying nor affirming, Mr. Froelich would turn his square, powerful back and march with even strides to the staircase that led to the cellar. Then, dizzy with our own conjuring, we would gather in the lot to add another page to the Froelich fable.

What invention! Like Hades, the Froelich lower depths were guarded by a monster, but one infinitely more horrible than the three-headed Cerberus. A plated creature, we decided, with claws made of broken soda bottles; fangs as long and gleaming as butcher knives, oozing poison; and a breath that scorched all living things. Oh, we had read our fairy tales! We could never have fashioned so fine a nightmare without the aid of those wonderful stories that are meant to beguile the tender years. When we had exhausted our powers of description, we would disperse and go our separate ways, ready to jump out of our skins if a cat crossed our paths.

And the fountainhead of all this gooseflesh was the father of the girl I loved!

I never really met Elsie — I merely became conscious of her. Since that pair of swaying pigtails traveled the same school route I did, I came to know them, expect them, and miss them when they were not there. I would walk behind and watch them swing in unison, two ropes of braided corn silk, each terminating in a butterfly of blue ribbon. They must have matched a nine-year-old's dream of beauty. The face came later. It was on one of those days when I was trailing her, enthralled, that she turned and fixed me with a stare that plainly said: "I know you're following me. I've known it all along."

The curious thing was that I had never followed her all the way. Somewhere en route I would be diverted by friends or a candy store or an impromptu game of Chinese handball. I was as yet a comparative newcomer to the neighborhood, but it was only a matter of time before I learned the awful truth. It was revealed to me the day that I did follow her pigtails all the way to my own house, to the very entrance of the Froelich cellar. I wanted to shout a warning, tell her to flee before a forked tongue licked out of the corridor and swept her into some awful maw. She stood there, however, plump and unafraid, waiting for me.

"I know you," she said.

I stared.

"You live on the third floor. Apartment Three-E."

I gaped.

"This is my father's house," she went on. "My father is the su-per-in-ten-dent." She unfurled the hyphenations like a royal flag.

There is a degree of awe that stuns fear, makes us approach what we would normally flee. I believed her. To the young it is not the enormity of a tale that suggests falsehood but the tone — and Pigtails' voice was matter-of-fact. She was telling the truth. Froelich was her father. She actually lived down there among the horrors. I suppose in that instant she became for me a creature of magical charm. Hers was the beauty that could enter smoky caves and bring forth the destroying dragon, docile and puppylike at her heels. Hers was the innocence that could allay the wrath of murderous kings, or worse than kings — Froelich. All that I had imperfectly taken from the Grimms was embodied in the half-frowning, pink-faced girl who invited my friendship.

"Do you want to play in my room?" she asked.

"Huh?"

"My father says it's all right," she assured me.

That should have been my cue for caution. I can't remember my precise reaction. I should think I appeared hopelessly stupid. I'm surprised now that Elsie didn't give me up on the spot.

"My father says it's all right for you to play with the toys, providing you don't break them," she continued.

"What toys?" I asked.

"You'll see."

"I have to go upstairs for a glass of milk," I said, grasping in my blankness an irrelevant straw.

"Well, after your milk."

"I don't think your father likes me," I said with more pertinence.

"It's *all right,* I tell you," she insisted. "You be down in ten minutes."

She turned and descended the steps.

I went up to my apartment and had my milk, behaving like one under a spell. Of course, I had no intention of obeying her command. Go down *there?* I would as soon have run naked into flames. Sooner. When I had finished my milk I went downstairs, trying to pretend that nothing had happened, that this was a day like any other. I would join the boys for a game of stickball and remember, if at all, the strange conversation with the Froelich girl as something not quite real.

Once in the street, I looked in the direction the boys usually gathered and saw three or four already busy with a ball, twirling a stick in the air. Then, against all inclination — under a spell, as I say — I moved in the other direction, toward the Froelich entrance.

Had she not been there, the episode would have ended that instant. I doubt that the spell would have lasted more than a few crucial moments. But she was there, hands on hips, an impatient expression on her pretty face. She compressed her lips and spoke with sharp distinctness.

"Come on!"

I came. I walked down the steps and entered the corridor, my flesh tingling.

She led me through a doorway into a maze of gray, harsh

walls, among ash cans, dumbwaiter shafts, fuse boxes. There was a curious smell about the place, a mixture of mildew and coal gas and something else — sulphur, maybe — that strongly hinted of the demonic. My glance darted crazily to dim corners, expecting at every step the heart-stopping growl of the guardian beast, the heavy, slithering movement.

"There's the boiler room," she pointed out, and I gazed into a sunken dungeon where a bloated black whale wallowed next to a pyramid of coal. The heat was overwhelming. We walked on. "And here's where I live," she said at last, opening a door very much like the door to our own place upstairs.

We entered the apartment, and I saw before me a gleaming white kitchen. Then there was another room, in which there was a massive round table covered by a great circle of yellowing lace, and then another room, with a wide bed and a tall chest of drawers. And then we stood at still another threshold.

"This is my room," she said proudly.

It was neither large nor small. Against one wall were a bed, a dresser, a chair. On the other three walls was an arrangement of shelves and pigeonholes bordering the stagelike floor, on which was set up a complete miniature village.

Everything was carved and lathed out of wood — the houses, the church with its delicate spire, the school with real light emanating from real windows, the policeman in the act of blowing his whistle, the cars, the trucks, the inhabitants. On the shelves were extras enough, I thought, to defeat boredom for a lifetime. It was plainly Creation, the First Day, and I beheld the wonder of it, stricken with admiration and envy.

"Do you know my name?" she asked.

"No."

"Elsie," she said. "And I know yours. It's Lenny. Now, if you want to play, you must promise one thing."

"What?"

"You must promise to do everything I say, because my father made all these toys in his shop, and I have everything just the way I want it and they're mine anyway."

Small thing — do everything she said! Why didn't I leave at that moment? I didn't because like every other fool I had to discover freedom by losing it. At the time, it didn't seem like such a great thing to promise. I wanted only to be allowed to stay, to look, to touch.

"I promise," I said.

"O.K.," she said, giving a little sigh of accomplishment. "Let's play."

Elsie squatted cross-legged on the floor. I got down beside her. In seconds we were lost in the busy manipulations of her private world. She had a natural sense of make-believe, and she ordered her subjects about with all the passion and shadings of an accomplished actress.

"You," she directed, "are driving this car. . . . Go ahead, take the car."

I put my hand on the car. Elsie rolled her blue eyes and sighed exaggeratedly. "Well, *move* it, you dope!"

I moved it.

"O.K., now," she continued. "I am this lady with the baby carriage and I'm crossing the street, see. The light is green. You're supposed to stop at the corner because the light is red for you. But you don't stop. You hit the baby carriage. . . . Go on — hit it."

I pushed the car against the baby carriage, and thereupon all hell broke loose. Elsie screamed that I had killed her baby. She called for help, the police. In a twinkling Elsie was the police. She changed her voice, propelled the policeman toward me, called me a bum in the name of the law and arrested me.

Traffic resumed. Women shopped. Children came out of school. Disobedient boys were punished. Bank robbers were foiled. All in all, a highly law-abiding, rigid, somehow feminine world began to emerge. With seriousness and subtlety Elsie imbued her toy village with life. Time and place out of mind, I knew of nothing but this hypnotic web of activity until I heard the front door open and close and heavy footsteps resound.

Froelich!

I had forgotten. I stared wildly at Elsie, seeking from her face some clue to my fate. The suspicion that I had been lured into the demon's cave by a pair of pigtails must have been in my mind, and I sat frozen in fear, waiting for the unimaginable.

Mr. Froelich appeared in the doorway of his daughter's room and looked down at both of us. He was vast. He filled the doorway. Seeing him for the first time at such close range, I could make out certain details that distance and apprehension had previously obscured. I noticed that he had a deep cleft in his chin. I noticed the porcelain blue of his eyes, the virile bristles of his mustache. Clamped in one side of his mouth was a short pipe. Looking at me, he emitted three contemplative puffs and then said: "I don't think you'll break any windows this way."

I could have swooned with relief.

"Oh, Papa, go away!" came snappishly from Elsie.

Mr. Froelich still looked at me, a slight smile forming

around the stem of his pipe. "Excuse me," he said, and disappeared from the doorway.

It was autumn when I made my first descent to the Froelich underworld. By the time winter came I had forsaken the upper spheres entirely. The boys on the block knew of my fantastic misalliance, and I'm sure I would have been scorned and abused except for the singular nature of my treason. I was, first of all, in league with Mr. Froelich, and this called for caution in their attitude, if not respect. And then, I shouldn't be surprised if they sensed the strangeness of my position; some of their silent aversion might well have been pity for the damned.

I had taken to calling for Elsie in the mornings to accompany her to school. This was at her insistence. "If I let you play with my toys for years and years, I guess you can walk with me to school." There was very little logic and less truth in her reasoning. She did not let me play with her toys — she merely used me as a live addition to her menagerie. But having let all my other friends go by default, I clung to Elsie with a child's undiscriminating need of companionship.

At any rate, I would call for her in the mornings. I would ring the bell of the Froelich apartment and Elsie would open the door for me. She never bothered to say hello. She merely turned around and went back to the kitchen, where she and her father were finishing their breakfast. I had long since learned that there was no mother to curb Elsie's tyrannical ways.

"My mother died when I was two years old," she had once informed me, as if this were another of her strange accomplishments.

The scene in the morning was always the same: Mr.

Froelich sitting at the kitchen table dressed in his overalls, his blue eyes impassive. His large hands rested on his knees. Deep-pitted and scoured, they might have been carved by their owner. My place was any convenient corner, elbows on table, chin on fists. In the warmth and brightness of the kitchen I would watch Elsie's father perform the ritual of plaiting her hair.

On the table were a hand towel, a brush, a comb and two blue ribbons. Elsie would take her position before her father, and then Mr. Froelich would begin to brush her hair with long, smooth strokes. Occasionally, without a word, he would hand the brush to me. I, duly initiated, would take it to the sink and allow just the right amount of water to run over it.

When the brushing was completed, Mr. Froelich would take the comb and with a single, incisive line divide Elsie's hair into two equal parts. For me that movement was like a note of unearthly music, which drugged my senses and left me a dreamy witness to what followed. Separating each half into three parts, Mr. Froelich proceeded to braid his daughter's hair into the two perfect pigtails that had ensnared my days. When he reached the end of each braid he would take up one of the ribbons, and although they always appeared to me too fragile to be handled by those thick fingers, the bows somehow always emerged crisp and feminine.

By the time the operation was finished I would be sunk in such a delicious lethargy that Mr. Froelich's sudden "So!" was like a frightening summons, jolting me out of my blissful, waking sleep. Elsie would then gulp the last of her milk, leaving a white crescent on her upper lip that she removed with a wipe of her tongue.

Mr. Froelich remained seated as we made for the door. Just as we were on the point of departing he would look at me with an unfathomable gaze and say, "Good-bye, sweetheart." This would make Elsie regard me with brazen eyes and then scream with laughter. Muffling her screams with both hands, she would flee out the door. I followed, burning with shame.

By midwinter all charm had departed from the toy village. Everything that had once captivated me was now merely boring. The policeman with his accursed whistle became a symbol of the stultification of my life. Elsie, for her part, never lagged in spirit. She hovered over her domain, arranging the wooden lives — and mine — with austerity and female purpose.

"What are you *doing?*" she would demand if by chance I set a piece to suit my fancy. "Are you crazy? That doesn't go there!"

"Yes, it does," I said.

"No, it doesn't."

"Why not?"

"Because it doesn't, stupid. You're not supposed to take anything unless you ask me first."

"You don't know everything," I would say bitterly.

"If you get fresh, I'll tell my father."

There it was, the ever-present threat. I withdrew, feeling a rebellious desire to plunge both hands into her maddeningly dull arrangements and scatter everything in one grand smash-up. But then I would glance at that imperious brow, the determined mouth, the eyes in which I had so often seen glints of latent savagery, and I would refrain. She was, after all, the daughter of Mr. Froelich, and that knowledge sat on my shoulder and whispered a constant warning in my ear. I saw myself chained by fear to this room, condemned to sit cross-legged forever, obeying the commands of Elsie Froelich.

I began to think. I thought of other days. I thought of stickball days, and the wild freedom and the friendly, sweating presence of other boys. I thought of the privet bush and the blood brotherhood of those who had suffered or almost suffered at the iron hands. Was it possible that the striding giant of those days was the same man who appeared at intervals before the door of Elsie's room, a newly carved piece in his hands, an uncertain smile on his lips?

"Now, what do you think this is?" he asked one day, offering a fire engine to the goddess.

Elsie looked at her father and then buried her derisive laughter in her hands.

"A monkey!" she screamed.

Mr. Froelich turned his eyes toward me, and I spied in them the patient sadness of one who finds no equity in his love.

"It's a fire engine," I finally said, hating Elsie for her pointless cruelty, hating Mr. Froelich for his limp sufferance.

"Oh, no, it's a monkey," she insisted, getting up and seizing the toy, which must have taken weeks of skillful labor to make. "Don't you see it's a monkey? Here's the head and here's the tail." Without a backward glance at her father she found a place for the fire engine, saying, "There!" And there it stayed, subject only to her decree.

All days became as one in the monotony of servitude. Plans for escape began to obsess me. I prayed for some horrible disease that would keep me in bed for weeks and weeks, a disease that would render me permanently contagious. I thought of telling my parents that I was being kept prisoner in the cellar of our own house, but I knew that if I did that, there would be an immediate outcry and interdiction. I would be forbidden to go near the place, and the vengeance of Froelich would be on all of us. I thought of a thousand different acts that might cause Elsie to tire of me, reject me, find me as hostile to her well-being as I found her to mine. But Elsie, like all first-class egotists, was as oblivious to my wave lengths as she was absorbed in her own. As for my getting too far out of line, she knew she could always correct that with one swipe of her paw.

Foolishly I thought I must *do* something to end my captivity. It never occurred to me that the answer might lie in doing nothing — absolutely nothing. And I doubt that that thought ever would have occurred to me except for the deluge of snow one night.

I remember waking that morning and seeing out my window the deep layer of snow piled in the street, banked against houses, shaping itself upon the contours of cars. What stays with me yet is the feeling of insulation imparted by that blanketing snowfall. Above all it was soundless — soundless in itself and insulating all other sounds.

Something of that feeling must have stayed with me when I went downstairs to call for Elsie. It stayed with me through the ceremony of her hair, through school, and after school as we trudged back to the apartment house. Paths had been shoveled during the morning hours, and the heaps of snow glittered invitingly. Boys plowed knee-deep in the whiteness, their shouts crashing like crystal in the winter air, then quickly dying against the muffling snow.

"Hurry up and have your milk and come right down," Elsie ordered as we separated at the cellar entrance.

I did as I was told. I went down to the cellar and to Elsie's room, where I took off my coat and sat on the floor, dumb as any of her baleful toys. She looked at me.

"What's the matter with you?" she asked.

"Nothing."

She began to play, assigning to me my role for the day. When she asked me to perform an action, I did it poorly, spiritlessly. I said nothing.

"What's the matter with you?" she asked again.

"Nothing. I don't feel like playing."

Now she looked carefully, her eyes weighing the strength of my declaration. "What do you want to do?"

"Nothing," I said.

Elsie put out a tentative hand, touched the fire engine, rolled it slowly back and forth as she considered her strategy. I sat staring dully at the floor.

"You got a stomachache?" she asked.

"No."

"A headache? Sometimes I get headaches."

"No," I said, prepared to go on saying no until both of us and all of Mr. Froelich's handiwork were dust.

Arranged on the floor was the day's pattern of Elsie's play — everything as she wanted it. The policeman here, the vehicles there, the schoolhouse, the people, the whole miserable cosmos. It was Elsie herself who sent the fire engine crashing into that sacred order, scattering pieces, even breaking a few. The devastation couldn't have been more appalling if it were life-size. I sat as though made of stone.

"*You* make a game," she said.

"I don't want to."

"What do you want to do?"

"Nothing."

Her lips pursed in sullen deliberation. She shook her head slowly from side to side, swinging her pigtails, increasing the tempo until one of the braided ropes whipped over her shoulder. This she seized, pulled at meanly, plucked the blue bow open and then sat chewing a tassel of hair. I glanced at her just in that instant when her face reflected the glow of a sudden thought.

"I know! You brush my hair."

Flushed with the success of my new-found perversity, I was at first prompted to say no, but an instant's reflection gave me pause. I thought of all the mornings when I had watched Mr. Froelich brush and brush, my eyes glazing with the delicious torpor brought on by the soft, sinuous, golden mass of hair. How often I had wanted to do that myself! To brush Elsie's hair, I had always felt, would be to steal the talisman of magic. Once I had done it, I would possess forever some secret power.

"O.K." I agreed.

Elsie went to get her brush and comb. She came back and sat on the floor, undoing her braids, and with a shake of her head spread loose her shoulder-length hair. I felt that I had passed over the forbidden threshold. An atmosphere of sacrilege hung in the air, as thick and voluptuous as incense. I took the brush she handed me and timidly touched it to her hair.

"Brush," she commanded.

I let the bristles slide down her head.

"Oh, not like that!" she said impatiently, taking the brush from me. "Like this." She showed me how to make the bristles bite.

I began to brush her hair. The curvatures set by the braiding smoothed out. Little crackles of electricity followed the path of the brush, seemed to flow through my arm, seemed to charge the room itself. I was spinning gold. I was working the secret charm. I don't know how long we sat there, but I do know that I did not hear the front door open and close as I usually did. I did not hear the heavy footsteps as I usually did. It was only when he was at the door of Elsie's room, his presence coming over us like nightfall in a forest, that we became aware of him. Elsie and I turned in the same instant.

Mr. Froelich's face was a rock. Betrayal was in his eyes, but he did not look at me. He bent the terrrible weight of his gaze on his daughter, stared at her until his very silence became a roar of accusation. Dimly then I must have understood what Elsie had done. Dimly it must have come to me that there are those who would destroy everything rather than give up a trifle they have once possessed. I turned to look at Elsie and saw her face wrinkle into a mask of wailing penitence. In another instant she flung herself at her father, burying her face in his overalls, howling like a witch at the stake.

Above her cries, above her perfidious hair, Mr. Froelich at last deigned to look at me. He made a single motion with his head. Go, it said. Freedom, it said.

I didn't hesitate. I gathered my things quickly. I slipped past the locked figures of father and daughter, let myself out of the apartment, wound my way through the underground maze, took one last glimpse of the boiler room with its slumbering whale. And then, running as though the legions of hell were behind me, I made straight for the white and wonderful world.

The Ride Back from Lenox

Dan Goodman lay awake, listening for sounds in the next room. He wondered what time it was. There was no sign of light on the Venetian blinds. His watch was on the night table beside him, but he felt disinclined to reach for it. If it was something like five o'clock, he didn't want to know. He would just as soon pretend it was two, that the squawk from Susan was caused by whatever dream might disturb the sleep of a six-months-old infant, and that she would ball herself into a corner of the crib and be silent for another four or five hours.

"Was it Susan?" Dan whispered, as Karen slipped back into bed.

"I thought you were asleep," Karen whispered back. "She was just tossing around. I think she'll sleep."

"How about Bobby?"

"Like a rock."

"Any idea of the time?" Dan asked.

"Five."

"Lord!"

"She'll sleep for at least another hour," Karen said.

They were both silent. Dan rubbed his foot along the sheet

and felt the grit of sand. It bothered him only a little. It used to bother him enormously when he was a kid. He could still remember standing on the bare floor of a summer place, and his mother shaking out the sheets before he got into bed.

Now brush the bottoms of your feet before you get into bed, or you'll have it all full of sand again.

Recalling that, Dan suddenly recalled the composite essence of beach and damp and salt. Some cell of memory retained the pure, early quality of it and gave it back to him at this moment. Curious. He always tried to catch it, coming to the shore for the first time after a year in the city, but the senses serving him now were obviously not the same that caught and kept that seaside odor.

Nothing, in fact, was the same. Certainly this vacation was a far cry from vacations he had enjoyed in the past. *Plus ça change, plus c'est la même chose.* For the French maybe. For Dan Goodman, things had changed, and changed to a point where there didn't seem to be a prayer of their ever being *la même chose.* Not that he was wringing his hands over the changes, but still it was on the side of prudence, not to mention sanity, to recognize these changes and bow before them.

Why, the very fact that they were spending their two weeks with Aunt Dora was a signal not merely of change but of capitulation. Poor Aunt Dora! If she knew what an awful compromise she represented. Perhaps she did and didn't care. She had her own compromises with loneliness to make, and four human beings under her roof precluded any search for motives.

It was Karen, finally, who made the decision.

"What shall we do then, just stay at home?"

"But Aunt Dora!" he groaned. "I warn you. Two solid weeks of health foods, canaries, and local news."

"And sunlight, and ocean, and damn little expense," Karen pointed out, inexorably. "If you have any other suggestion about where we can afford to take the children for two weeks, I'd be glad to listen. We ought to be grateful she asked us."

"She's been asking us for eight years."

"It took two children to make us accept. At least we'll be able to go out a few evenings and know the children are in good hands."

That, of course, kicked out the center pole of any protest, and his resistance collapsed.

And, naturally, Aunt Dora was marvelous with the kids, and the kids were marvelous with Aunt Dora. After one week, Bobby looked like a Cherokee full of buffalo meat. Susan had in Aunt Dora an absolute sponge, one which soaked up every variety of dampness as if it were desert rain. As for their freedom — they had an embarrassment of it! Aunt Dora was for shooing them out of the house every night. . . . "It's your vacation, too, and you should make the most of it. They have lovely dances at the hotel. There are movies in town. Don't you worry about me!"

The hotel had a four-piece band that played rock 'n' roll to teen-agers. The movies in town showed calculated or unintentional horrors. So it was mainly walks in the evenings, which, despite Aunt Dora's assurances, were trammeled by a feeling of guilt. If a gorgeous sunset on the bay or a freshening breeze from the oceanside stirred them to some vague spontaneity, a vision of Aunt Dora in frantic crisis would cut across their mood, leaving it dead.

The truth was that they were not enjoying themselves. Some interesting people might have rescued them from dullness, but interesting people gravitated to interesting places, and whatever virtues this little seaside community might have, interest was not one of them.

"You asleep?" Dan asked.

"No," Karen said.

The walls of Aunt Dora's house had the effect of magnifying sound, and after a week of it Dan and Karen fell into whispers the moment they closed the door of their room.

"I have an idea," Dan said, sitting up.

"What?"

"Let's get dressed and take a walk on the beach."

"Now?"

"Now. Let's watch the sun come up. Are you game?"

"I'm game," said Karen, "but suppose one of the children . . . ?"

"Aunt Dora's here."

"She'd be scared out of her wits if she happened to peek in here."

"We'll leave a note tacked to the door. I'll just say we went to watch the sun come up. It's as simple as that."

"But suppose . . ."

"Suppose," Dan interrupted, "we do just one thing on this vacation that we're likely to remember."

"All right."

They switched on a light and dressed. Stealthily, with a smothered flashlight, they inspected each room. Aunt Dora signalized consent with her even-spaced, bubbling snore. The children were sound asleep in the other room. Dan and Karen walked out of the house, easing the door shut behind them.

The house was situated one block from the beach. They walked in that direction, breathing the cool, damp air. The street lamps were still on, but a pre-dawn glimmer was already questioning the lamps with gray authority. Sleep pervaded the street as strongly as it did the house, and Dan and Karen continued in their constraint of silence, distrusting the use of their voices in this odd light. Dan finally cleared his throat, as if to test the volume of sound.

"I am reminded," he said. "Air Force. Miami Beach. Reveille. They lined us up for roll call at about this hour, and there was a breeze coming off the ocean. I recall thinking to myself that I would make it a practice in my lifetime to watch the sun come up."

"I feel as if I could lean on the air and sleep," Karen said.

Dan turned his head and looked at her. She had put on the same white blouse and gray slacks that she wore the previous evening. Her hastily combed hair was wreathed in a nimbus of stray filaments. It suddenly struck Dan that Karen looked different. He had never before seen her in such a light, no cosmetics, her skin pallid and scored slightly at the mouth and eyes. It wasn't that it made her look any older; rather as if some preliminary touches had been tried for an amateur role of a middle-aged woman. One knew, of course, how young she was, how fresh beneath the artifice, and therefore found the incongruity amusing.

They reached the beach and began walking toward the water's edge where firmer sand would give them a better footing. At intervals, wire trash cans tipped rakishly in the sand. The lifeboat hung suspended from a beach davit, ghostly white. A complete overcast of stratiform clouds covered the sky, and the beach in either direction dimmed away in mist.

"Not so promising," Dan said, his words sounding precise and tiny against the drumming surf. "If those clouds over there break, though, you'll have a really dramatic sunrise."

"Is what I feel rain or mist?" Karen asked.

"A little of both, I think."

"Do you think it'll rain?"

"No more than this," Dan said. "Does it bother you?"

"No. It's refreshing. Do you have your watch?"

"Yes," said Dan. "It's five-thirty. What time do you think we should be back?"

"Oh, no later than a quarter after six. Susan is usually up by six-thirty."

"You don't fully trust Aunt Dora, do you?" Dan asked.

"I do," Karen replied. "I still think it will be a shock for her, not finding us there. I'd like to avoid that."

"She'll live," Dan said. "Aunt Dora's a durable piece of goods."

"How long has she been living here?" Karen asked.

"God knows! Years and years! Ever since Uncle Harry died. I can only date it by the fact that I was just starting high school then. I can remember being led up to Uncle Harry's bed some days before he died. I didn't realize it, but it was a family farewell. Grim ritual. In spite of all that pain, he had the presence of mind to ask if I had started high school yet."

"Poor Aunt Dora!" Karen said. "And she's been living alone all these years. There must have been money."

"Insurance," Dan said. "Some real estate. I think she still collects rent from some buildings in Philly. It's always been assumed by the family that Aunt Dora was loaded and queer. Not crazy queer, funny queer. You know, crank foods and birds all over the house."

"She only has two, and they're caged."

"I know," Dan said, smiling. "Family myth. She's neither loaded nor queer. But still, you never get over an early notion. That's why I find it so strange, spending a vacation in her house. It's a sort of retreat. Second line of defense."

"Who's attacking?" Karen asked.

"Fixed income," Dan said. "Two kids. Inflation."

"What would you have had?" Karen asked.

Dan looked down at the tips of his tennis shoes flinging a little plume of sand with each step.

"Am I alone in this?" he asked. "We *are* bored, aren't we? Or is it just me?"

"Dan, we're bored at home, too, at times."

"Right! True! That's why being bored on one's vacation is a touch too much."

"But, darling, where could we have gone with two children?"

Dan lifted both arms and waggled his hands. He knew. He knew. He semaphored his intimate knowledge of every variation of the argument. The places to which they couldn't go; the places to which they didn't want to go; the places which wouldn't have them. Several years ago, when Bobby was two and Susan unborn, they returned to a resort in the Berkshires that had meant a great deal to them. It seemed simple enough. If they couldn't manage a baby-sitter, they would take turns going to the music festival. It was a hellish embarrassment. Not only did neither of them get to a single concert, but it took all their resourcefulness and energy to keep from being regarded as a pair of inconsiderate pests. Parents who had made other provisions for their children felt — and rightly, Dan claimed — that they shouldn't have to endure the inconvenience and annoyance of someone else's child. And so the desirable places were even less possible than the undesirable ones. The proximity of enjoyment only underlined their loss of freedom.

Nor was it solely a matter of vacations. The pattern of

their lives had undergone a change, the nature of which emerged unmistakably in the last year or two. Impulse had given way to necessity. Of course they could still manage an occasional dinner in the city, but time was no longer the obliging medium through which talk or silence might drift toward some unexpected view. Time was a taximeter ticking off a baby-sitter's fee, a parking lot's charge. Friends, old and new, were determined by subtle levels of mutuality, and they now found themselves left only with those whose pressures and concessions matched their own.

Dan was willing to admit that there was nothing remarkable in all of this. It happened to millions. But somehow universality didn't mitigate the individual case. He felt himself engaged in a curious contest.

"We'll go as far as the rock jetty and then turn back," Dan said.

"All right," Karen agreed.

The light rain had ceased, but the mist had thickened. They could see only a few hundred feet ahead. Above, the cloud cover remained unbroken, and it didn't appear at all likely that they would have a sunrise to see. The ocean was to their left, and along the margin, where waves cast the water's rejects, there was an unusually large collection of shells. They had noticed it at the beginning of their walk, but it didn't seem particularly significant. As they continued their walk, however, the area of shells widened, became more dense until now it covered that portion of the beach near the water like vast, stippled carpet.

"What on earth is that?" Karen asked.

"Damned if I know," Dan replied.

They moved closer.

"Clams," Dan said. "Little ones. There must be millions of them!"

"Are they dead?" Karen asked.

"I have no idea. Looks like it. Don't clams bubble or something when they're alive?"

He picked up one of the clams and pried apart the shells. A few drops of seawater spilled from the hollow. He dropped the separate halves.

"They're dead, all right. I have never in my life seen so many of anything at one time. It just goes on and on."

They walked at the periphery of the belt, and occasionally one of the clams would crush beneath their shoes with pathetic fragility.

"Ugh!" Karen said, grimacing. "Let's move away."

They moved back and stood looking at the sea-strewn profligacy. There was something uneasily compelling in the sight of so many dead organisms. The compact of their mass death gave them an elegiac importance, as if the sea had assembled them on the shore for a brief, formal ceremony of mourning.

"It's biblical," Dan said. " 'The sea shall give up its dead.' What do you suppose happened?"

"Some sort of plague," Karen suggested. "Perhaps the life chain was disturbed. Plankton."

"What plankton?"

"I don't know. Isn't plankton terribly important?"

Dan laughed. "Terribly," he said.

"What will happen to them?" Karen asked.

"I imagine they'll all be washed back into the sea when the tide comes in," Dan said.

"What time is it?" Karen asked.

"Five to six."

"Let's go back."

They started back, Karen walking on the outside, away from the clams. There didn't seem to be anything further to say about the phenomenon. They both shared the feeling that they had come upon it by accident, almost intrusively, and that any further comment would lack relevance or proportion.

"Do you remember the Berkshires?" Dan asked, after a few moments of silence. "I mean the first time."

"Of course," Karen said.

"I keep thinking of that night ride back from Lenox," Dan mused. "Getting crocked on brandy in the car. Slugging it right out of the bottle."

"It was cold that night," Karen reminded him.

"So it was. Condensation on the windshield. I had to use the wipers. How we found the lodge, I'll *never* know."

He looked at Karen. Her eyes met his in a quick assertion of memory.

"We were drunk," she said.

Dan grinned. "Were we? Not very. I have a distinct recollection of everything that happened."

"So do I," Karen said. "Why should you think I'd forget?"

"I didn't say you forgot."

"This isn't the first time you've mentioned the ride back from Lenox," Karen said.

"Do you mind my mentioning it?"

"No."

"No, you're right," Dan said. "I keep coming back to that. It's just that time really stopped there. For half an hour, we were immortal. You know, I sometimes think that's what these ancient mysteries were all about. Drunkenness and frenzy under the stars. But at least you were a creature alive on earth and not a flat dumb surface pasted with timetables, wet diapers, and bills!"

"Oh, Dan," Karen murmured. She leaned toward Dan. She took his arm and pressed it tightly against the flank of her body. "Do you resent the children terribly?" she asked.

"What nonsense!"

"Don't say 'what nonsense'. *I* resent them a little at times."

The automatic force of denial suddenly spent itself in Dan. He did resent. Not exactly the children, whom of course he loved, but . . . *Yes,* the children! Whom else? He loved and resented. He resented the greedy, mindless, draining encroachments they made. He had been prepared to give whatever was reasonable: strength; time; spirit; love. But it was unreasonable! If you wanted to do the job properly, it was a piecemeal surrender of every right.

"Don't get the idea that I don't love my children," he said.

"I know you do," said Karen.

"But they shouldn't be absolutely everything."

"No, they shouldn't," Karen agreed.

"But they are."

"Almost," Karen said.

She released his arm. The separation seemed more than physical.

"Why should it be that way?" Dan asked.

"I don't know," Karen replied. "Perhaps because we have nothing to oppose them. We're ordinary people. Neither of us will ever be very important."

Dan turned to Karen in astonishment. For an instant, he saw clearly into their separate minds. He perceived the distance and direction they had traveled. His Karen! She had left him — how long ago? — and had gone on alone in the busy resignation of things as they must be. He felt deserted, betrayed.

"So we must give it all to them," he said.

"I don't think of it like that," Karen said.

In a sudden impulse, Dan reached out and seized Karen. He wanted to rivet her to the spot, stop her relentless trudging toward Aunt Dora's house, and morning bottles, and death.

"How much *do* we have for ourselves?" he demanded.

"As much as ever," she said.

"Will we ever have the Berkshires again?'"

"No," Karen said. "Not like that. I wouldn't want it that way again. It would be foolish and false. We'd be acting and we'd know it, and that would spoil it. Don't you see?"

They trudged in silence to the wooden ramp that led from the beach. There they paused and emptied their sneakers of sand. Dan straightened up. He gave a little snort of laughter and shook his head. They had both announced things that should make a change in their lives, but he knew that lives don't change. They go on. At other times, in other moods, Karen would relent, and she would want the charm and hunger of their early days as much as he did. Certain of this, Dan held out his hands to her. Karen smiled, yielded to his embrace.

His arms around her waist, hers around his neck, they faced in opposite directions. Dan saw gray ocean and cathedral clouds through a break in the overcast . . . Karen was looking at her watch.

Each Man in His Time

HAL NEWMAN steered through the automatic coin booth, tossed a dime into the catcher, and was greenly thanked on his way out. It was early, not yet ten. The morning sun was brilliant, and as the car moved along in the shadow of the New York side splinters of golden light shot from the Jersey palisades. In the center of Hal's field of vision was the bridge, defining space with such flawless symmetry that it gave the impression of having grown there, naturally, out of millennial forces of need and balance.

"Glorious day," Hal observed.

"Glorious," Stella echoed. She sat in the open car with her head reclining against the back rest. Her eyes were closed. A kerchief protected her hair from the wind's buffeting. Narrowly framed and without makeup, Stella's face had the molded serenity of a death mask.

Hal glanced at his wife. He thought he detected a touch of pink at the base of her nostrils.

"Are you catching a cold by any chance?" he asked.

"Possibly," Stella answered.

Christ! he thought. *In June!*

"I do wish you had said something," he rebuked her. "We

certainly don't have to be driving with the top down. For that matter, there was no crying need for you to come along today. I could have managed."

"If I were to stop functioning every time I felt a cold coming on . . ." she said.

"True," Hal agreed. "You've got a point there. You're a champion cold-catcher."

Stella opened her eyes and turned toward Hal. "It's not my idea of fun," she said.

"I was only kidding," Hal apologized.

He was not only kidding. Stella was great at catching colds. She caught them in all seasons, in all weather. She wore a catarrhal rawness on the wings of her nose as other women wore pastel lipsticks and black eye shadow. Nor was Hal offering second thoughts when he said he could have managed without her. While still in the house, he had suggested she might wish to utilize this Sunday in a different way. As for himself, the straightening up of the stock and the bookkeeping that had to be done were, at the worst, minor. He could easily manage. But he didn't insist. The custom of her assistance, like the regularity of her colds, was a price his patience had learned to pay for all past loyalty and sacrifice.

Now that the store (in its fourth year) was a solid, profitable enterprise, it would have smacked of the grossest ingratitude even to hint that her help wasn't needed and welcomed. To begin with, she loved the place, lined as it was with paperbacks from all the publishers and dispensing day-long music of her own choosing. It was, she claimed, a haven; and although she had never extended the claim quite that far, Hal knew that she also looked upon it as a kind of tabernacle at which they could celebrate the miracle of their redemption.

Redemption, of course, brought up the question of money, the never-to-be-forgotten money, the money needed to build the tabernacle. That had come from Stella's bone-dry, skeptical father, every blessed, interest-free cent of it. For Stella's sake, of course, since she didn't seem to have enough good sense to walk out of a bad marriage; and however quickly the debt had been repaid, the watermark "For Stella's Sake" remained spectrally ingrained on every order form and bank deposit slip.

"We'll have to take good care of you when we get home," Hal said, feeling compunctious. "Aspirins, hot tea, and the Sunday paper."

Stella smiled, dipped her head toward Hal's shoulder. "Darling," she said affectionately. "I'm perfectly all right . . . I was just thinking that I forgot to tell Diane what to make for lunch. It'll surely be franks and beans again."

Their daughter, Diane, was thirteen; their son, Marc, five — an age spread which revealed something of the uncertainties that had beset their lives. But since things seemed determined to work out reasonably well, they could count Diane's early maturity among their latter-day blessings.

"It won't kill them," Hal said. "They eat damn well all week. Besides we just had breakfast. We may be home before they even think of lunch."

"Oh, *please* let it take longer than that!" Stella implored. "I can't stand to face a multiple-choice Sunday. All I want is for someone to serve *me* a tuna on toast and a cup of coffee."

"That can be arranged," Hal said.

As they approached the Dyckman Street section, Hal glanced up and spied the Cloisters museum. He rarely came this way any longer during daylight hours, and when he did he was generally too preoccupied to notice anything. But this was a day of piercing green and blue and gold, and the Romanesque lines of that once-familiar structure reasserted itself with startling beauty against the summer sky.

The Cloisters! Lord, the time he had spent there! With Stella during the early years, and then alone — so many times! That had been *his* haven, that repository of religious relics sitting atop a promontory opposite the Jersey cliffs. How often he had been solaced by the bleeding unicorn and wooden saints pointing rapturously to Heaven! — how often during those years of writing books that endlessly began and never ended.

Years of piddling jobs, no jobs, non-commitment, saving himself for the Big Thing. The Cloisters had been his shade and water during that parched wasteland of years. It had comforted him, and confirmed him, and even at times restored him. Often he had confessed to all but himself that he did not have it in him to be what he wanted to be, and he would come to the Cloisters for the last awful confession. There it was that he found new resolution for the illusory goal. Something about the place. The stimulating mixture of death and art, perhaps.

Well — and who could ever have thought that he would become so bored with it? So bored, indeed, that he could barely get through a fifteen-minute tour without being overwhelmed by complete enervation. The pietàs and reliquaries pressed on his eyelids like sleep. The faded tapestries affected him so that he couldn't look at them without a mounting impulse to scream his tedium at the wall-eyed kings and conquerors.

That was something he'd never told Stella, his boredom with the Cloisters. It bored him even now to think of mentioning it. Then why mention it? She undoubtedly knew. They never went, that was all. After years of pilgrimage, they ceased to go and never a word said. Just as they had ceased frequenting the other museums, the little movie houses, the little restaurants, the little galleries, the little shops.

Hal's glance fell on the fuel indicator. The needle rested on E.

"Oh, great!"

"What happened?" Stella asked.

"We're out of gas."

"Isn't there a station a little further on?"

"I hope they're open."

They were open. Hal pulled in. He told the attendant to fill it up, congratulating himself on having refrained from pointing out that automobiles ran on gas, and that someone who drove the blasted thing six days a week should have made it second nature by this time to keep the tank full. To make sure he wouldn't lapse into secondary irritations, Hal got out of the car and walked into the station where they kept the cigarette machine. After receiving his pack of cigarettes, he turned, and as he did so he found himself staring at a boy he had thought to be dead for the last twenty years!

The boy was standing next to one of the pumps, wearing the uniform of a station attendant, but — my God! — was it possible for anyone to look so much like Jerry Kramer and not *be* Jerry Kramer? For one eerie moment Hal lost focus on two decades of history, and he was almost ready to march over to where that boy stood and demand an explanation for the long imposture. But then the boy turned, and of course it was not Jerry Kramer. The face was broader, the eyes not so dark, the features less handsome. Of course Jerry was dead; had been dead since a particular twin-engine bomber went down in the Pacific.

Hal paid for the gas and drove away from the station. He drove in silence for a few minutes, then he said, "Did I ever tell you about Jerry Kramer?"

"No," Stella answered. "Who is Jerry Kramer?"

"*Was,*" Hal said. "Jerry died in the war. In the Pacific. He was a pilot."

"Oh? . . . No, you never mentioned him before. Friend of yours?"

"Uh-huh."

"What made you think of him?"

"There was a fellow back there at the gas station who looked so much like Jerry that it made my hair stand on end."

"Why didn't you point him out?" Stella asked.

Hal shrugged. "What for? You didn't know Jerry. It wouldn't have meant anything to you."

"Did Jerry mean something to you?" she asked.

"Well — yes, of course, else why should I have mentioned him?"

"Did you know him a long time?"

"My whole life, you might say," Hal replied. "That is, until he was killed."

Stella raised herself to an upright position. She tucked a finger into each side of the kerchief and pulled back, exposing more of her face. It was not a handsome face; it had no single feature whose dominance drew the eye away from the plainness of all the others; but one could imagine a certain feminine insistence when these same features had been younger, more animated, more intent upon calling attention to themselves.

"Now I find that very odd," she said. "You've talked so much about your past that it hardly seems possible you could have avoided mentioning Jerry Kramer, who, you say, meant something to you, who you knew your whole life."

Hal smiled. "It is odd," he granted, "but somehow I never thought Jerry would have interested you."

"Is that why you never mentioned him?"

"No. Not exactly. Frankly, I don't know why. Possibly because he died in the war. Out of sight, out of mind. I guess really it's because his life had so little connection with what's happened to me since."

"Were you fond of him?" Stella asked.

Hal considered. He tipped his head to one side, shrugged. "That's a tough one," he said. "Yes and no. Fond? Certainly not *fond*. But I liked Jerry. You see, his mother and my mother were good friends. We were sort of thrown together from the beginning. We just accepted each other. It never occurred to us not to. Each of us was part of the scene, like our parents and the homes we lived in."

"Did he bully you?" Stella asked.

Hal looked up at the sky, and then brought his gaze down slowly until it came to rest on Stella. The expression on his face balanced cautiously between irritation and forbearance. "Now what in hell made you ask a question like that?" he asked softly. "Why should he have bullied me? And what makes you think I would have let him had he tried?"

"My darling!" Stella rushed to apologize. "I'm sorry. I just thought — well, the fact that you never mentioned Jerry Kramer before made me think there might have been something unpleasant in the background. You know how kids are — someone's always tormenting someone."

"Jerry Kramer never tormented me," Hal made clear, each word as neatly formed and separately nested as an ice cube.

Stella pressed against his arm. "I'm sorry," she repeated. "Please tell me about Jerry. What sort of boy was he?"

"A sort of boy with all the usual equipment," Hal said laconically.

"Hal, please —"

Hal closed his eyes briefly and nodded once. The gesture was by way of breaking off an old thread that he might have woven into an argument. He wanted no more of that. He had woven so many arguments — out of nothing, out of gossamer — that it seemed for a time in their lives that they had nothing but the weaving of arguments. It was their only sustaining activity, their only mutuality. But that was done with. He had vowed that that would be done with.

"Well," he said, "let's see. Jerry. What can I tell you about Jerry. I guess the most important fact about Jerry was that he was handsome. Extremely. Like one of those young men by Andrea del Sarto. Half seraph, half devil. Deep-set, black eyes. A fine, straight nose. A mouth adapted to laughter or scorn." Hal paused and glanced at Stella with a smile. He went on: "I'm sure you've heard this from me before, but at the risk of repeating myself I'll restate an old theory of mine. It's this: very handsome people — like Fitzgerald's rich — are different from you and me. They *do* possess and enjoy early. I don't know whether that makes them hard or soft, but it does give them a great advantage. They cease wondering who they are at a much earlier age. They are handsome — and that seems to be enough."

"Oh, Hal!" Stella cried deprecatingly.

"You don't believe it?"

"Nooo! . . . Did Jerry possess and enjoy early?"

"Yes."

"I take it he was very successful with the girls," Stella said.

"Very," Hal said. "He had his pick."

"And did that make you unhappy?"

"The normal amount of jealousy, I suppose. That's to be expected, is it not?"

"Perfectly," said Stella. "But is that how Jerry spent all his time? Was he interested in anything besides girls?"

"Oh, yes," Hal replied, nodding reflectively. "All the two-fisted, red-blooded American things. Playing football, crashing parties, knowing the latest dance steps, and also being well versed in certain in-group subtleties."

"Oh? That sounds very interesting. Such as?"

Hal laughed and shook his head. "Damned if I remember," he said. "It's difficult to recall now . . . Let's see . . . Well, there was Al Jolson. Yes. Believe it or not, Al Jolson, who *I* considered the paragon of cornballs, but who apparently enjoyed a twilight vogue among the in-groupers. For them Jolson had style, *éclat.* Don't ask me why. You know how those things are: the right people decide that it's so, and, by God, it's so! You were judged according to the amount of enthusiasm you could pump up for Al Jolson. And cars. And dance bands. Two more items among the lowbrow *avant garde.* If you didn't know why a Packard was to be infinitely preferred to, say, a Buick, you were pretty damn square; and if you couldn't catch the essential difference between Tommy Dorsey and Benny Goodman, you were utterly hopeless. Things like that."

Stella looked at Hal with a purse-lipped little smile. "And were you utterly hopeless?" she asked.

"Utterly," he said. "But of course I didn't see it that way. I regarded myself as way above it. Aloof. I even let Jerry know on several occasions how funny I thought it all was, his standards of trivia. I, you see, was already convinced that mine was to be a higher destiny. I read books."

"And now you regret it all," Stella said.

"On the contrary," Hal returned. "I didn't realize it at the time, but I was getting my early merchandise training. Now I'm in the business of books."

Stella slid down again into a more protected position in the car. She made no reply to Hal's last statement. She had learned to disregard the occasional seepage that showed along the seams of their repaired life.

Hal exited at Seventy-ninth Street and drove crosstown toward the park. The Newman store was on the east side of the city. Hal's decision to use the West Side Drive was a mere roundabout to catch a little of the loveliness of the day in a nicer setting.

At this hour of the morning there was a freshness even in the city; a soft, fragrant scent that Hal recognized as a cue to memory, a stimulus to revive other Junes. But Hal no longer encouraged these chain reaction nostalgias. They were useful, perhaps, for writing books, not selling them.

Jerry Kramer, however, was not so easily put out of mind. It was not only the shock of seeing a stranger who bore such a striking resemblance to Jerry that stayed with Hal, but the revived shock of first learning of Jerry's death. That news had come to him by way of two oceans and a continent, when he was himself tucked safely away in a headquarters corner of London, a post he had never sought, but one he was happy enough to enjoy when it had fallen his way.

He had learned by mail that Jerry had died a hero; shot down by enemy ground fire while returning from a mission. Those deep-set, dark eyes were gone from the world forever; that charmed, del Sarto handsomeness. And what did Hal Newman feel on learning the tragic news? Hal Newman felt a sneaking, secret gladness that Jerry would not be coming back with his hero's teeth gleaming, and his officer's cap at a rakish angle, and his rows of well-earned ribbons, and his easy assumption radiant with a new sheen of glamour.

He felt all this, and at the same time he felt overwhelmed with guilt and sorrow. Death was a ludicrous price for Jerry to pay for his swagger and his showoff stunts. Jerry was meant to live. Jerry was meant to become a successful but small-time salesman; to grow fat and bald and have the marvelous promise of his youth come to nothing. There was every likelihood that this would happen, because for all his charm Jerry was only passably clever, only fitfully determined. He was just a good-looking kid with a penchant for enjoying life.

Those enjoyments! To make the high school football team. Jerry made it — a third-stringer, at best. Hal could remember going to one of Jerry's games and seeing him trot out on the field, almost comic in his bulky armor, surrounded by teammates with legs like tree trunks. Hal could recall shuddering at the thought of Jerry in the fray. He would be broken like a twig. But Jerry was indeed called from the bench, and he took his place in the backfield, and he was hit by a bull from the opposing side, and he managed to survive.

Jerry played in two games the whole season, but he had his letter — a blood-red A on a refulgent white sweater. The swagger of it!

And the girls. The rumored girls and the real girls. The lost, sullen daughters of candy store owners. Looking back,

Hal could plainly see the furtive shoddiness of those conquests, but in looking back he also caught the lurking flavor of Lilith, the ineffaceable one, the night demon known to the fraternity of Jerrys and missed forever by the oddball Hals. Curious. With the death and diminution of so much, one would think that this particular memory would have lost its sting; but as Hal well knew it is not the object itself but the hellfire of adolescent imagination that burns in the mind. It doesn't make a difference how intrinsically unimportant these lost opportunities are: the time for such intensities comes only once, and when they are missed they are missed for eternity.

There was a dance, Hal recalled. Oh, a real swank dance. At the Waldorf. Some organization to which their parents belonged, and since dances were for Hal infrequent, and swank dances a fairy-tale event, he had looked forward to it for weeks in advance. Formal clothes were not required, but he had precipitated a family crisis by demanding a suit somewhat more appropriate to the occasion, a double-breasted, navy blue suit; and a new pair of black shoes; and a new white shirt; and a new, carefully selected tie. And he had gone to Jerry's home the evening of the dance, because a group of the younger people were to proceed to the hotel in someone's car. He was early. Jerry was still dressing.

Hal could vividly recall Jerry as he put on a pair of socks, each of which had a hole in a different place, one at the heel, and one at the toe. The shirt Jerry selected was pink. Pink! An old shirt, if one looked closely enough, frayed at the collar. The tie was black, knitted, and Jerry performed such complicated maneuvers with its knot that only an abbreviated pendant was left hanging. But there was a pin to hold the tie in place, and when Jerry buttoned his singlebreasted suit every item in his attire contributed to a perfect harmony of color and proportion.

Jerry was a virtuoso of minor effects, but these effects rendered him sharp and original for every occasion. At the dance, he chose only the intimidating beauties, and he executed a step known as the "Westchester," a gliding, dipping routine which required (as all dances did and do require) not only a mastery of movements, but a willingness to take in dead earnest the rhythms and hesitations which give a dance its style. So Jerry enjoyed a personal triumph, holding the loveliest girls in his arms and making them props for his own performance. The dance band and the perfume-scented air existed for *him,* and the affair at the Waldorf became for Jerry what such affairs were supposed to be — a joyous interlude at which the greed of youth was fed to satiety.

Jerry played at life a little above his head. He was not really a football player, yet he was on the team. He was not made of heroic stuff, yet he died a hero. It was merely a question of enjoyment. If one was alive and there were girls and sports and wars, then why not try to take each at its best?

Hal Newman had managed to persuade himself that he was superior to this, because Hal Newman was bidding for something else. One day he would fashion his immortality out of all he had missed.

When they arrived at the store, Stella immediately began working on the ledger entries. Hal busied himself with filling in and straightening the racks. The stock room was piled with cartons he hadn't been able to get to during the week. Methodically Hal slit the tape and ripped open the flaps of a few cartons, taking out neat stacks of paperbacks whose position in the store would be determined by title, by price, by author, and by that whim of the publisher which set the mode of sex or seriousness on each book. He switched on the tape recorder, and the quartet took up at the point where it had been silenced the previous evening.

The store was fairly long and not so narrow that it couldn't conveniently accommodate a center row of revolving racks on which the fast-moving titles were displayed. Shelves covered the walls from floor to ceiling along the length of either side of the store, and these presented an unbroken facade of books, each book a different title, and many titles replaced each week as fresh floods poured from the presses. He didn't always think so, but now Hal could see nothing but lunatic conceit in any man's wish to add a drop to this ocean.

This thought was one Hal often popped into his dry consciousness, much as he might have popped a hard candy into his mouth, to relieve the dryness. But this time the thought became an irritant. It was as if it were making contact with a freshly sprouted canker sore. Hal didn't have to search long for the cause of the canker. He hadn't thought of Jerry Kramer for years. Such a sudden and strong dose was bound to produce a reaction. The odd assortment of guilt and grievance had worked a chemistry in the blood.

He wondered if it would have surprised a revenant Jerry to wander in here and find middle-aged, mustached Hal Newman — still slim, surprisingly well-preserved, albeit rather faded — arranging the writing of other men for easy sale. Hardly. He would probably say: *"Pretty good. Nice setup! Making any dough?"*

A lost fragment of conversation came back to Hal:

"What are you going to do, Jerry?"

"Hell, who knows? Play the horses most likely. How about you?"

"I think I might try writing."

"Yeah? No kidding? That's O.K. You make a lot of dough if you hit."

Everything was "O.K." with Jerry. It was neither good nor bad: it just *was*. If it looked appealing, one sampled it, put it on, made love to it, used it with full enjoyment and no question. If it was unappealing, one wished it luck.

"Good luck to you, Hal, with your wife and your life."

Since Hal could not exorcise the ghost of Jerry, he thought of the full-blown, sumptuous women Jerry would have loved had he lived; women with never a cold, but who employed every device of cosmetics to enhance their attraction, and who would not hesitate to use their intelligence to serve their womanhood. He thought of all the dance steps since the "Westchester" that Jerry would have mastered with facile grace. He thought of all the opportunities to make money that Jerry would have seized with uncomplicated directness, and of the pleasurable, uncomplicated ways that Jerry would have spent it. Married, no doubt, in time; with children; for there was no life experience that Jerry would have denied himself; and none that he would have clung to after it had ceased to please him.

As he thought of these things, there began to build up in Hal's mind an increment of unused time whose substance and size filled him with an old panic. This was the same panic that had afflicted him years ago, when he still had the major portion of his life to live, and the dread of not living it well had haunted his days and nights.

He had not lived it well — not at all — but it was not

the knowledge of failure that clutched at his throat. It was something else. Jerry? No, not Jerry. Millions of Jerrys had been slain, and if the quantity of their unlived lives had ever washed back over the world mankind would have been drowned long ago. No, it was not his own unheroic life nor Jerry's heroic death that created this sudden terror, but the chilling thought that at bottom it all came to the same thing, that none of it made the slightest difference.

But surely, *surely,* it must make a difference what men did. It was only the doing that distinguished the quick from the dead. It was only the speed of earth that held it to its course around the sun . . . The senseless terror increased, and Hal felt that at any moment the planet on which he stood might lurch, might fall back into the sun and be consumed. Something had to be done to hold the earth to its course . . . *something* . . .

"Stella!" he cried with unexpected suddenness.

Stella, seated at the desk at the checkout counter, literally jumped for fright.

"What!"

"I'm sorry," Hal said. "I didn't mean to startle you."

"Hal, you idiot!" Stella snapped, genuinely angry. *"Damn* you! You scared the life out of me. I thought you had a stroke or something. What is it?"

"I just had an idea."

"It had better be a good one."

"It is. Listen. What would you think of opening another store? We've got a successful operation here, and I don't think it's by pure accident. We've created an atmosphere, people like it. I know something about book merchandising by this time and we've got credit — "

"Are you serious?"

"Absolutely! Look, our debts are paid off. I know I'm good for a sizable loan at the bank. Suppliers have already told me they'll back me to the hilt if I want to expand. This store is very nice, but it's no more than a living. Why not make money? Why on earth not?"

Stella looked at her husband. Her pocketbook stood beside her on the desk, a white blossom of tissue flowering up from its open mouth. She plucked one and touched it to her nose.

"I have no objection to money, dear," she said. "None at all. But don't you think it's rather risky?"

"No," Hal answered, steady as a gyroscope with the spin of enthusiasm he had given himself. "We can incorporate. No matter what happens to the other store, it won't affect this one. And what can possibly happen? We know how to pick locations. We won't overextend the operation. It will be just a matter of repeating the experience of this store. Don't you think it's a good idea?"

"Yes-s," Stella said dubiously. "Yes, I suppose it is, but I thought — "

"You thought what?"

"I thought you were content with just *this.*"

"Yes, I know that's what you thought," Hal said. "And that's what I thought *I* thought. But should I be? Should I be content with just this?"

"Darling, that's such a peculiar way of putting it," Stella laughed. "You either are or you aren't. There's no morality involved. Only you can decide whether you're satisfied or not. Frankly, I'm a little surprised. You've never said anything about this before, but you must have been thinking about it. These ideas don't just come from the blue."

"This one did," Hal assured her. "The wild blue."

"Well," said Stella, "I don't want to throw cold water on it. We don't have to decide right away, do we? I mean, there's no desperate rush . . ."

"No — no desperate rush."

"We can talk about it," Stella recommended, looking not displeased with the prospect of talking about it.

"We can talk about it," Hal agreed. "It will take some talking."

Hal rid himself of the last of the books he was holding and returned to the stock room. There were many cartons still to be opened, but he felt no urgency about the job. The atmosphere of the stock room was tranquil, compounded of stillness and paper and dust. He slit open a carton and folded back the flaps. Then he scooped out a batch of books, holding them cradled in his arms, bringing them close to his nose and sniffing the friendly bouquet of wood pulp and printer's ink.

He knew they would never open another store. Stella didn't want it, and he couldn't blame her. She had been frightened too often to venture willingly one step beyond the known zone of safety. And in truth Hal wasn't sure that he wanted it himself. The fear that had panicked him into this proposal was passing, and he could no sooner see himself in the role of free-swinging entrepreneur than Stella could.

Perhaps Stella was right. Perhaps he was content with just this. That thought drifted mockingly through his mind as he turned toward the store, but as he viewed the vault of paperback books and Stella sitting there at the desk, aureoled against the front display window, Hal Newman felt neither contentment nor dismay but the inexorable order of the scene. It was as if this had been ordained from the day of his birth, and he had worked all these years to bring about the final consummation. Its perfection was its rightness, and recognizing this Hal at last accepted it.

As he passed from the stock room to the store, it occurred to Hal that the perfection of Jerry Kramer's life was that he had never once departed from the rightness of his style.

Come to the Fair

BOBBY DEMEREST sat cross-legged on the first landing and stared down at the screen door of the porch. Bobby was eleven years old and skinny as a stylite. He wore just the bottoms of his seersucker pajamas, and his eyes held a brooding, angry look. To be made to go to bed when voices in and out of the house leaped like jets of festive color was calculated cruelty and nothing less. He had fought well, employed the whole bag of tricks, but in the end his father had trampled bull-like among the tender shoots of his mother's psychology and ordered him off. So he had made his withdrawal in sullenness and now sat in the semi-darkness, his forehead pressed between two posts of the bannister, rebelliously awake.

Below was the large room which served as kitchen and dining room. To the left were the sink, the stove, the refrigerator, all lacquered blue by the moonlight which came through the kitchen window. In the center of the room was an oblique slash of yellow made by the porch light filtering through the screen door. The rest of the room was hidden in darkness.

Bobby listened to the voices on the porch with at best a half-hearted interest. As he listened, he watched the August-mad moths batter themselves against the globe of the porch light. He was tired and could easily have slept, but to go back to his own room would be a surrender of he knew not what point of honor.

"At this time of summer, I start wishing for fall," he heard his mother say. "Really, I've had enough heat."

"I have a distinct recollection . . ." his father began.

"Yes, I know," interrupted his mother. "I'm sure I must have longed for summer in February. It just seems to me that the seasons are overlong."

"Winter, perhaps," said Aunt Rhoda, "but not summer. I was made for heat. I think if I had the opportunity to live in the tropics . . ."

"Would you?" pounced Mr. Thompson, who visited his sister three houses away precisely on the weekends that Aunt Rhoda came to visit them.

"I would, indeed!" she answered, firmly. "I don't know if there are any statistics to prove this, but I feel sure that the nearer you get to the equator the happier people are. It's in the northern latitudes that you get progress and neurosis."

"How about the Eskimos?" asked Mr. Thompson. "They seem happy enough."

"Isn't that odd!" exclaimed Aunt Rhoda. "When you said 'Eskimos,' I instantly thought of them as tropical people."

Mr. Thompson laughed. "Perhaps what you admire is the primitive life," he said.

Thus the conversation went on in its empty fashion, accompanied by the clink of ice in glasses. For Bobby it was typical of this whole maddening summer at the shore. What seemed like several lifetimes ago, they had made the long automobile trip from the city, coming to this house which distilled its own resinous and hostile odors, and in which almost nude bodies perpetually paraded in a sheen of sun-tan oil, flopping sandals, and trailing bath towels.

He hated it. At least in the city when his parents had guests they would be gone in the morning. Here he had awakened many times to find some man snoring in a cot by the window in his room. And of course there was the matter of friends. He had none here. He wouldn't dream of making any. Donald was his only, his true friend, and he had been compelled to part with him because of the crazy notion on the part of his parents that he would enjoy himself at this place.

Far from enjoying himself, his days were a stretch of bright desolation broken intermittently by a weekend invasion of adults. Being an only child, he wasn't even afforded the diversion of sibling strife. There was just the beach club which his father had joined where there were a pool, handball courts, a pavilion, and a section of private beach. He went there every day with a ball and gloves, but he seldom found someone to play with. The kids of his own age were a strangely inert breed who trooped after their mothers like tame cats, and the few men who might be around during the week played with a pounding fury that squelched even the hope of participation.

Condemned to this isolation, he became a listener and a watcher. He found corners where he could observe without being observed. At the beach club, he had his private post atop the lockers. He had found it one day when, flayed by boredom, he climbed a wooden ladder at the side of the pavilion simply because it was there. Having climbed it, he found himself on the roof of the pavilion, directly behind which were the lockers. The roofs of the lockers themselves were flat, incapable of hiding a mouse, except for the first row which carried out the decorative green trellis edging the pavilion. Here, flat on his belly against the hot tar, he could peer through the cubicles formed by the trellis and into that open space at the top of the locker doors.

For the most part, he saw nothing. When he did see something, it was only heads. The head of a woman applying makeup. The head of a man talking to himself. But he would watch for hours, because sometimes he would witness an anomaly of behavior which left him in a state of pure wonderment.

Like the time he saw that lady perform her curious pantomine before the mirror. He had been watching her comb her hair, her expression set routinely to the purpose of her task. Suddenly, as though something in the mirror had moved her to love, her face was transformed into a mask of indescribable longing. Eyes half closed, she moved slowly toward her own reflection until her lips touched the surface of the glass. There they lingered for several yielding and passionate seconds. As suddenly as it had come, so it passed, and she briskly finished the combing of her hair, opened the locker door, squinted in the sunlight, waved to someone at the end of the row of lockers, and strode off, slapping her bathing cap against her heavy thigh with masculine abruptness.

It puzzled him, that scene. It came back to him at odd moments, and the feeling that prevailed in him was that he had witnessed something less funny than it seemed.

"This ice bucket is a puddle," Bobby heard his mother say.

"I don't think the trays have had time to freeze," said his father.

"I'll see," said Aunt Rhoda.

"Let me," offered Mr. Thompson.

"We do need another bottle of ginger ale," said his mother.

"I'll get the ice cubes, and you can bring the ginger ale," said Aunt Rhoda.

They came through the screen door, one merged silhouette.

"The bottles are under the sink, aren't they?" Aunt Rhoda called, her voice beginning to hush.

"Yes," came back.

Bobby waited for the spurt of light as the refrigerator door opened. He watched his aunt pry loose the tray.

"Not quite," he heard her whisper. "The centers are still watery, but it will have to do."

The refrigerator door closed, and that corner of the room was plunged into an even deeper darkness. There was a montage of sounds: bottles rattling; the bony crack of ice cubes being broken from their nests; the rustle of bodies. Bobby wasn't sure he heard the word, it was so low and furtive.

"Darling!"

There by the window, like black cutouts against dark blue pasteboard, he saw the profiles of Aunt Rhoda and Mr. Thompson.

"No, Ralph, please," murmured his aunt.

"Darling!" Mr. Thompson repeated.

"Lipstick," cautioned Aunt Rhoda.

"Rhoda, Rhoda, Rhoda!" anguished Mr. Thompson, running the syllables together in a perfectly absurd fashion.

Aunt Rhoda then made a crooning, dream-like noise. "Sweet," she said. "We can't. The others . . ."

The bulky silhouette disengaged. Aunt Rhoda and Mr. Thompson became two people. The screen door opened and Aunt Rhoda walked out first, saying in an astonishingly businesslike voice:

"I'm afraid these ice cubes are hollow."

"So is life," his father returned, cheerfully.

"Shall I resent that?" said his mother.

"Why, I think you should," said Aunt Rhoda.

Bobby didn't wait to hear any more. He got up and groped his way back to his room. He stood hesitant in the darkness, not quite knowing what final act to commit that would signalize his disgust and emptiness. He felt his way along the bureau, the wall, and came across his box of things which stood in the corner. He reached down and picked up the fielder's glove he had never had occasion to use here. Slipping it on his hand, he punched the center to a smooth, symmetrical hollow. Then he brought the glove up to his face and breathed in the oil-rubbed leather as if it were a field of flowers.

At last he got into bed, sliding one arm beneath the pillow and turning on his right side. He knew he would soon sleep for there was a drone of somnolence in his head. Before sleep, however, he wanted to think once of the scene in the kitchen. He wondered what strange complicity his aunt and Mr. Thompson shared that they should breathe such hasty guilt at each other in a darkened room. Particularly he thought of Mr. Thompson's abandoned little cry of *"Rhoda, Rhoda, Rhoda!"* and it shocked him in an indefinable way that one adult should utter and the other accept so ludicrous a sound. Fascinatedly, Bobby repeated it to himself, aping the painful cadence of Mr. Thompson's voice. "Rota-rota-rota-rota . . ." he chanted to himself, until the name lost its meaning and form and became no more than a string of verbal beads threaded swiftly and mindlessly by the movement of his lips.

The following day, Sunday, was savagely bright. Not a cloud, not a wisp of haze to obscure the polished brass of the sun.

"I've got a tennis date," Mr. Demerest announced, as soon as breakfast was over. He cast a look at Bobby. "Want to come?"

Bobby shook his head. "I'm going to the pool," he said, hoping the refusal would burn a mordant scar in his father's heart. Dearly would he have loved to go, even if only to watch, but true belligerents accept no compromise. The war he had declared against his father and mother for bringing him to this friendless place had in common with real war that it could lose the ardor of its original cause without lessening the intensity of combat.

"Not alone," ruled Mrs. Demerest. "You'll have to wait for me."

"You take hours and hours and hours," Bobby protested, his voice rising dangerously.

"Ralph and I are going to the club," said Aunt Rhoda. "He can come with us. I'll keep an eye on him."

"I don't want him near the water for at least another hour," said Mrs. Demerest.

"I'm gonna play handball anyway," growled Bobby.

Mr. Thompson arrived shortly after, looking rather silly in white duck shorts and a striped jersey. The three of them left for the beach club, and on the way there Mr. Thompson had an insane fit of jollity. He sang a patter song from Gilbert and Sullivan replete with gestures and an English accent. Aunt Rhoda thought it hilarious and laughed much too loud and too long. Clearly they were both afflicted with the same disease of irrationality. Bobby was relieved when they reached the club and he could separate from them.

He went directly to the handball courts and saw in a glance that there would be no game for him today. The usual Sunday contingent of thick-muscled men were out there, batting the small, hard, rubber ball against the wall with a force that would have shattered every bone in his hand. Disgruntledly he threw his own ball against the wall of one of the vacant courts a few times and then left. He walked to the pavilion and from there could see his aunt and Mr. Thompson indolently stretched on beach chairs. He knew that if he joined them they would ask him a few spuriously cheerful questions and then go back to their deadly conversation. Without another thought, he turned and marched straight to the ladder and climbed to the roof of the pavilion.

The tar of the roof was so hot that it fairly scorched his flesh when he stretched out behind the green trellis. After a few moments, he got used to it and there was a voluptuous pleasure in feeling the heat penetrate his bones. He lay first on his back, his eyes closed against the glare of the sun. Then, slowly, like a chicken on a spit, he turned over on his stomach, propped his chin on his hands, and looked down through the squares of the trellis.

There was nothing. The lockers within his view were all closed, and only a voice further down humming in a low, preoccupied way gave evidence of human habitation. The core of discontent within him was untouchable, but he allowed himself for the moment to enjoy the smell of tar and the drowsy ambience of heat. He laid his head on his arm, closed his eyes, and began to sing the song he had learned that last term in school:

> *"The sun is a-shining to welcome the day,*
> *Heigh-ho, come to the Fair. . . ."*

He first heard their voices as they came up the side aisle, a man and a woman, and by the time he raised himself to peer through the trellis they were in sight. They walked slowly, as if performing a ceremony in tribute to the woman's grotesque appearance. The smock-like dress she wore ballooned out around her stomach, and she swayed like an overloaded haycart on a bumpy road. Bobby studied her face to see if she wore an expression suitable to her hideous condition — intense depression, anguish — but instead he saw a pleasant round face, sparkling eyes, and black hair neatly and simply combed. Beside her, the man looked as lean and brown as a coolie.

She was carrying a child in her belly. This Bobby knew, but like all the information tendered by his mother it raised many more questions than it answered. He could only think of himself in a similar predicament — bearer or borne — and either situation filled him with horror.

"The locker's like a steam bath," said the man. "Let it air out for a moment."

The woman leaned back against the wall and put both her hands flatly against her swollen belly.

"It must be sleeping," she said.

"I wish the hell we'd get back to the city," the man said, irritably. "Supposing you're off by a couple of days. I wouldn't trust them to remove a splinter in the hospital they've got here."

"You're not going to be the traditional male, are you, darling?" asked the woman.

She entered the locker and lowered herself to the bench like a blind man groping for a seat. She uttered a luxurious and weary sigh.

"Put on my sandals, you poor man," she said.

The man kneeled and removed the flat-heeled shoes and socks she was wearing. As he began to put on the beach sandals, the woman gave a little cry of amusement.

"That was a fifty yard punt," she said.

The man put his hand on the woman's stomach.

"*Hey!*" cautioned the woman, nodding her head toward the aisle.

The man leaned backward and looked both ways.

"There's no one around," he said, and returned his hand to her stomach.

They both remained motionless, heads inclined sideways, two people listening to the tick of a hidden clock. Suddenly the man's hand jerked away — precisely as if he had touched a hot stove.

"The beast!" he said.

"Oh . . . oh . . . oh!" The woman laughed ponderously, spasmodically, writhing about in unbearable glee. "I . . . can't . . . laugh," she gasped.

"Well, stop, for God's sake!" said the man.

The woman's laughter subsided, and she gave both her hands to the man, who pulled her gently to her feet. They gathered their beach chairs, their beach umbrella, their draw-string bags and towels, and, closing the door, they walked away in the same ceremoniously measured pace.

Bobby turned over on his back and lay quietly for several moments. Then he got up and began to walk toward the ladder in a swaying waddle.

That evening Mr. Thompson came to dinner. Bobby suspected something was up. His mother had spread the linen tablecloth instead of the usual plastic one. A big bowl of flowers was placed in the center of the table. There was a palpable hum of excitement in the air.

"What's the matter?" he asked.

"Nothing, dear," answered his mother, smiling mysteriously at his father. "Mr. Thompson is coming to dinner."

Aunt Rhoda came down, fastening an earring into place. Dressed in a blue gown that showed her tanned shoulders to advantage, she presented a picture of nervous radiance. Alternately she pressed the fingers of one hand with those of the other.

"You look lovely," said his mother.

Aunt Rhoda gave a quick, doubtful smile. She turned to his father, who was trying to fit a dark bottle into the refrigerator.

"George," she began, uncertainly, "I have a favor to ask . . ."

"At your service," he answered, brightly.

"That's precisely what I mean," said Aunt Rhoda. *"Don't* be at my service. You're a sweet, noble man, but, please, this once, no heavy-handed humor, no speeches, no epigrams. Just let things take their course naturally."

Mr. Demerest raised his eyebrows and shrugged innocently. "Silent as the tomb," he said.

"What's the *matter?"* Bobby demanded again, feeling sure there was going to be another of those secretive parties whose preparations went on under his nose but from whose joys he was eternally excluded.

"There is nothing the matter," repeated his mother. "I just want you to be on your very best behavior tonight. If you'll promise me . . ."

"You're going to have a party, that's what," Bobby began, his voice shrill with accusation.

"Why, yes, we may have a party," said his mother, "but you'll be there."

"Oh, Lord," murmured Aunt Rhoda, "it's going to be ghastly. I just know it is."

So it went, taut as a wire, everyone busy with some concern that stayed just out of sight and sound. Mr. Thompson arrived at last, dressed in a white jacket, and looking, oddly, as if he were afflicted with the same nervous disorder. His father mixed highballs, and he and Mr. Thompson went out on the porch for a while. Then dinner was finally ready, and they sat down at the table and plunged their spoons into the grapefruits as if *they* were the ghosts that were haunting them.

"Before you know it summer will be over," said his father, inconsequently.

Mr. Thompson raised his head like an animal scenting danger. He held his spoon with a chunk of grapefruit in it midway between the table and his mouth.

"Since you are Rhoda's nearest relatives," he began, and the words were like a dreadful invocation for everyone became deadly still, "I guess — well, I guess you should be the first to know . . ."

Mr. Thompson was somehow prevented from finishing what he had to say. Or maybe he did say it, but whatever it was it became completely tangled in the melee that followed.

"Oh, Rhoda!" cried his mother, getting up and kissing Rhoda.

"Well, Ralph . . . !" said his father, getting up and pumping Mr. Thompson's hand.

"It was only this afternoon. . . ." said Mr. Thompson.

"Only this afternoon," chided Aunt Rhoda.

"This calls for a celebration, and I just happen to have . . ." said his father, going to the refrigerator.

"Ralph, I can't tell you how delighted . . ." cried his mother, kissing Mr. Thompson.

Bobby looked on this riot of movement, heard this truncated gibberish, and felt within him the first bubble of an uncontrollable ferment. Something wonderful had happened. A great joy. It shone in everyone's face. But he was never, never to know. Life was a marvelous cake surrounded by the impenetrable bodies of adults.

"Well, Bobby," said his mother, "congratulate Mr. Thompson. You're going to have a new uncle. Shake his hand."

Reluctantly Bobby stuck out his hand, and Mr. Thompson seized it in his great, moist palm. It was a most undignified grasp, trapping all his fingers in an awkward, painful way.

"Lemme *go!"* snarled Bobby, jerking back his hand.

"Bobby!" came from his mother. "What on *earth* is the matter with you? You apologize to Mr. Thompson this instant!"

"Oh, that's all right," said Mr. Thompson, attempting to put his hand on Bobby's head.

Bobby took a vicious swipe at the hand.

"Lemme alone, you jerk!"

Mr. Demerest moved in like a policeman.

"Now, that's enough from *you!* Up to your room! March!"

Bobby retreated before his father's earnest threat. He turned around and stumbled to the staircase in a burning haze of tears. He climbed the staircase, trying to stomp a hole in each step, and when he arrived at his room he slammed the door behind him, flung himself on the bed, and screamed his fury into the cool, muffling chenille.

How long he cried, he did not know. Vaguely he remembered a knocking at the door, and a voice (it sounded like Aunt Rhoda's) asking a question he did not hear and would not answer if he did. When he got up from the bed and walked to the window, the sky was almost black. Pretty soon, he knew, his mother would come, and, after some more scolding, she would take him downstairs to finish his dinner.

He wasn't angry anymore. Tears had dissolved his anger into melancholy. He put his elbows on the windowsill and rested his chin on his hands. Slowly, sadly, as if it were a dirge, he sang to himself:

> *"The folks are all singing so merry and gay,*
> *Heigh-ho, come to the Fair. . . ."*

He could see them, the fabled folks, dressed in some sort of costume and singing a clandestine song not meant for his ears.

> *"All the stalls on the green*
> *Are as fine as can be,*

With trinkets and tokens
So pretty to see.
So it's come then, maidens and men,
To the Fair in the pride of the morning."

What stalls? What *were* stalls? And trinkets and tokens? And what, for that matter, was a Fair? Why were things so everlastingly shrouded in mystery? And what morning would he ever awaken to join the maidens and men who sang in the pride of their knowing?

Summer Place

He couldn't remember having been sent on the errand, or what he was supposed to buy, but there he was in the supermarket, standing in line. In front of him was Mrs. Stevens, the tall lady with the sick boy who lived in the shingle house on the other side of the hedge, and she was talking to the clerk in her stiff-lipped manner. He felt none of his usual impatience to get out, but the person behind him kept pushing at that one spot on his shoulder, whispering, "Hey . . . hey . . . hey." He tried to shift his position, but the hand remained, pushed him harder, and finally a voice whispered in his ear . . . "You wanna go, or not?"

Dick opened his eyes and felt his heart pound against the mattress for fright.

"What's the matter?" he whined.

His brother Walt straightened up and stepped back. He was wearing just his shorts, and his tanned body looked threatening in the yellow light. Beyond Walt, on the shelf, the little hurricane lamp was lit. It gave their room an atmosphere of crisis.

"It's five-thirty," Walt said. "You forget?"

He didn't speak in a whisper, but his voice was carefully

modulated. Then Dick remembered. He remembered the previous evening, the conversation just before sleep, the astonishing offer.

"No," he answered, "I didn't forget. Shall I get dressed now?"

Walt nodded. "Sure you're not too sleepy?" he asked. "Maybe you'd rather sleep?"

Dick kicked off the sheet and put both feet on the straw matting. He groped for his socks and moccasins. "No," he said. "I'm O.K." He found a sock, but his fingers betrayed him. They fumbled drunkenly, unable to perform the simplest task. Walt came over and took the sock out of his hand.

"You don't need socks," he said. "Just put on the moccasins."

Dick slipped his feet into the moccasins and began to shuffle out of the room.

"Where are you going?" Walt asked.

"To the bathroom," Dick mumbled.

Walt had his jeans on by this time. He stood there regarding Dick, his hands on his hips.

"To brush your teeth, I suppose?" he asked.

"No," said Dick.

Walt shook his head. "Anything you got to do you can do after we get clear of the house. You go in the bathroom now and start splashing around, and you'll have everybody up. What kind of soldier are you?"

"I'm no soldier," Dick said, resentfully. He felt then like asserting what he was usually at great pains to minimize. The seven-year spread of their ages seemed vast in the half-lit room. Walt loomed big and was full of a harsh impatience. Being treated at this sinister hour with the equality he always campaigned for made him wish to crawl into his nine years as into a soft blanket.

How differently his mother or father would have treated him! They would have coaxed him out of sleep with patience and tenderness. They would have taken him by the hand and led him to the bathroom so that he wouldn't stub his toe, or, as was once shamefully the case, use the clothes hamper for a toilet.

"Well, are you going to stand there all day?" Walt asked. "Get dressed."

Dick took off his pajamas and reached for his clothes. Walt crossed the room and drew aside the curtain. A queer shade of gray entered the room. Dick had never seen its like before. "This is dawn," he thought, repeating the word Walt had used last night, and he was taken with a shiver of guilt and terror. He knew they were doing something their parents would be furious about. He wasn't scared for himself, because his age was his shield, but the inevitable showdown between Walt and Dad showed on the horizon like a lightning-lit thunderhead.

Instinct told him that this whole business was related somehow to last night's argument. He thought the word "argument" to himself as he might have "walk" or "supper." It aroused no particular reprobation in his mind. Arguments were part of his parents' mode of life. They started out of the ripeness of time and circumstance, were conducted in his presence with formal coldness, and then, when it was assumed that he was asleep, they would rise like surf on a windy day, sending muffled breakers against his closed door and occasionally casting up a word white with violence.

Being at this summer place decreased the number of arguments but increased the intensity of each. His father came out only for weekends. Saturday night there was usually a big party, and on Sunday an argument that started in the early afternoon and continued until late at night. Last night, Saturday, there was no party. During the week, Dick had heard his mother tell his father over the telephone that his precious customers could do their swilling elsewhere one week. All arguments revolved around Dad and his customers in one way or another. His mother hated them . . . "every gross, stupid, paralyzing one of them!"

"You like good clothes, don't you?" was his father's retort. "And a choice spot on the Cape for the summer?"

"I'd live in a hovel not to endure those pigs!"

"Keep it up. You may get your wish."

"At least I'll be able to choose my own company."

"Your own company! Who? Fakes? Queers? Leeches? Why don't you get smart? They'd drop you in a minute if it wasn't for my money."

Of the many inexplicable things about his family, Dick counted the behavior of Walt at these moments as the darkest and most troubling. Having absolute freedom of movement, Walt would nevertheless choose the environs of the house whenever an argument started. Dick would find him pacing the porch, roaming up and down the staircases, moving about, generally, like a caged tiger. Friends would drive up and honk their horns, and Walt would go out and exchange a few words with them. After a moment, they would drive off and Walt would return to the house to resume his pacing. There was nothing to be read from those brown eyes which at other times gave such clear signals of mood. Like the tiger's, they showed neither hatred nor fear, but only a cold, passionless withdrawal.

Last night Walt had paced and paced while the voices rose

and fell in tireless monotony. And finally he came into the room they shared and switched on the hurricane lamp. Dick was not asleep, but he pretended to be. By sound he followed Walt's movements about the room. He visualized him throwing his jeans over a chair, stripping off his T-shirt, going to the closet and fussing with his fishing tackle. When he heard the creak of Walt's ship-style bed, Dick opened his eyes.

Walt was stretched out, his hands folded beneath his head. Against the dark paneling of the wall, his profile showed as sharp and immobile as stone. There was no flicker of life on his features, but Dick knew that his brother was *listening*. He listened with his whole body, with all his nerves, as though to lose a decibel of the vicious rhythm would destroy him. And when the voices were no longer to be heard, Walt still listened, as one listens for the pebble dropped into a bottomless well.

Dick watched his brother, wondering what terrible secret lay at the heart of his silence. Outside a muted chorus of crickets and one shrill leader began to counterpoint each other. Dick's attention strayed to the seesaw of sound, letting it rock his mind like a hammock until sleep was only a step away.

"You awake, Dick?"

The words flared like a sudden light. At first Dick thought that someone else had uttered them. Once in bed, Walt hardly ever spoke. And when there had been an argument, it was as if all speech had been sealed in an iron vault.

"Dick?"

It *was* Walt, still lying so, with his hands under his head.

"Yeah?" Dick answered.

"I'm going fishing tomorrow," Walt said to the ceiling. "Real early. At dawn. You wanna come?"

"Me?"

"You're always crying you wanna go fishing with me, so here's your chance. Mr. Mills down at the wharf says the fluke run early. Yes or no?"

"Did Mom say it's O.K.?"

"I didn't ask her."

Then Dick knew that Walt was putting him to a test, and that if he failed, Walt would consign him to hopeless infancy for all time.

"I'll come," Dick said.

"O.K.," said Walt. "I'll wake you up." And he turned over on his side.

They left the house through the kitchen, pausing there to put cold cuts and bread and fruit into a paper bag. Walt held the screen door so it wouldn't bang. They walked to the tool shed where Walt kept his bait — angleworms bedded in seaweed. Dick carried one of the fishing rods with studied nonchalance, but all the while delighting in the weight and spring of it. After picking up the bait, they started down the dirt road that led to the inlet.

It was a warm morning, but long, nervous shivers coursed through Dick's body. Everything seemed altered in the pale blue light. The trunks of the trees were almost black, and every leaf stamped its green intensity in the air. Dick walked behind Walt in a kind of dew-soaked lethargy. Deliberately he would put his face in the way of an overhanging branch and let the chilly moistness trail across his eyes, his cheeks. Once, when a pheasant startled him with its loud thrashing, Dick turned his gaze away from Walt and accidentally ran the tip of the fishing rod into his brother's back. He halted, waiting to be accused of clumsiness, but

Walt merely glanced over his shoulder and continued walking.

The inlet surprised Dick. Beach, water, wharf, everything seemed to lie under a spell. No ripple or noise disturbed the vast serenity. On each piling of the wharf sat a motionless gull, its beak buried in its feathers. It was as if they had intruded upon a scene not meant for their eyes, a gigantic slumber they would be rash to disturb.

Their rowboat, a gift from Mother to Walt and fancifully named Nausicaä by her, was tethered to the beach with a lead weight. Walt walked straight to the boat and put in all his gear. He motioned to Dick to do the same. Then he removed his moccasins and rolled up his jeans.

"Get in," he ordered Dick.

Dick got in, and Walt shoved off, hopping in himself when the boat was afloat. As soon as he was in, Walt picked up the oars and began to row. He rowed with an easy, strong stroke, dipping the blades just right and making the boat leap ahead with each pull.

"I'm going to row to deep water," he said. "It'll take about fifteen minutes. You hungry?"

Dick shrugged. He hadn't thought about food, but now that Walt mentioned it Dick felt his stomach twitch. He reached for the brown paper bag and began to investigate.

"Make me a ham sandwich," Walt said.

"There's no butter," said Dick, after rummaging around.

"Tough," said Walt. "Didn't you ever eat a sandwich without butter?"

They each had a sandwich and an apple, and then Walt continued rowing out past the wharf, into deep water. The sun was up now, turning the water to jade. A blunt-nosed trawler came toward them, and two fishermen in canary-colored oilskins waved to them as they passed. Dick waved back.

"I guess this is all right," Walt finally announced, and began to tie the extra length of rope to the lead weight. He tossed the weight overboard and played out the rope. "Can you bait your own hook?" he asked Dick.

"Uh-huh," said Dick, but when it came to cutting the wiggling worms and impaling them on the hook, he made a queasy mess of it. Walt took it over and baited both their hooks.

"Cast out," Walt instructed. His own cast described a clean arc, but Dick's snapped short and plopped in the water.

"That's O.K.," said Walt. "It doesn't make a difference."

The waves of the trawler reached them then, and their boat rose and dipped, rose and dipped. Dick looked at Walt, wondering whether he could risk a smile. Before he could decide, however, it was Walt who smiled, a rather awkward, reticent smile that seemed to take the whole strange morning into account.

"Dad's going to raise hell when we get back," he said.

"Maybe he'll see the boat gone at the beach, and he'll know we went fishing," Dick offered, hopefully.

"Sure," Walt said, ironically. "That'll square everything." His gaze went out toward their lines, and then quickly back to Dick, where it rested in a half-humorous way for a moment before he spoke. "Do you think a bell is going to ring when you've hooked one?" he asked.

Dick shot a wild glance at his float and saw it bob under once — twice. Panicked, he gave a tremendous heave on his rod and began to reel in. "That's the way," Walt said, calmly. "Rip it out of his mouth." He took the rod away from Dick, reeled it in, rebaited the hook, and cast out again. "Now, look," he explained, "when you've got a nibble, you give it five seconds, and then you pull like this . . . see? Just enough. Think you can do that?"

Dick nodded, and Walt handed the rod back to him. He then reached into his jeans and pulled out a crushed pack of cigarettes. He lit a match and cupped it expertly in his hands. Dick looked steadfastly at his float as his brother applied the flame to his cigarette. Walt's smoking was not just simple disobedience; it was a breach of honor. "I know you can smoke as much as you please behind my back," their mother had said. "I have no way of stopping you. But I'd rather you didn't. I'd rather you would wait until you're eighteen before you start. Can I have your promise on that?" Walt had given his promise, and if he broke it on occasion it was only because that occasion wanted some equalizing act of dishonor. Dick noticed that Walt smoked on mornings after a bad fight.

"You hear anything last night?" Walt suddenly asked.

"You mean the crickets?" asked Dick.

Walt shook his head. "No, I don't mean the crickets."

"Hear anything where?" Dick asked. "In the house?"

"Jesus, you can be such a stupid little bastard," Walt said, wearily. "Of course in the house. Where do you think I mean — in Africa?"

"You mean Mom and Dad?" Dick said, uncertainly. They had never spoken of it before. It was there, unalterably, from the beginning of time, like the gold-fretted, antique clock his mother took with her wherever they made their residence. And it was, however wrong, stamped with a higher rightness by reason of its familiarity.

"I mean Mom and Dad," said Walt.

"They were having an argument," Dick stated.

Walt lifted his pole, waited, then reeled in some line. "That's right," he said. "An argument. I'm surprised you know it has a name. You usually look six million miles away whenever they square off. Talk about bliss!" The mingled contempt and anger on his face dropped swiftly, as though a sudden voice had counseled him. He spoke again, quietly. "They've been arguing a long time. Long as I can remember. If it's not about people, then it's about things; if it's not about things, then it's about places. They have a real talent for it. By the law of averages, you'd think they'd agree about something. But they never do!"

Dick wondered whether he was expected to say something. He would have liked to offer a helpful suggestion, not for his sake, or for his parents', but for Walt, who looked isolated in his hurt. He could do nothing, however, but stare at an oarlock and feel a resentment against his mother and father.

"It's no one's fault," Walt went on. He sat hunched forward, his gaze on the water. A slight breeze had come up, and a pleasant, liquid sound caressed the boat. "I think you ought to understand that it's no one's fault. Dad has his good points; Mom has hers. They just don't get along, that's all."

Dick tried to be everything at once: glum, sagacious, sympathetic, angry. If he could make his face a composite of all things, Walt might find a portion of the one needful to the moment. He promised himself a program of coercion. Hunger strikes, irregularities, disappearances, all sorts of strange eruptions whenever an argument took place. The power of frailty swelled in him, and he knew for a certainty he could bring his parents to their knees with this most versatile of weapons.

"Suppose," Walt asked, making the question sound innocuous, "suppose you had to live with either Mom or Dad, which one would you pick?"

Dick shrugged. "I don't know," he said.

"Well, which one do you like better?"

"I like them both."

Walt bit the corner of his lip. He played his line for time. "Sure," he said. "I know you like them both, but don't you like one just a little bit more than the other?"

"Which one do you like better?" Dick asked.

"It doesn't make a difference which one I like better," Walt said. "I can take care of myself."

"I can take care of myself, too," Dick retorted.

Walt turned his gaze away from the water and looked at Dick. "All right," he said. "I like Dad better."

Dick had never known his brother deliberately to lie — even when the moral stain of the lie would be infinitesimal compared to the explosive consequences of telling the truth. But he was lying now. Dick knew it, and that knowledge made him all caution. A shadow of significance touched the edge of his mind.

"I like Dad, too," he said.

"Better than Mom?"

Dick was silent.

Walt flipped his cigarette into the water. They both watched it ride on the ripples.

"Look," said Walt, "Mom and Dad are going to get a divorce. That's what they were talking about last night. Do you know what a divorce is?"

Dick nodded his head.

"Good," said Walt. "At least I don't have to explain that. They're going to be real clever about it. They're going to feed you the idea with an eyedropper — a little each day. That's Mom's jerky psychology. Instead of giving you the whole business all at once, she's going to 'accustom' you to it. Well, O.K., now you're accustomed. You don't have to wonder what the hell they're talking about when they start working on you."

Dick kept his eyes riveted on the oarlock. Once, to cure him of fear of the dark, Walt had dragged him to the threshold of a darkened room. He had kicked and screamed and, at the last, bit Walt's hand so hard that it bled.

"What's a divorce?" he asked.

Walt's face clouded with anger. "For Pete's sake! You just told me you knew what a divorce is."

"What's a divorce?" Dick repeated, sullenly.

"A divorce is when two people separate. Mom and Dad are going to separate. They're going to live in different houses."

"Where are you going to live?" Dick asked.

"With Dad."

"Where?"

"How do I know? Somewhere. In a house."

"Where am I going to live?"

"With Mom."

"Will I ever see you?"

"Sure. We can see each other as much as we like. The whole business is just for Mom and Dad's sake. They're not happy together. Now, listen, you gotta promise me that you won't tell them that I told you. I only told you because I didn't want you to get the same slow poison I got. If you tell them, so help me God, I'll never speak to you again!"

"I won't tell," said Dick.

They stayed out on the water until the sun was almost directly overhead. Walt caught three flatfish that churned the water when they came to the surface, flashed agonizingly in the sun, and then lay panting their life out on the floor of the boat. When they were dead, Walt strung them together and hung them over the side in the water.

"That'll keep them fresh," he explained.

They ate the rest of the food, and Walt smoked two more cigarettes. Finally Walt looked at his watch and said, "I guess we better get back." He hauled in the anchor and set the oars in the locks. As soon as he began to row, Dick reached out with both hands and seized his wrist.

"What's that for?" Walt asked.

Dick said nothing. He pulled at his brother's wrist with dumb, maniacal strength.

"Cut it out!" Walt snapped.

But Dick held on, his eyes sightless and unheeding. The rim of his compressed lips was white with the strain. Walt released the oar and tried to free his arm — but without violence, without anger.

"What's the matter, Dick?" he asked, quietly.

Dick didn't answer. He only held on as though all time could be stayed if only he could stay it now. Then Walt twisted his wrist, and Dick realized that his strength was not enough. He let go. Walt reached out and put his hand compassionately on Dick's knee.

"We have to go back," he said.

People were on the beach when they got there, but not their parents. Walt carried the fishing rods and the three fish he had caught. They walked in silence up the little dirt road and came in view of the house. Their mother was standing on the porch wearing a red bandana and a red polka-dot dress. Their father was on the lawn, in shorts, his arm raised in a gesture that was half-salutation, half-menace.

Dick walked behind Walt, in an agony to know where to rest his gaze, until finally it fell on the three dead fish that dangled from the end of Walt's line. He watched them slowly revolve in the sunlight, one after the other, as if they were playing a stately, lunatic game.

Playgrounds, Parties, and the Primordial Molecule

WALTER awoke with a jolt when Ralph piped, matutinal and loud: "Where the hell is the bottle?"

Amy, also awakened, sucked in her breath, trying to judge whether that volume of sound penetrated the thin walls of the apartment.

"*Your* fault!" she whispered to Walter. "Entirely your fault!"

Walter, his feet on the floor, sat for a moment and tried to catch the shape of those evanescent profundities which came to him upon awakening. Always upon awakening — or just before falling asleep. He had tried to work the phenomenon up to some metaphysical law, but the thing fell apart for want of concrete examples. It was good as far as it went, but as far as it went wasn't even to first base on the way to the Absolute. . . . "Near the twilight zone of nothingness, our minds are prepared to receive the ineffable Truth of the Universe," he had once said. "What truth?" he was asked. "I said *ineffable,*" was his retort — but that was strictly a dodge.

"I've never heard him use that word before," Walter said.

"But he's heard *you* use it," Amy said. "Countless times."

At least Walter knew what bottle. Ralph, being three, was in the animistic stage. The distinction between things and people was clearly defined but not altogether separate. Things, of course, didn't answer back, but that didn't prevent one from having a nice talk. Last evening, before falling asleep, Ralph had a nice talk with an empty bottle of Chablis, '51. Inferior stuff. The Chablis was a variation of the milk bottles, the Seven-Ups, the Cokes, the Schweppes'. The child just took a shine to empty bottles, and he lined them up in front of him when he ate, deployed them on the floor when he played, and took them to bed with him. Last night, it was the Chablis, and when Walter went into his room about nine to remove it, Ralph was asleep with one arm over the bottle, like a miniature Bowery character.

"Young man," said Walter, entering Ralph's room, "I don't ever want to hear you use that word again."

Ralph was standing in his crib. He beamed. He stretched out his arms. He was ready for the day. Seeing that readiness, Walter felt as he did when, years ago, the sergeant ordered double time on the last mile of the twenty-mile hike — full kit.

"Where's Mommie?" Ralph asked.

"Sleeping," said Walter. "C'mon, we'll go in the kitchen." Walter carried his son into the kitchen. He looked at the fireman-red electric clock on the wall. "My God!" he whispered. "Six-thirty! . . . Now, look, boy!" he said to Ralph, his voice querulous with self-pity. "Now just you look, boy . . . !"

"What did the hippopotamus say to me?" Ralph asked, referring to last night's bedtime improvisation.

"He said you should go back to bed and sleep some more," Walter essayed.

Ralph said nothing. Walter sat Ralph in his chair. It was

his plan to get a glass of warm milk in the boy. That sometimes produced a soporific effect. But Ralph wasn't having any.

"Djoos," he said . . . Which meant "orange juice" . . . which meant no dice on getting back to sleep.

Walter squeezed orange juice. He looked as if sleep had crumpled him like a wad of paper. His mind was an inlet of quayside water: calm, oily, bearing on its surface the flotsam of dreams and memory.

Last night the Steins had dropped over at nine-thirty. Just like that. They talked until eleven-thirty. One would think that two hours of conversation would leave some residue. Walter tried, but all he could recall was a still life of Joe sitting in the easy chair, one leg slung over the armrest, eating pretzel sticks and drinking scotch highballs. Vera was caught in the pose of leaning towards Amy and saying something with bright inanity.

Quite suddenly the projector began to turn, and the whole Stein episode came to life. Joe Stein was being his phlegmatic, irritatingly down-to-earth self. If there was anything, Walter thought (using the back of the spoon to squash the pulp through the strainer) — if there was anything in life which dropped drops of acid into his soul, it was talking to the kind of guy who hung you up on a semantic peg when he bloody well knew what you were talking about. That was Joe Stein. That was Joe to a T.

The point he had tried to make was, perhaps, not a simple one, but certainly not beyond Joe Stein's Ph.D. brain. Man, for all the camouflage of his multiple civilizations and mountainous artifacts, was born of this earth; which was, in turn, born of that sun; which was, in *its* turn, part of the Galaxy, which . . . ad infinitum. Therefore, talking of art, or religion, or divine intuitions (which, as it happened, they *were* talking about), it was entirely conceivable that some unusually sensitive person might fetch out of the tension of his being a truth as significant as anything coming from test tubes or atom smashers.

"Such as what truth?" Joe asked.

"Such as Shakespeare," Walter answered.

Joe shrugged as a bookie might, being asked to consider the aesthetics of horseflesh.

"The unity of art approximates the unity of the cosmos," Walter tried again.

"Yuh got me," said Joe.

Now Joe knew what he was talking about. He deliberately took the stand that if you're going to equate A to B, you must have a common denominator for both. Which was all right for arithmetic, but when supposedly intelligent people got together and conversed . . .

"Where's Mommie?" Ralph asked.

Walter turned and looked at the beautiful round face of his son. It wasn't that he had forgotten his presence. That was impossible, since the child was right there. What had happened was that form of lateral blindness which is the result of concentrating too much on the center stage of one's own thoughts. In a flash of prescience, Walter saw his son twenty years hence . . . "What have you ever given me? . . . Whenever I tried to reach you, you were miles away, thinking your own thoughts . . . Did you ever concern yourself with what *I* was thinking . . . ?"

"Here," said Walter, setting the glass of juice on the Baby Butler and kissing the firm, fat, brown cheek, "is a delicious glass of orange juice. Do you want a couple of straws? Shall I make you a special thing with the straws?"

Ralph nodded. Walter telescoped one straw into the other and gave Ralph an absurdly long object to sip through. Ralph was delighted.

"How about a nice boiled egg?" Walter asked.

Ralph nodded without interrupting his sipping.

"O.K.," said Walter, "I'll make you a nice boiled egg, because an egg is very good for you — and I love you. Is that fair?"

He must never forget that nothing is lost in the mind of a child. The silent, somber father in the kitchen squeezing orange juice might very well become a focal point of the neurotic pattern . . . ("Well, Dr. Bergmanthal, my father was a rather uncommunicative man . . .")

"Who are you going to play with in the playground today?" Walter asked. "Do you think Jimmy will be there? How old is Jimmy anyway? Do you know how old Jimmy is?"

"Jimmy hits Katherine?" Ralph said.

"Does he? That isn't nice."

"What does the hippopotamus say?" Ralph asked.

"The hippopotamus says that Ralphie is a nice boy," Walter said.

"Is Jimmy a nice boy?" Ralph asked.

"Not if he hits Katherine."

"What does the hippopotamus say to Katherine?"

"I didn't know the hippopotamus was talking to Katherine," Walter said, depositing an egg in a pot of water and turning on the range.

"What's he say?" Ralph insisted.

"He says Katherine is a nice girl."

"Does the hippopotamus like me?"

. . . The trouble with talking to people like Joe Stein was that you got sucked into a conversational Gresham's Law.

Bad intentions drove out good motivations. Actually, when he came to think of it, he never did get around to making his point. His point, simply, was that the molecules of the human body contain the secret of the universe. They must. It was clear as the nose on Joe's face. Human substance is a refinement of earth, which goes back to the etcetera. Attraction, repulsion, suspension — the body (which of course includes the brain) is microcosm of the heavens. Therefore — and here was the point he was *really* trying to make — art is not a fortuitous, questionable thing, but the most direct and pure expression of the indwelling cosmos. (God! His brain was clear now!) . . . Beethoven and Rembrandt were not merely masters of form, but intuitionists of the Galactic Harmonies. Immortal, let us say, not merely because their creations are enjoyed by the ages, but because the unity and grace of their creations approximate a greater Unity and Grace! It is the primordial molecule within us which responds. . . .

Try to get all of that out in a conversation with Joe Stein! Or anyone else, for that matter. The first thing you get thrown at you is to define your terms.

"Daddy, you read me this story."

Ralph held a book in his hand. Ralph, seated in his chair, was banked on all sides with empty cans, empty bottles, books, toys, and uncategorized oddments.

"What story is that?" Walter took the book. "*Lollie the Llama,*" he read. "O.K.," said Walter, "Let's read this book." He read: " 'Once upon a time there was a llama by the name of Lollie . . .' "

Amy entered the kitchen just as Walter was finishing the story of Lollie the Llama.

"You're sitting with your bare feet again," she said. "You're never really rid of athlete's foot, and you insist upon traipsing around the house without slippers. I mean, after all, do you *want* Ralph, or me, to pick it up?"

Amy looked in the pot, which had been going at a slow boil for an unspecified time. She turned off the gas, ran cold water over the egg, cracked the shell, and then wrapped it in aluminum foil and put it in the refrigerator.

"Hard as a rock . . . Please go and put your slippers on — and for *Pete's* sake comb your hair! You look like something out of a Mack Sennett comedy."

"Aggressive this morning, aren't we?" Walter said.

"No, darling, not aggressive," Amy answered. "I don't see why men feel they have the right to go around looking a fright while women are expected to look like . . . like . . ."

"Sylphs in the Sunday supplement," Walter offered.

"Exactly."

"Which would make a good sequel to Lollie the Llama," Walter said, walking out of the kitchen.

Walter went to the bedroom and got his slippers and robe. He then went to the bathroom and brushed his teeth and combed his hair. Looking at his face in the mirror, he observed the faint smile of satisfaction on his lips. This morning, boiling an egg for his son, he had finally hit upon the shining argument. When lucidity comes, dear Horatio . . . All he had to do was remember the few salient features . . . the body as a microcosm of the heavens . . . Beethoven and Rembrandt, and that business about the harmonies . . . the primordial molecule responding to great art.

Walter returned to the kitchen looking quite neat.

"That's better," said Amy. "Just look at Daddy — doesn't he look handsome now?"

Ralph gave Walter a great look of wonder, saw nothing unusual, and went back to his endless arrangement of bottles.

"How are we going to divide the day?" Walter asked.

"You take Ralph down to the playground, while I clean up," Amy proposed. "I'll do part of the shopping this morning. You'll have to go out later this afternoon and get some special things from the German delicatessen. Those imported biscuits. I think I'll make that clam dip this evening. Everybody likes it, and it's easy to make."

"How many people are coming?" Walter asked.

"If I've told you once, I've told you a dozen times," Amy said, exasperatedly. "What do you think about when I talk to you? I'm not going to tell you again."

"Let's see . . ." Walter mused. "Harriet and George, naturally. Dottie and Jack, at a hazard. Anyone else?"

"Just your brother and sister-in-law."

"Oh . . . You know these Saturday night shindigs have been going down at a steady rate," Walter said. "In quality, I mean. I can remember the time when we used to talk about Proust and politics. Now it's all dirty jokes and how's-your-business-these-days. I think we've exhausted each other's pitiful store of borrowed ideas."

"People who talk about art incessantly suffer from arrested development," Amy retorted.

"True," said Walter. "Even very true. But coming of age is so boring. I grant you that one can't go on talking about Proust forever, but what's the alternative? Business conditions, real estate, and babies."

"I should think you would have had your fill last night with Joe Stein," Amy said.

Walter smiled. "Joe is a polarized jerk who shoots to the other end of an argument as a matter of principle. He'd rather be perverse than President. He knew *exactly* what I was talking about, but he'd be tortured on the rack before admitting it. Here — see if this makes any sense to you . . ."

"Daddy . . ." said Ralph.

"What, boy-o?"

"Daddy . . ."

"*Yes,* sweetie?"

"Daddy . . ."

"He doesn't want you to keep talking," Amy said.

"Well, that's too bad," said Walter. "That is just too bad."

"Daddy . . ."

"How would you like to be left out of a conversation?" Amy asked.

"I'll include him in," said Walter. "Here, son, see if this makes any sense to you . . . the human body is no more than a microcosm of the heavens. Within each of us dwells the divine sense of the universe. Therefore . . ."

"Mommie!" Ralph cried.

"Oh, cut it out, Walter!" Amy snapped. "Are you deliberately teasing the child?"

"Mommie . . ."

"Yes, my sweet pancake. Come on, I know what's troubling you. Let's leave Daddy to his divine universe."

Amy hoisted Ralph out of his chair. The child lay his head on his mother's shoulder. Carried out of the kitchen, he looked at Walter with eyes that were serene and ungloating in their victory.

The bacon crumbled under Walter's fork. He took a piece of bread and mopped it up together with the egg yolk. He slumped in his chair. His eyes squinted as if he were trying to bring into focus some far-distant object. It was a squint of the psyche, really, coming to the surface.

There must be, he was thinking, something to this waking up business. Upon the moment of awakening, in that instant before the mind has a chance to throw the switch on the circuits of its personal history, then, perhaps, it is at one with the perfect consciousness of pure being. Momentarily devoid of its accidental accretions, the mind is suddenly made aware of . . .

Walter groped. Walter strained. Like a man going hand over hand up a rope, Walter reached the limits of imagination. Exhausted and wistful, he gazed at the refulgent and unattainable peak — and once again descended.

The playground was a geometry of steel, concrete, and wood in which the young dashed about, miraculously avoiding broken bones. Ralph clambered up the slide, stood fearlessly at the top, turned around, and took a belly-whopper down — backwards. Walter caught him at the bottom.

"Let's play on the monkey-bars," Walter suggested.

"No!"

Ralph squirmed free, raced around to the steps, and repeated the performance.

"Let's play ball," Walter pleaded. "Here, I have the ball. C'mon, we'll have a nice catch."

"All right . . . Ooh! Here comes Katherine and her Daddy."

Ralph spread his arms and ran toward Katherine, screeching like a Sioux. Katherine, seeing him come, also spread her arms and ran, screeching at a different pitch. Both fathers stood rooted, envisioning blood and tears. Within a millimeter of impact, they stopped and looked at each other.

"I got a bottle in my house," said Ralph.

"I'm going on the swings," said Katherine.

They turned away from each other and walked back to their respective fathers.

" 'Morning," said Walter.

" 'Morning," said the other.

The two men were Saturday morning acquaintances. Katherine's father's name was Fred. Ralph and Katherine began to chase each other around in a slow circle.

"These kids," said Fred.

Walter smiled. "Yeah," he said.

"Miracle they don't break their necks."

"Mine almost did," said Walter. "Went up the slide there and did acrobatics on top. Don't know where they get their nerve."

Fred shook his head. "Crazy," he said.

"I think I'd go nuts if I had to be out here every day of the week," said Walter. "I don't know how the women do it."

"You can say that again," said Fred. "I'd go out of my mind."

The two men stood with their hands shoved in their pockets. They made a pretense of watching the children.

"My wife tells me a couple of delinquents tried to break open the coin box in the laundry room," said Walter.

"Yeah," said Fred. "Heard that. If I got my hands on the little bastards, I'd go over 'em with a lead pipe. Too much coddling these days. I don't go for this psychology stuff."

Walter wondered whether the man wasn't right. He himself felt murderous impulses against the blue jeans marauders, but he also distrusted someone who "didn't go for this psychology stuff."

"Oh, the world's in fine shape," he said.

"Yeah," said Fred. "Great."

"Hydrogen bombs," said Walter.

Fred glanced sideways at him. Walter, holding a rolled-up *Times* in one hand, slapped it into the palm of the other.

"See where they let go with another blast," he said.

"Uh-huh," said Fred. "Boy."

"Terrific," said Walter. "Gives me the creeps. I just can't conceive of that much power."

"Beats me," said Fred.

"Megatons," said Walter. "One million tons of TNT." He sighed, shook his head. "They say that's what's always happening on the sun."

"What's that?"

"Atomic explosions. They say the sun is just an atomic furnace."

"That so?" said Fred. "Could be."

"Yep," said Walter. "Supposedly that's how this miserable old earth came into being. One of those explosions lost its equilibrium and went shooting off into space. Stopped finally, began revolving around the sun, and cooled off."

Katherine's father shifted uncomfortably. It was written on his face in quiet, skeptical lines . . . "How the hell do *you* know, mister?" . . . He called to his daughter: "Hey, Kath, I thought you wanted to go on the swings."

"I'm going on the swings!" screamed Katherine.

"I want to go on the swings, Daddy," screamed Ralph.

"We have to go help Mommie in the store," Walter lied.

"No!" Ralph's face screwed up for tears. "Swings!"

Walter squatted and circled an arm around Ralph. "How about that piece of chocolate?" he wheedled.

Ralph weighed the two temptations. He looked at Katherine. "Gonna get chawklit," he said.

Walter walked out of the playground with Ralph. The mock orange trees in the chained-off area were in blossom.

That, too, thought Walter, was spoken for in the ball of flaming gas streaking around its parent sun. That and Katherine's father. Infinite and inexplicable were the ways of the primordial molecule.

The time between Ralph's dinner and the arrival of guests was a Sisyphean labor. Walter and Amy rolled up the dishes and magazines only to have toys and bottles roll down. Ralph, of course, was cranky, because he sensed he was being given the brush. Amy's face reflected the three-way tension of clam dip, getting dressed, and straightening up. Walter was seized with a vacuity as powerful as drunkenness.

"Read him one of his books," Amy instructed, her voice vibrating with control.

Walter took Ralph in hand and began to read a book. Ralph, his legs encased in bunny-cute pajamas, teed off and kicked the book half across the room. Walter faced Ralph around and gave him a lecture on cooperation. Ralph, slithering off like an eel, spat his detestation of "cooperation."

"All right, then, young man," said Walter. "To bed."

Ralph yelled as if he were being butchered. Walter laid the hand of authority on the bunny's backside. Rebellion became heartbreak, and Walter lifted Ralph out of his crib, hating all people who came to other people's houses on Saturday evening. He crooned in Ralph's ear, promising Persian gardens on the morrow. Ralph was finally placated with four Band-Aids wrapped around four separate fingers and an empty milk bottle.

The dinner dishes were cleaned. The exhaust fan blew the odor of liver-and-onions out of the kitchen. Toys were picked up off the floor, magazines and papers disposed of, and a preparatory calm settled over the apartment. Ralph went into the kitchen and opened a cabinet.

"We have half a bottle of scotch, three-quarters of gin, and some bourbon," he reported to Amy. "Do you think that will be enough?"

"You should know," said Amy, struggling upward into a dress. "Zip me up."

Walter zipped and went back to the kitchen. He tried carefully to calculate the drinking habits of his guests. He figured he would just make it if he took his brother circumspectly aside. Walter went back to the living room. He stuffed tobacco in his pipe and sucked on a flame.

The revelations of the day hung in his mind like smoke in an airless room. They had neither shape nor movement, but they were there . . . Beethoven and Rembrandt . . . the primordial molecule . . . Yes . . . A new idea began to germinate in Walter's mind: If it was true that the human composition contained within it the secret of the universe, was it not also possible that man has always been striving toward union with that secret? The hydrogen bomb, for example, not as the final boom, but the irresistible yearning of man to rejoin his origins. Yes! Walter perceived the link between philosophy and science in this sunburst of an idea. It was magnificent! . . . Man inexorably bent upon blowing himself back to his cosmic beginnings. It was — what was the word? — teleological . . . it was *the* teleological significance of man's history on earth.

Walter wondered whether it was possible, at his age and everything, to embark on a philosophical work. The title composed itself: The Teleological Significance of the Nuclear Age . . . "Since man first turned his eyes upward to observe the sun, the moon, and the stars, he has wondered . . ."

The doorbell rang.

"That's probably Dottie and Jack," Amy called. "I'll be out in a minute."

Walter opened the door. Dottie and Jack entered.

"Hi, Walt." . . . " 'Lo, Dottie, Jack. Come on in. Amy'll be out in a minute." . . . "How's Ralphie?" . . . "Hi, Amy, take your time." . . . "What'll it be? Scotch? Bourbon? Sit down, for goodness' sake. Oops, there's the door again. 'Scuse me." . . . "Hi, Walt." . . . "Come on in." . . . "Where's Amy? How's Ralphie?" . . . "Sit down, for goodness' sake . . ."

By nine, everyone was seated with a glass in hand or on a table. Peanuts were being nibbled. The prologue of parking difficulties and baby-sitters had been uttered. The accustomed hiatus presented itself. Walter spoke:

"You know," he said casually, "a thought occurred to me today . . ."

"Let me interrupt you for just a second, Walt," said George. "I know I'll forget this if I don't spill it right away. My lawyer called me up to tell me this one. Will what you had to say hold for a minute, Walt?"

"Sure," said Walt.

"Well," said George, "here was this beautiful blonde going cross-country on a Greyhound bus . . ."

Walter sat with his scotch and soda held before his face. Slowly he revolved the glass. Pinpoints of light exploded in the amber liquid, betokening immutable laws in the eternal quest for unity.

Mr. Isaacs

OLD Mr. Isaacs sits by the stone urn in front of the apartment house in all seasons, in almost all weather. He sits in a wooden folding chair which is placed there by his daughter, who has no time, no patience, and very little money. Like a straw doll whose stuffing has been pulled thin in spots, he bends, sags, but keeps a pair of blue, observant eyes fastened upon the world around him.

The people of the street have become accustomed to seeing him. In winter, they expect to find him there, shapeless in layers of old clothing — for he would freeze to death, sitting hours, unmoving, unless his daughter swathed him in God-knows-what: castoffs, towels, an overcoat so bleached of color that one takes it for whatever light is upon it. In frightful coldness, Mr. Isaacs can be seen gazing at the curb, as if some memory has projected itself there. A watery pendant forms at the end of his nose, freezes, and becomes an icicle. If he has a handkerchief, it is so buried in the recesses of his clothing that he has neither the strength nor the dexterity to find it. So the icicle forms, and a distant observer might think there is a diamond embedded in the face of the old man who has just turned his head toward the sun.

During the day, the life of women and children swirls

around Mr. Isaacs. Children too young for school, too old for immobility, run screaming past him, having no more regard for his presence than for the huge stone urn which decorates the front of the house. Occasionally one of the children will observe a movement and, arrested in flight, will pause for a moment before the old man. At opposite poles of life, the two will stare at each other, one not having learned the dissimulation called politeness, the other having forgotten it, and for a moment there is an exchange of beautiful blankness between them.

After three o'clock, a fury seizes the street. The older ones come out of school, and a look of caution comes over the features of Mr. Isaacs. The dream passes from his eyes, and they take on the sharpness of one who has lived in danger all his life.

He must watch the skaters. The skaters take him as a natural hazard, bearing down like an avalanche, then veering sharp, as they would around a hydrant or baby carriage. Mr. Isaacs shows no sign of panic during these moments of jeopardy. He begins to nod his head, holds his cane more tightly, and when one of the skaters splays out like a crab, clutching the air, going down, ripping pants, knees, elbows, Mr. Isaacs still sits nodding his head with mechanical dispassion. The smooth, brown cane he carries is by his side — almost as if it hadn't moved.

Then there are the ball players. This madness takes the form of pounding a rubber ball against the side of the house. Here again is a presumption of accuracy on the part of the boys which sets Mr. Isaacs to nodding his head and clutching his cane. Finally the ball will thud harmlessly into his many-layered armor of rags.

" 'Scuse me" is all that can be spared, for the game is

fiercely competitive, and Mr. Isaacs so feebly alive that he can't be credited with much feeling.

Mr. Isaacs will then jab his cane like a sword in the direction of his tormentors.

"Hey, look, the old guy wants to talk to you."

So the young one approaches, half-curious, half-annoyed, bouncing his ball and waiting for the formulation of some half-dead complaint.

"How old are you?" Mr. Isaacs asks. His voice is surprising. It is not as one would expect it, like gravel rattling around at the bottom of a rusty barrel. It is deep and smooth, almost as if Mr. Isaacs were an orator in his day and has kept this attribute as a memento of the art.

"Eight," the boy will say, or "Ten," or "Thirteen."

Mr. Isaacs nods again. He lifts his head to the boy, revealing a face over which the flesh has grown tighter and tighter with the years. Lined, sere, but with a tautness which gives a severe aquilinity to his nose and the waxen incipience of a smile to his lips.

"Someday you will be the President of the United States," Mr. Isaacs informs the boy, with such solemn certitude that the youngster's brow furrows in bewilderment. Without alteration of expression, Mr. Isaacs indicates a section of the wall well out of range. "Is there something wrong with over there?" he asks. "There's no one sitting over there you can hit with your ball, is that the trouble? Do an old man a favor. Take your friends over there to play."

All of this is intoned in the same, rich, musical voice. The boy backs away, taking fright from something behind the words spoken with senile gentleness. The lashless blue eyes follow the boy's retreat without humor, without rancor, without forgiveness.

Everybody who lives in the same apartment house with Mr. Isaacs knows a little something about him. He is the albatross hung about the neck of his ponderously overburdened daughter — and she is not the sort to take even ordinary burdens lightly.

"What can I do? Put him in a home? Even a home wants money, and for the poorhouse I'm not ready yet."

She has a natural sense of the dramatic, assuming a pose and expression the medieval painters would have given their souls to capture. Her two hands nested in her lap like a pair of obese doves, her head tilted at the angle of resignation, her eyes half-closed against the implacability of fate.

"I don't understand it," she confides to her friends and neighbors. "Here is a man who worked his whole life in the garment trade. A skilled operator. Good money I know he made. It comes time for him to retire . . . not a cent! Where did it all go? On his family he didn't spend it. *This* I can tell you!"

Often Mr. Isaacs is present when his daughter brings up these mysterious questions of the past. It is as if he does not hear her words. He does not hear most of the words his daughter utters, groans, shrieks, weeps. They are wind on the surface of a sea whose calm depths Mr. Isaacs cleaves with submarine thoughts.

"Ideas he had," accuses the daughter, turning to him with a scorn all the more complete for its blindness. "Ask him."

No one asks Mr. Isaacs. It is known that he was active in the union when it was no more than a harassed little cluster of immigrants seeking to turn stones into bread. It is known that all the early criers for justice became big men, important men, men to whom the presidents of companies offered cigars, spoke respectfully. Not Mr. Isaacs. When the great struggle was about to bear fruit, he withered on the vine, lost interest, became once again an operator on dresses whose seniority assured him almost a full year's work.

"What are you always thinking about?" yells the daughter when the repeated thrusts of her scorn blunt themselves against the blue-eyed, nodding insentience.

"Shall I go to my room?" asks Mr. Isaacs.

"Go . . . !"

But she has nowhere to consign him. He is too meek for hell, too secretive for heaven. He must stay here, in the room her two sons occupied before they rushed out like a pair of convicts in a prison break.

"Leave him alone," says the son-in-law, from behind his paper. The noise disturbs him; also, a little, his conscience. It was the old man, after all, who got him his job in the dress house.

So there is quiet.

What is he thinking? He does not think. There is no sequence to the pictures that slide across his mind. But the pictures are bright, although they lead to nothing, form no pattern of which Mr. Isaacs would care to say: "This is my life."

Today is an autumn day, full of clouds, presaging the season Mr. Isaacs may not survive. The shadows of clouds stimulate one set of memories; the sunlight another. Sitting in the folding chair beside the stone urn, Mr. Isaacs feels the warmth of the sun on his face and hands, and the sensation travels like an electric signal, crossing and recrossing nerves, until it comes upon the one scene it is meant to illuminate.

This is the courtyard of his father's house in Warsaw. His father is wealthy in the sense merchant Jews were allowed to become wealthy in Poland. There are a carriage and two horses in the rear of the courtyard, and the smell of the beasts and their manure mingles with the smell of cooking. On Sunday his father receives guests, and the huge wooden table in the courtyard is covered with a tablecloth like a mantle of snow. The back door of the kitchen opens upon the courtyard, and from it issue his mother and two servants carrying bowls, platters, tureens, all steaming, all redolent. They are placed on the table, their covers are removed, and a cloud of smoke like the cry "Hosannah!" rises and wafts this way and that as the breeze takes it. Just then the sun comes out, striking the glazed, bellied flanks of the bowls, and the refulgence is such as though God Himself cast down one beam of benevolence to make all present remember this day.

"Well, Mr. Isaacs . . . ?"

Mr. Isaacs looks up slowly. Vaguely he recognizes the woman before him. She is someone who lives in this house and must touch him with a word whenever she passes.

"I was sleeping," says Mr. Isaacs.

The woman looks up at the sky. "Pretty soon it'll be winter," she predicts.

Mr. Isaacs nods.

The woman shifts her bundle from one arm to the other and cautions: "Don't catch cold."

Mr. Isaacs fumbles in his mind for the pleasantness which pointless words have shoved aside. What was it? He cannot remember. A cloud covers the sun and grayness rushes into the street like a river.

Gray is the window which stands like a dirty sentinel at the end of the line of sewing machines. It offers no light, only casts a gray diffusion in its immediate vicinity. In the late afternoons of fall and winter, it becomes opaque black reflecting the yellow lights within the shop.

Here within his circle of yellow light, feeding fabric which flows in waves through his machine, he is at home. This varnished pine table, the bobbins, the spools of thread, the sewing machine with its coating of oil, the fabrics of cotton, wool, rayon, silk, jersey, faille . . . all of this combines to create a dry, friendly odor in the nostrils. His ears are attuned to the drone of two dozen machines. Occasionally the forelady comes to gather up his work. She counts the pieces, snips a thread, and carries it off as if it were her own billowing child. At noon, he unwraps a sandwich of salami. Tonight there will be chicken soup thick with noodles and white pieces of meat. Between the familiarity of meals and the familiarity of work there is a sense of eternity.

But the calm must be shaken. He has sworn to do something, and today it must be done. He is going to speak to his employer, the dwarfish Mr. Krakow, whose strength is the strength of ten because his heart is totally impure. He is going to say: "Give me a little more money, Mr. Krakow. Two dollars. With fourteen dollars a week I can live; with twelve I cannot." He has rehearsed the scene so often that he has come to know Mr. Krakow quite well. He is a good businessman, a man with a rough sense of justice who knows the value of a good workman. Therefore he will answer: "All right, Isaacs, but let me see *work!*" Ah, he will show him work. It is settled. He gets up from his chair. Weintraub, who sits to his left and is apprised of his plans, raises his head. His mouth hangs open, and if wordless supplication had the power of human arms Isaacs would remain pinned to his chair.

He is in the office of Mr. Krakow only a short time. Nothing much is said, but inside his flesh, where it cannot show, he has been raked by the claws of arrogance. An ugly fang has pierced his heart. He sits down again at his machine. His gaze wanders to the window, and he finds there is nothing friendly in its somber filth. He turns to his machine and begins to work, but the fabric which flows through his hands is repugnant to him. He is a savage, and he is stitching the flesh of his enemy.

In the afternoon, the mothers come down with their infants and baby carriages. They stand in the sunlight, close to Mr. Isaacs, and talk. He hears their conversation but gives no sign of it. Their voices fly above him like birds calling to each other from different trees.

"I don't know what to buy. . . . Meat. Joe only likes meat. . . . I think she is catching cold. . . . Maybe it's adenoids. . . . She always sleeps with her mouth open. . . . Are you going shopping now? . . . Yes. . . . Come. . . . Hello, Mr. Isaacs. How are you feeling? . . . Isn't it a beautiful day? . . ."

Now he is aware that his daughter is standing next to him. She does not seem to notice him, but looks up and down the street as though it were a ship and she its commander. This way to the beauty parlor, the movies, the house of a friend; that way to the market, the shoe store, the dry cleaning store. Life is kept in balance by the choice of her direction.

"Are you all right, Pa?" she asks, her glance still ranging the street.

"Yes."

"Are you warm enough?"

He nods.

"I'm going shopping now."

She leaves his side, and for several seconds Mr. Isaacs fumbles with the skeins of past and present. His daughter's voice confuses him. It is not his wife's voice, yet beneath the sound of its own quality lie the same inflections.

Deliberately Mr. Isaacs invokes memory, and he is like a man stumbling around in the darkened rooms of his own house. Hannah is dead, this much he knows, but the transition from her life to her death is only the last in a series of gradations. He tries to think of Hannah and sees countless wax-filled glasses in which the Friday flame of holiness burns. He sees the porcelain-top kitchen table gleam dully under the ceiling light. On the center of the table is an ancient silver tray, a clean napkin, and a bread. He sees laundry dampened and rolled, waiting for the iron that heats on the stove.

They are in the kitchen. Somehow all their evenings are spent in the kitchen. The other room, the one with the leather davenport, the arm chair, the massive circular table, will last a thousand years, for its dark austerity does not invite ease-taking and the reading of a paper. So it is in the kitchen that he reads his newspaper, while Hannah unrolls a shirt and spreads it on the ironing board. She takes the iron from the stove and holds it close to her face, judging by its heat whether it is ready. She applies it to the shirt, and there is the expected and comforting hiss of steam.

When the doorbell rings he goes to the door and in the dim corridor sees a familiar face. He steps out into the corridor, closing the door quietly behind him, and there in the conspiratorial darkness, amidst the commingled smells of a dozen different suppers, the visitor addresses him in a voice that is both question and challenge.

"You heard?"

"Yes," says Mr. Isaacs.

"He fired me."

"I know. Don't worry. He will have to take you back. He will have to take you back and pay you all the money you lost when he signs with the union."

"When will that be?"

"Soon," says Mr. Isaacs.

"A week? Two? Three? The rent is paid for the month . . . but food?"

Mr. Isaacs reaches into his pocket and brings out his leather purse with the snap fastener. He gives the man five dollars.

"I will pay you back."

"I know."

"As soon as I'm working again."

"I know."

"Good night, Isaacs."

"Good night."

He returns to the kitchen, picks up his paper, and sits down again. Hannah has finished the shirt. She closes all the buttons, folds it neatly, and lays it on the mound of ironed things. Out of the corner of his eye, he watches her hand reach for the next article of clothing. It is pink, something of hers, a petticoat, and when the iron touches it there is a sibilance of steam and one spoken word — as heavy and purposeful as the iron itself.

"*Narr!*" says Hannah. . . . "Fool."

Toward six o'clock, the atmosphere of the street changes. The skaters and the ball players have departed. Here and there a window opens and a shrill voice cries: "Sidneeee! . . . *Sid*-ney!" There is a slight chill in the air. The sun has passed over the roof beneath which Mr. Isaacs sits, and a straight band of gold stretches out along the upper stories of the tenement opposite.

Pretty soon Mr. Isaacs's son-in-law will walk up the street with his evening newspaper folded under his arm, his heavy face darkened by a day's growth of beard. He will come up to Mr. Isaacs and halt there with the saturnine patience of a hospital attendant. If Mr. Isaacs is sleeping, he will tap him on the shoulder. If he is awake, he will simply nod. Then he will assist Mr. Isaacs to his feet, and with one hand under the old man's arm and the other holding the folding chair they will proceed into the courtyard littered with the day's leavings of candy wrappers, fruit cores and circulars.

They will walk up the staircase, pausing at each landing for Mr. Isaacs to catch his breath. They will come to the second floor where there is a window with a pane of stained glass. It is an oddity in the building, this pane of colored glass. No other window has it. And it is here, every evening, that Mr. Isaacs repeats the same words to himself. He cannot remember what it was that first began the ritual, but when his gaze falls upon the pane of stained glass, he asks:

"What am I waiting for?"

For it is Mr. Isaacs's notion that he is holding off death by a daily act of will. Nor does death importune, but keeps with him like a friendly dog, pausing when he pauses, and going when he goes. It crouches beside him in the living room, its muzzle resting on his shoe. It follows him into the bedroom and watches as he labors with buttons and sleeves. Then, in the isolation of his room, Mr. Isaacs feels free to address his companion in the manner lonely people adopt towards domesticated pets.

"What am I waiting for?" he repeats.

There is no time, only distance, and his own life has

receded so far that all perspective is lost. Joseph in the pit, Moses striking the rock, his father's courtyard in Warsaw, Mr. Krakow's medium-priced line of garments — they are all story-pictures painted on the curving wall of memory.

Now he composes his body for sleep, or death — he knows not which. Often it is for death he decides, but in the moment of choice a figure springs up and stares at him with frightened eyes. It is a shabby figure, pathetic, neither old nor young, but one whose story is so unique, so full of failures close to Mr. Isaacs's heart, so devoid of triumphs, that Mr. Isaacs feels toward it a great compassion — and would linger one more day in a world that contains its presence.

Jingle Bells

"You ought to be ashamed of yourself," said his mother, and Fred Kramer had no doubt that he should. He was thirteen. If he lacked a natural instinct for the obligations of family, he had certainly been informed of them often enough. "You'll just have to take our word for it," his father added, supplementing moral argument with authority. "I should think a boy of your age wouldn't have to be told his duty to his grandparents."

Fred was rather ashamed, but this shame only acted to increase his aversion to the visit. The aversion was something he couldn't control. He had barricaded himself behind a series of flimsy excuses, only to have them knocked down with a single word of reproof.

"They don't want to see me," he groused. "Half the time they don't even know if I'm in the room or not." The last part of his statement had a mendacious claim to truth. Time and presence operated unevenly in the minds of the old people.

"But don't you want to see *them?*"

An outright "No" would have been honest, but it would have violated the code of Right and Wrong. It was Wrong not to want to see one's grandparents, and although his mother and dad knew perfectly well that he didn't want to see them, they kept up the nagging pretense that something other than simple distaste was at the base of his reluctance.

"Five days a week is enough basketball, I should think," said his mother.

Fred didn't particularly want to play basketball. Not since that skinny creep, Len Allister, had made his appearance in the schoolyard. Len was a long articulation of elbows and knees, each of them metal-tipped and lusting for the face and ribs of Fred Kramer. It was weeks since he had gone to the schoolyard, but Fred saw no reason to remove that obsolete item from the barter shelf. In the business of emotional bargaining, it was necessary to keep on hand a sacrifice inventory.

The truth? Fred didn't know himself. Oh, yes, he did, in a way, but it was in a way that he couldn't express. It was there, in the back of his head, in that dead-letter file of unexplained sensation. He thought of his grandmother, and his lips recollected the contact of a cheek tumid and oversoft, like a saturated sponge. And, like a sponge, he had only to touch it for the tears to flow. They seemed to come without the grimace or cause of grief. The seamed face and childishly innocent eyes remained as fixed as a mask, but the tears would come, as if a disembodied memory dwelt inside of her.

He thought of his grandparents, and his nostrils flinched at an odor that was neither good nor bad, pungent nor bland. Rags, perhaps. Old rags which had lain in an attic and in which mice had nested. It pervaded that room at the shore where they lived. It seemed to come from the yellowing piece of lace that covered the ancient sewing machine, from the enormous, dead eye of the television set; it came even from the grapes his grandmother would occasionally set before him on a dish, grapes that it gagged him to eat, feeling, as he did, that he was partaking of the decaying mold of the room.

His grandfather had not completely lost the habit of communication, asking the same questions each time, saying the same things . . . "You like school?" . . . "How old are you now?" . . . "He looks a little like Charley." . . . rubbing his arthritic hands on his mirror-smooth pants. But despite his addled propensity for talk, he shared the puppet-like quiescence of the old lady that lived in the room with him. It was impossible for Fred to think of them as husband and wife. They seemed so oblivious to each other, so enveloped in separate dreams.

"And besides," continued Mr. Kramer, "it's about time you learned there are some things you have to do whether you want to or not."

"Well, I'm *go*ing," Fred muttered.

There was something in the way his father admonished him that made Fred look at him. A hint of irony clung to the corners of his mouth. Sympathy? Falseness? His father caught his glance, held it for a moment, then squared his shoulders in his customary manner and looked away.

Mrs. Kramer appeared from the kitchen carrying a brown paper bag in which were contained the various things the old people liked to eat. She had prepared them the previous evening — stewed fruit, boiled beef, a cake made with many eggs.

"You'd better wear your mackinaw," she said to Fred. "It's chilly."

Fred sat alone in the back of the car. His mother and father sat up front. During the first ten minutes of the drive, he contrived a position which might have served as a classic model of discomfort. His shoulders substituted for his bottom on the seat of the car, and his bottom hung unsupported in space. His knees, pressed against the front seat, formed the other end of his cantilevered tension.

He indulged his fantasies lazily, letting his favorite of the apocalyptic letter to the Kremlin shade off into a misinformed bit of sex with the dark-haired Sandra who lived in the private house up the street. Conversation from up front filtered back to him on another wavelength, disturbing his private reception, and only occasionally becoming intelligible.

". . . four children and not one who will take them in," his mother was saying.

"Four!" his father scoffed. "One is living in Canada. The other is out on the Coast. As between you and Charley, I might ask how many rooms does he have in *his* house? Twelve? Thirteen? From a practical point of view . . ."

"Practical! From a practical point of view, I suppose they should be put in a gas chamber. From a practical point of view life itself makes no sense."

When the pain in the back of his neck became unbearable, Fred straightened up and gazed out of the window.

"How old is Grandpa?" he asked.

There was no doubt that his mother knew to the day, but she looked down into her lap and appeared to think about it.

"Eighty-four," she said at last.

"And Grandma?"

"You've got a head like a pin," she said. "Don't you remember the party we had in May for her eightieth birthday?"

Fred remembered the party. He hadn't quite realized it

was a birthday party. The celebration had overtones of some sort of wedding. He and his cousin Paul had mixed four different kinds of soda in tall glasses and plopped in their huge scoops of sherbet. It tasted lousy, Fred recalled. He was beginning to feel a little carsick. He rolled down the window.

"There's nothing a person can do gracefully any more," he heard his father say. "Neither live nor die."

"Selfishness," said his mother.

"Come on now . . ."

"If I had my way . . ."

"If you had your way! Don't talk like a child. In the natural order of things, it's the old who must be sacrificed. The Eskimos . . ."

"Oh, shut up! The *Eskimos!*"

"What about the Eskimos?" Fred asked.

"Nothing about the Eskimos," his mother answered. "Some of your father's ancestors were Eskimos."

Fred grinned. "Yeah! No kidding?"

His father scratched himself with one finger above the right ear. He reached into the side pocket of his coat and extracted a cigarette.

"You're not going to smoke that, are you?" Fred asked.

"Excuse me," said Mr. Kramer, "I forgot."

Cigarette smoke in the car was *the* specific for making Fred ill.

Fred's senses sharpened suddenly at the sight of the ack-ack battery off to the right. The trim khaki-colored guns and radar screens evoked a montage of black puffs in the air and doomed planes streaking earthward, trailing smoke and flame. Aside from the guns, which were always a thrilling sight, Fred knew that they were coming to the best part of the ride.

In a few minutes, they would be on the bridge — and then the water!

Since the day was bright with October brightness, the water of the bay flashed gold. Two men were fishing from the bridge, the steel of their poles adding to the general coruscation. Scattered at their feet were glistening patches of seaweed. The gulls hovered on spread swings, their bellies enamel white, their industrious heads turning this way and that. Fred rolled the car window down all the way and stuck his head out. He heard the concert of hoarse gull cries.

Invariably, when he came upon this sight, the same thing happened. He repeated the words "Jingle Bells" to himself, and this code summoned the image of four rosy-cheeked children riding in a horse-drawn sleigh over a field of snow. The book containing the songs and illustrations had eroded out of existence years ago (so he had mauled it in talismanic love), but he had only to say the words and he was instantly transported to that awesome brink of discovery. Sun-drenched it was, murmurous, and full of nameless portents. They were riding, he knew, to the world outside his room, outside his house. It was the world on the other side of the hill where they were going, and there, gathered as if for a hero's welcome, were all the things that would ever happen to Fred Kramer.

Since that first afflatus, Fred discovered that other unexpected sights and sounds could touch it off. The sight of the bay on the way to his grandparents', for example. And when it came, he would sit transfixed, his mouth slightly open, for all the world a dull boy in a fit of vacancy.

The first half-hour of these visits was almost bearable. His mother and father would pump cheer and life into the room, stirring up the old people, rousing them from their torpor with family jokes and a special kind of banter.

"Still going for a swim every morning?" Mr. Kramer asked his father-in-law.

The old man nodded. He began to rub his thighs with the palms of his hands. Fred always wondered whether it was his hands or legs that ached.

"Every morning," he replied. "Seven o'clock. Then I run up and down the beach."

"You think you're kidding," said Mr. Kramer, turning to each one in the room to emphasize his seriousness. "I read an article in the paper not so long ago about a man over eighty who belonged to one of these Polar Clubs. Went bathing every day — sun, snow, or hail!"

Fred wondered why his father should seem so unlike himself when he was with the old people. Ordinarily balanced and uncondescending, he would, in their presence, lose his poise and give way to clownishness.

"How are the meals, Mama?" Mrs. Kramer asked.

The old lady made a gesture . . . Not good, not bad.

"Do you get enough? . . . Papa?"

"Sure enough. How much can an old man eat?"

Fred watched a familiar expression pass across his mother's face. Guilt, irritation. They needled her, the old people. In a thousand ways, they let her know they'd be happier living with her. Fred knew by heart his mother's monologue of self-laceration. It always came to the same impasse.

"How about your own?" his father would ask.

"They are my own!" she would cry.

But that's where it would end; for the choice, Fred knew, was between himself and them. He felt no compunction that the decision was, would ever be, in his favor. He thought it was for the reason that his parents, no more than he, did not want their home infused with the staleness which identified this room. He had convinced himself that if they should ever come to live in his house, the walls would instantly turn to this pale, institutional blue and cracked linoleum would take the place of the carpets.

"Come on," said his mother. "The meat is warmed up."

She went to a drawer and took out a tablecloth. She laid two places, and the old people obediently sat down. They were docile and expectant, like well-behaved children.

"Why only two?" the old lady asked. "Aren't you going to eat?"

"Don't be silly," said Mrs. Kramer. "We had our lunch."

They ate slowly, spilling the juice of the stewed fruit, relishing the beef too obviously. The old man picked up his head and looked at Fred. He touched his beef with his fork.

"A piece of boiled beef?"

Fred recoiled in horror. "No," he said. "I don't like that kind of meat."

The old man shrugged. "It's very tasty," he said.

Mrs. Kramer served tea for everyone. Fred refused to touch his. He picked up his piece of cake with his hand and ate it that way. He intercepted one swift, angry glance from his mother. When the meal was over, she cleaned the dishes, surreptitiously picking other things from the cupboard that looked in need of a cleaning.

"Was Charley here this week?" she asked.

"Charley?" echoed the old lady.

"This week?" said the old man.

They both pondered on the unitless flow of time.

"No," the old man said at last. "I don't think he was here this week. Maybe last week."

"Is the television set working all right?" Mr. Kramer asked.

They both nodded.

"If anything goes wrong with it, I want you to let me know right away," Mr. Kramer said, forcefully. "I'll see that a good mechanic comes to fix it. You've got to be careful with these guys. They'd steal your eyeteeth."

Fred squirmed. His father's best intentions had the ludicrous effect of a grown man blowing soap bubbles.

"Here," said the old man, rubbing his thighs again. "Here's where it hurts."

Mrs. Kramer inclined her head to one side. Her eyes filmed over pensively, as if she were hearing the first strains of a familiar, sad piece of music.

"The doctor says it's nothing."

"It doesn't hurt him," the old man said. "For him, it's nothing."

"He's not your age, either," Mrs. Kramer said.

The old man nodded.

"It's a beautiful day out," Mr. Kramer interjected. "Why do you sit cooped up in the house this way? Come on, we'll go for a drive."

The two old people smiled and sat unmoving.

"It's too tiring for them," said Mrs. Kramer.

Then they were all silent, and Fred knew that the second phase of the visit had begun. An invisible presence entered the room, and now they would all sit and contemplate this presence. The long silences were not as awkward as long silences might be, because the presence was there to relieve the necessity of speech.

His grandmother and grandfather sat at either end of the kitchen table nodding mysterious affirmations. His mother sat near them, trying to pick out of the abundance of language those few possible words which would distract their inward gaze. His father sat near a window, looking out, drumming his fingernails on the pane, emitting long sighs which terminated in off-key melodies from *Carmen.* And Fred himself sat drowning in boredom and watching the tableau recede from him, as if it were painted on a retractable wall. Minute after minute it would go on, until Fred felt that all, parents and grandparents, would simply dwindle out of existence by a uniform act of will. And then someone spoke, his grandmother, and the still began to move.

"My last few years could have been happy," she said.

"Mamma!" Mrs. Kramer implored wearily.

"Don't listen to her," said the old man.

Then Fred heard his grandmother speak his mother's name. "Ruth," she said, in a voice so feeble yet so eerily compelling that Fred felt the goose bumps rise on his flesh. He saw his mother get up and go to his grandmother, embrace her, bend her head to receive a secret. All Fred could make out was a low sibilance that passed between his mother and grandmother.

He had never witnessed such behavior before, yet what struck him most was the familiarity of the scene. It came out of his own past. Just so his mother had whispered to him, covering him with the protective integument of love. To find this act repeated here, under these circumstances, filled him with bewilderment. There was a treachery in it. The pattern of solicitude which defined his life had shifted, and he suddenly found himself among people whose history was not his own.

The hand touching his shoulder startled him, coming unexpectedly and seemingly part of this frightening charade. It was his father. Mr. Kramer's face was composed and expressionless. He had both their coats over his arm, and with a motion of his head he indicated that he wanted Fred to walk outside. Fred did so, glancing around once and seeing his mother and grandmother still locked in that dreadful, swaying pose.

In the hall, Mr. Kramer said, "We'll take a walk."

They left the house and walked toward the boardwalk. The air wasn't cold, but Fred shivered after the overheated room and general oppressiveness.

"What's the matter with Grandma?" he asked.

"What do you think is the matter with her?" his father returned, rather strangely.

"She's old, I guess," Fred said.

"Isn't that enough?" asked his father.

It wasn't enough. Even if he was willing to accept it as an explanation of his grandmother's behavior, it didn't explain his mother's.

They walked up the incline to the boardwalk, and then crossed over to look at the ocean. The beach was an expanse of light gray powder shot with brilliants. Wind had smoothed the surface so that it gave the appearance of having been swept with a gigantic broom.

"I never saw the beach like this," Fred said.

"This is the best time of year," said his father. "Come on, let's walk on the beach."

Fred thought it odd that he should suggest this, but he liked the idea. They walked down a flight of steps and trudged over toward the surf where the sand offered a better footing.

"It's warmer near the ocean during the late fall and winter," Mr. Kramer remarked. "Water doesn't get as cold as land."

"I thought it would be colder," Fred said.

"Most people do."

"Is Grandma sick?" Fred asked.

"No. She's very old."

"Is she scared of something?"

"I guess so."

"Of what?"

"Of dying, perhaps."

"Is she going to die?"

"Yes. Of course. Everybody must get old and die."

This wasn't news to Fred, but it was the first time in his life that someone was confronted with the actuality of the event. What troubled him was not that his grandmother would soon die, but the apparent helplessness of everyone around her. Particularly his mother. Death, his father had offhandedly declared, must come, but there was something arbitrary and mean about its coming in the face of so much bitter disapproval. This was a preemption of authority he didn't like.

"Is Mom scared?" he asked.

"Yes . . . no. Very sorry, let's say." Mr. Kramer stooped and picked up a shell, trying unsuccessfully to scale it over the water. "Don't think too much about it," he said. "When I was your age — no, older, I guess — anyway, I used to think a great deal about death. Since that time, I've become a dozen different people and I haven't died yet. It's no use worrying about death, because the person who does the worrying is not the person who's going to die." He turned to Fred. "That doesn't make much sense, does it?"

Fred shook his head.

"No," Mr. Kramer agreed. "The important thing is not to think about it too much. No one really understands it."

They walked in silence for a while. Fred found himself thinking of the way his grandmother had whispered her terrible, fearful secret to his mother.

"They're like babies now," he said.

"Yes," said Mr. Kramer. "I guess you could say that."

Then Fred felt the chill of knowledge, but it was not the knowledge of death. The condition of his grandparents was too remote to be real, but the condition of his parents presented him with a sudden view of pathos. To be old, as his parents were old, meant to bear the extremes of either side of life. It meant to understand and comfort the afflictions of infancy and decrepitude, to give one's ear to the frightened whisper, and this, Fred realized, was a burden.

"We'd better be getting back," his father said.

They turned around and began walking back to the house.

"The shore is loveliest at this time of year," Mr. Kramer said, as they entered the room.

Everything had returned to normal. The old people were drinking tea again. Fred saw that his grandmother was once more her blank, wrinkled, half-smiling self. His grandfather was rubbing his thighs.

"What time is it?" Mrs. Kramer asked.

"Almost four-thirty," Mr. Kramer told her.

"We'll have to be getting back," she said. "I must prepare dinner, and Fred has homework to do."

"Do you like school?" the old man asked Fred.

"Sure," said Fred.

They lingered for another thirty minutes, and then they began to put on their clothes.

"Next week we'll come early to pick you up, and you'll spend the day at our house," said Mrs. Kramer. "Charley and the family will be there."

"Good, good," said the old man.

Everybody seemed happy. There was even a note of festivity. A crisis had passed. There was a great deal of kissing and hand-shaking, and then they left.

On the way back, no one spoke much. Mrs. Kramer asked whether they would like the sliced cold roast, or the meat diced up and fried with potatoes and onions. Fred and his father decided they would like the diced-up meat.

They came to the bridge again. Now there was a deep-toned somberness over the bay. The fishermen were gone, having left withered clumps of seaweed as a memento. One lonely-looking fishing boat puttered toward the bridge.

Fred felt drowsy. He thrust his hands into his coat pockets and hunched up in the back seat. This was the moment when he had planned to give himself over to thoughts of death. The death of his mother, his father, himself, but no sooner did he begin to probe at the rim of darkness than the image of the four children in a sleigh rose up in his mind — and Fred gave himself over instead to his private vision of joy.

Happy Birthday

THE woman at the perfume counter asked George Mariner what sort of girl his wife was. "I mean," she quickly amended, "is she blonde or brunette?"

"Brunette, I guess," George answered.

"Would you say that she's conservative or — ah — experimental in her tastes?"

George wondered whether his own person represented something of an answer to that question.

"On the whole conservative, I would say," George answered.

"Well, this is very nice . . ."

She tipped a flask and rubbed the glass stopper on the back of her hand. Then she waved her hand back and forth and brought it directly under George's nose.

"Dry," she said, "and subtle."

George could detect no difference between this one and the last, which the woman had designated as "Gay."

"Tell you what," George said, "I think I'll skip perfumes. They're tricky. Like ties. You never can buy them for someone else. I'll get her Berenson's book on art instead."

George nodded pleasantly to the woman and walked out of the department store. He had added that last bit about

Berenson because of the flicker of contempt that passed over her face when she knew that she wasn't going to make the sale. Berenson would hold her, the painted stick!

Paula's birthdays were a curse. Paula didn't know it, of course, seeing only the careful wrapping paper, the ribbons, the gifts that were as much a matter of spiritual parturition as taste. Once a year, he had to go into an empathic trance and come up with something which was not only true to the basic Paula, but which was also a significant advance in his understanding of her complicated and sensitive nature.

Last year the item which bore the burden of his regard was a piece of sculpture in sandstone. A cat. George recalled his presumptuous swagger about the thing. He was not merely right, he felt; he was years ahead of himself. The cat represented a double gift. There was its own voluptuous self (Baudelaire's cat, he meant to call it), and there was also his palpable discrimination. To Paula, one was as valuable as the other.

Paula unwrapped it on her birthday morning and stood with clasped hands trying to breathe rapture into herself. It had failed. Why? George couldn't say. By a hair, no doubt, but to fail by a hair is even worse than an out-and-out blooper. Such a failure imposes duplicity on both giver and receiver. The one tries to pretend that it wasn't really a failure; the other tries to pretend that he isn't aware of the disappointment. There are smiles, excessive assurances, awkward silences, and finally, inevitably, drawn by a power greater than caution or love, the passing remark that blows it all to hell.

"Sleepy little thing."

"Sleepy?"

"You know — somnolent — like a cat."

"You said sleepy. Torpor rather than vitality, right?"

"Darling, why are you being so sensitive?"

"I wonder." He changed his tack and looked rueful. "You know," he said, "it's just amazing how different it looked when I bought it. I would have staked my life on its being a little masterpiece. Now . . ."

"Now. . . ?"

"The wish was father to the thought. I can see that it's sleepy."

Paula embraced him compassionately — as one does the beloved who has committed a venial error. Their pose was symbolical: joined physically and looking in opposite directions. He was thinking that his ruse had worked as well as perversity could wish. By falsely admitting it was a lemon, he gave her the right to fall in his arms and sorrow for him. He now had a choice of squaring off and defending his honest opinion, or letting the whole thing go by default. With an inward sigh, he reminded himself that it *was* her birthday.

Weaving in and out of streets, George juggled the idea of handing Paula a gift certificate. ("Let's face it, honey, it *is* the thought rather than the gift, and my thoughts simply don't measure up.") The gambit wasn't as impossible as it sounded — provided he could bring it off without irony. Very unlikely. She'd recognize it for what it was: withdrawal rather than surrender; and then there'd be a mountainous fuss about the death of love.

Wearily, not knowing how he got there, George noticed that he was on Sixth Avenue. *Sixth,* for Pete's sake! You could turn this whole avenue upside down and shake out all its pockets and still not find anything that would please Paula.

He passed a fruit store. There was a crate of persimmons standing at a forty-five degree angle. Paula loved persimmons. . . . "So exotic. That marvelous color, etc. . . ." Well, how about a whole crate of persimmons? You can't have too much of a good thing. Besides, what a deal Paula could make of it with her friends! . . . "Guess what George gave me for my birthday! No, no . . . *guess!* Persimmons! A whole crate of persimmons! Wasn't that imaginative!"

The very idea of it made George roll his tongue around in his mouth. He never could understand Paula's enthusiasm for persimmons. Every time he ate one, he felt as though he had had his mouth sprayed with rock-wool insulation. George ended his thoughts on persimmons as he came to a halt in front of an art store.

As an art store, it was unquestionably second, or third, rate. The show-window was a hodge-podge of prints. George spotted the usual Chagalls, Matisses, Braques, and Picassos. How wearisome these prints were becoming! You saw them all over town. They had ceased to be representations of art. They were more like institutionalized posters. An army recruiting billboard or a Nedick's trademark would have as much effect on him.

Dulled by surfeit, George felt nothing at the sight of the particular print in the far left corner. He looked at it, knew that he had never seen it before, but nothing of importance announced itself to his eye. Then, as though an invisible hand had been turning the lens of his attention, George finally *saw* it.

It was Japanese. The subject was two peasant figures, a man and a woman, hurrying across a wooden bridge towards what seemed like a little village. The colors were buff, green, and yellow.

George walked into the shop.

"I'd like to see that Japanese print you've got in the window," he requested.

"Which Japanese print?"

The man wore an eyeshade on his forehead and a look of asperity around his mouth. His manner was plainly expressive of the fact that he needed you like a hole in the head.

(Great, thought George. Just what I needed.)

"The one without a name," George said.

The man looked at him with turgid, expressionless eyes. "None of them have names," he said.

"That a fact?" said George, smiling.

"If you'll point out the one . . ."

"Now we're getting somewhere."

The man looked up at the ceiling quickly, as if he had spotted something crawling there. "Look, mister . . ." he began, then drew back his irritation turtle-fashion. "Show me which one," he muttered.

They both stepped outside the shop, and George pointed to the print. The man nodded, and they walked back inside. There was a sliding panel arrangement in the partition at the back of the showcase. The man slid this open, stuck an arm inside, and brought out the print.

"Sixty-five dollars," he said. "Framed."

"Do I have to take that particular frame?" George asked.

"It's the only print I got," the man said. "I bought it at an auction, so it's got to be sold that way."

"I see. Do you mind if I take it over there, under a good light? I'd like to examine it for a few moments. In spite of everything, there's a possibility I may buy it."

The man relinquished the print and walked away from George. George propped the print against a stack of frames, stepped back a pace, and looked at it carefully.

It was lovely. The original (one could assume the colors

were even better on that) must be an incredibly delicate thing. There was humor in it, the distant, scurrying humor of two people trying to beat out an imminent shower. And the colors were as aqueous and gentle as only the Japanese could make them. George fell in love with it. He knew that he could look at it a thousand times, and it would never lose completely its first enchantment.

So much for *his* thoughts. Now about Paula . . .

George spread out before his mind's eye a hasty inventory of her likes and dislikes. Prints, per se, were highly questionable. (Here he could agree with her. Even when they were good, they were done to death.) But assuming it escaped the curse of banality, as this one did, how about the thing in itself? Was it art? — in Paula's sense. Was it something one would want to hang in his (her) home?

Questions began to pelt his mind. It was, after all, only a print. No matter how good, it was no more than decorative. It had little artistic value outside of its possible integration into a roomful of other things. This brought up the matter of wall space and harmonization of colors. It certainly wouldn't do in the bedroom, the kitchen, the breakfast room, or the foyer. This left — as he very well knew from the beginning — only the living room. And the furnishings of the living room were to Paula what viscera were to a surgeon; an organic arrangement of the beautifully functional and functionally beautiful; an evolution of artifacts tested against every caprice and comparison, and against which there was no appeal.

Simply and starkly, if he bought the print it would mean that Paula would either have to rearrange all the pictures, or replace one with this. George felt a tingle compounded out of crisis and challenge. In six years of marriage, he had never forced an issue of taste to a victorious conclusion. At the beginning, he was only too happy to let Paula have her way in the house. Traditionally this was the woman's province, and besides he secretly believed that Paula's sweet obsessiveness about their possessions was based on a desire to make things lovely for *him!*

Later, when he learned that Paula's obsessiveness was neither sweet nor particularly concerned with him, he would have willingly stepped aside and left her a clear field. But that, of course, wouldn't do either. To have one's way naturally implied having one's way *over* someone else. When Paula bought a lamp or discussed a book, she did not look for fatuous assent but intelligent concurrence. And if his intelligence didn't lead to concurrence, then it was held up by the scruff of the neck, like a supposedly housebroken pup guilty of a nasty relapse.

And when, still later, he chose to stand his ground, he found himself assuming all the awkward and galling postures of defense. It was Paula who was reasonable and patient, and he who committed the gaucheries of emotional imbalance. It was Paula who bore with sufferance his "I don't give a damns!" At such moments, she looked at him as if he had suddenly appeared in a lion's pelt with club — and that look assuaged his feelings more than a river of expiatory tears.

Gripping the picture, George turned it to yet another angle and gave it a last scrutiny. He knew that he was committed, and knowing this looked upon his action in a retrospective light, clearing all questions with his conscience and examining his motives for seeds of remorse.

Did he like the picture? Unreservedly! . . . Did he think it would fit in subjectwise? colorwise? Absolutely! . . . Did he *really* feel that Paula would like it? Well, if she didn't then six years of straining at affinities had produced nothing but a marital hernia.

George walked over to the man with the eyeshade.

"How much did you say this was?"

"Sixty-five dollars."

"Kind of high for a print, isn't it?"

The man performed a highly indifferent shrug. "There are less than a hundred of those in the whole United States," he said. "That was made in Paris. It took seven separate plates to get all the colors. If you don't think it's worth it, that's O.K., don't buy it."

George shook his head, smiling. "I don't know which is more irresistible, your salesmanship or the picture. I'll take it. Wrap it up, please."

George entered the apartment carrying the framed print wrapped in brown paper. Ordinarily he was at great pains to conceal his gift until the following morning — Paula's birthday morning. The idea of all that ceremonious pussyfooting didn't appeal to him this year.

"Good heavens, darling, what's that?" Paula asked.

"Your birthday present," he answered, kissing her.

"My . . . !"

"Couldn't very well sneak this one in, could I? I'll just put it in the closet, and we'll forget about it until tomorrow morning."

George went to the bathroom and washed up. He sat down at the dinette table and sipped the tomato juice. From where he sat, he could see Paula at the stove, her back toward him. A line of astonishment extended from the nape of her neck downward to the last vertebra.

"What's that I smell?" George asked.

"Food."

"Marvelous!"

Paula came into the dinette carrying a casserole. She set it down on a hot plate. Some sort of meat preparation simmered in brown gravy. There were rolls, peas, baked potatoes, and salad. Paula looked as if she were listening to a faint, scratching noise somewhere in the apartment. She sat down opposite George.

"Please help yourself," she said.

"Thank you. Smells divine."

"A recipe . . ." Paula uttered vaguely. "George, is that a picture?"

"Yes, darling, it is. Naturally I would rather have kept the sort of thing it was a surprise, but as you see that was impossible."

"A print?"

George laughed. "Well, hardly an original."

They ate.

"It's quite large," Paula said. She looked tense.

"Not very. I mean, as prints go."

"You must have selected it some time ago. It's framed, isn't it?"

"Yes, it is. That's the best part of it. I never saw the thing before tonight. Walked past a shop on Sixth Avenue, and there it was! I took one look at it and knew it was for you. But listen, if we start talking about it now, it will take the edge off it by tomorrow. Just forget it's there."

Paula seemed to be playing a game with the meat on her plate. She moved the pieces around from one spot to another without bringing any to her mouth.

"I wish I hadn't seen it," she said.

"So do I," said George.

"I'm wondering where we'll put it."

"On the wall, darling."

Paula lifted her head and looked at George beseechingly. She might have been imploring him to step back from the edge of a cliff where he seemed to want to want to cavort, like a college boy on a dare. George returned her look with blind cheerfulness.

"George, why are you doing this?"

"Doing what?"

"This!"

"Buying you a birthday present?"

"You know how particular I am about things for the house. What if I don't like it?"

"Ah, but you will! It's lovely!"

"But supposing I don't?"

"I'll be very disappointed."

"Can it be exchanged?"

"No."

Paula moved her food around on the plate again. George thought he saw her hand tremble.

"You want to provoke something, don't you?" she said, almost in a whisper.

"I beg your pardon?"

Paula put down her fork and clenched her hands in her lap. She leaned tautly toward George.

"You've done this deliberately to hurt me!"

George couldn't prevent a smile. His imagination had been so good that this scene had the familiar ring of having been enacted before.

"You're so sure you won't like it?"

"Yes!"

"Why?"

"Because you have no taste! You're a fine, intelligent, considerate man, but you have no real taste for things of this sort! It's no crime, my darling, but for God's sake, *recognize* it!"

As an illuminating aside, it occurred to George that they had at last achieved that mature level of communication Paula had always clamored for.

"Great to get it off your chest, isn't it?" he said. "I know just how you feel."

At eleven, Paula took a warm bath. The "walk" George announced he was going to take after dinner had developed into an ominously long absence. There had been neither flame nor ice. George had simply stated that he thought she was wrong. He thought his taste was quite good. Not as good as hers, of course, but certainly adequate for his own needs. The valedictory blandness he had put into that remark she interpreted as hurt pride.

Paula felt chilled, one of those bone-deep chills that even a warm bath couldn't reach. She put on the plaid robe George had given her long ago. She never cared for it. It made her look unfeminine . . . "Like a sorority-house matron," was her own description.

The picture! Paula suddenly reminded herself that the cause of it all was crouching there in the closet like a malignant beast. A nervous pride flared up in her again . . . Crush her! Cast her out! She could not be untrue to her deepest instincts! Surely if George were the man she thought him to be, he would understand this!

Paula got the picture from the closet and brought it into the living room. She tore off the paper as if it were hateful flesh. Then she held the picture away from her, arm's length, and looked at it under the direct glare of a lamp.

She held it so, looking, until her arms were tired. At last she set it down on the couch and began to walk slowly about the room, gazing at it from every conceivable angle. It was nice. It was very nice. The colors were miraculously suited to the room. Paula suddenly recalled that it was *George* who had found it, and, forgetting, she half-turned to express her delight. Her movement ended abruptly with the terrified realization that she was alone.

Chateaubriand

MR. ARNOLD SOMER, wearing a Burberry coat and a green hat, glanced through the Radio City arcade and decided to watch the skaters for a while. Except for his severely casual attire, there was nothing about him that might have excited attention. His height was average; his physique questionable beneath that massive concealment of coat; his face long and grave. It wouldn't have surprised one to learn that Mr. Somer was suffering from a duodenal ulcer. Actually he wasn't.

What did set off Mr. Somer from the intent humanity around him was his particular lack of intent. He strolled rather than walked. He was unburdened by package, parcel, portfolio or sample case. He kept his hands in his pockets. Time was obviously no great wind in Mr. Somer's sails. The handsome stores in the arcade attracted his eye, and he paused before each one to inspect the merchandise or service offered behind the impeccable plate glass. *Paris Illustré*, he read, and wondered whether he might like to go to Paris. It was doubtful. Marvelous place, he had heard, great food, but could anything really be better than that place on Third Avenue? Or the one on Ninth? Mr. Somer's own opinion was that excellence had a vanishing point beyond which it was a waste of money to venture. He was a hedonist with limitations.

At the skating rink, Mr. Somer watched a long-limbed girl with a notion of a skirt execute several stuttering steps forward before swooping into a long, graceful glide. Very much like a bird, he thought, beating its wings clumsily until it caught the air, then rewarding itself for the effort by soaring miles. He smiled. The simile pleased him.

Mr. Somer's mind, however, was only partially occupied with the skaters below. A glance at his watch informed him that it was almost four. That left him an hour and a half more. Like a person dividing a cake into segments, he apportioned the remaining time into a visit to George's bar, the picking up of his car at the mid-town garage, and the drive downtown. Practice had perfected these divisions to split-second timing. After all, he'd been doing it for almost a year now. Not once had he arrived late at that building on Hudson Street, and, more important, never had he cheated himself of his own precious time.

Still with the deliberate ease of a pensioner, Mr. Somer departed from the rink and continued to stroll toward Sixth Avenue. Some days ago he had decided to have a new suit, so he chose that street where he knew there were several of the better shops. He merely intended to look at fabrics, style. A friend of his had pretty much convinced him of the foolishness of buying ready-mades at nearly a hundred when for another fifty he could get a custom-tailored suit. "No two bodies are alike," his friend had said, "so how can these factory-produced jobs possibly fit you right." It made sense. The friend had recommended the tailor, and Mr. Somer had made up his mind.

He spent about fifteen minutes looking at models displayed in the windows and finally decided he would have a dark blue suit with a pin stripe. Of course that would necessitate the purchase of at least a half dozen appropriate ties, but since, on the same principle of diminishing returns, he never spent more than five dollars for a tie, the whole deal could be kept within reasonable limits. Mentally, Mr. Somer began choosing the ties.

George's bar on Sixth Avenue was a good example of its type. Entering it from a sunny street, you had to stand still for several seconds to accustom yourself to the mahogany gloom. Bottle-tops from the bar threw silver winks, and the odor was a spectrum with strong detergent on one end and orange blossom on the other.

Mr. Somer, not yet in full possession of his sight, made his way to the bar by familiarity and straddled a stool. George swam up out of the murk and gave the section of the bar before Mr. Somer an unnecessary wipe.

"Hello, George," said Mr. Somer.

"Hello, Arnold," said George.

The first name basis was at Mr. Somer's insistence. Not that he was unduly given to egalitarian practices, but George was so clearly a person of parts that it seemed quite in order.

George was a thin man of about fifty with a protruding Adam's apple, white hair, and sharp blue eyes. The thing Mr. Somer most admired about George was his voice. It was an unusual voice, abnormally deep, resonant. When he spoke, you got the feeling that each of his words had been mulled in a dark wine.

"What'll it be?" George asked. "Something new again?"

"*Is* there anything new?" Mr. Somer asked.

"I was thinking about it," said George. "Have I ever made you a pousse-café?"

"I don't think so," said Mr. Somer. "What is it?"

"Different liqueurs . . . in a glass like this . . ." George reached around and brought forth a pony glass.

"Uh-uh. No. I'm sure you never made that. I'll try it."

George gathered all the ingredients and set them on the bar. There was only one other customer in the place, a chap at the end of the bar, but he was in occult communion with his drink and needed no attention. One by one, George tipped in the grenadine, the crème de cacao, the cordial, the crème yvette, the brandy, until the glass was a lovely striation of colors.

"Drink it slowly," George instructed.

Mr. Somer lifted the glass to his lips and felt as if he were being made love to in several different languages.

"Delicious!" he pronounced. "You'll have to teach me how to make this one."

"I'll write it out for you," George said.

After the first sip, the two men relaxed in the manner of friends completely at ease in each other's company. Their conversation was obviously a continuation of some previous day's talk.

"That's life," said George.

"Well, I never claimed to be the world's greatest businessman," Mr. Somer said, immediately catching the import of George's platitude. "Money didn't mean anything to me. Not then."

"But was your wife in business with you from the start?" George asked.

"God, no!" answered Mr. Somer. "The whole thing happened within the last few years. Do you know anything about food brokerage?"

"Not a thing."

"Well, it's a tough business," said Mr. Somer. "You can

take my word for it. You're only working with a few accounts to begin with, and if you lose one . . . That's what happened to me, you see. I lost an account. Best one I had. It was a matter of cutting down on expenses, and since we didn't have any children, I asked Jean — my wife— if she would mind pitching in. You know, office work and things, until I got on my feet again."

George nodded. "That's how it began," he said.

"That's how it began," Mr. Somer echoed.

"Did you have any suspicion before that time?" asked George.

Mr. Somer wrinkled his brow and groped backward to the past. "Hm-m-m, not really," he decided. "Oh, of course, when you look back on things, you can pick out incidents, indications, but if you had asked me three years ago . . ." Mr. Somer shook his head. "No. I don't think she knew herself."

"Just had the instinct, eh?" said George.

Mr. Somer funneled an ironic smile down into the pony glass. "Instinct?" he queried. "Yes, I suppose so." He looked up at George with the confidence of a man who knows he will not be misunderstood. "I try not to be bitter," he said. "Frankly, it was ruthlessness. The tiger tasting blood."

"What did she do?" asked George.

Mr. Somer didn't answer immediately. He picked up the pony glass and held it before his eye, squinting through the amber brandy. "I couldn't single out any particular thing," he said, somewhat dreamily. "It was just the way she did it. Ruthless." He hesitated a moment, as though in search of some more apt word, but he merely repeated "ruthless" and finished his pousse-café.

"Another?" asked George.

Mr. Somer looked at his watch. "All right," he said.

As George prepared the drink, Mr. Somer was suddenly reminded of the fact that he didn't have a pair of black shoes. He'd always worn some variety of brown. He would certainly need a black pair to go with that dark blue suit. Happy thought, those shoes, for now he could visualize himself fully attired in his new ensemble. It gave him a sense of completion.

"Incidentally," he said, "I tried that cheese last night."

"The Edam? How'd you like it?"

"Good," said Mr. Somer. "Very good. You know, it's a funny thing, but I'm rediscovering my sense of taste. That cheese, for example. I had it with port, as you suggested, and it was . . ." Mr. Somer did something with his fingers which would have been universally understood. The quintessential squeezed between thumb and forefinger. "Never had cheese in the house when my wife was at home," he said. "Not *real* cheese."

"Americans don't know how to eat," said George, setting the fresh pousse-café before Mr. Somer. "They stuff themselves. Don't taste a thing."

Mr. Somer leaned closer to the bar, propped his elbows, interlaced his fingers over his drink as if he were forming a niche for an icon. The corners of his mouth struggled against an unseemly smile, but no amount of control could fully conceal the felicity that radiated out from his long sallow features. He looked like a man in love.

"There are so many good things in the world," he said. "I'm just finding that out."

Mr. Somer left George's bar at a quarter to five and went straight to the garage. He got his car and began to drive downtown. The last half-hour of George's sonorities still echoed in his head. The man's voice was so hypnotically attractive that he could just go on listening to him talk about nothing at all. But, of course, George was too intelligent a person to talk about nothing at all, and therefore he had been forced to feed him topics. Thus the business of his personal life, which Mr. Somer mildly regretted. No need to have told him about that, and, if he did, there was certainly no compulsion to tell the truth.

Well, not entirely the truth. That bit about his asking Jean to come downtown to give him a hand. That was a lie. He hadn't asked her at all. When she heard about his losing that biscuit account, she simply appeared at the office the next day with a hanger for her coat and a pair of plastic sleeves.

It was strange — strange beyond all understanding. True, their life had been a scratchy affair up until that point, but he had never detected an undercurrent of resentment in Jean. Nor did he take her appearance in the office as anything more than a desire to help. Looking back on it, he could only assume that she had spent those quiet evenings at home planning down to the minutest detail her course of action in the emergency she must have counted as inevitable. Either that, or she did indeed have a natural genius.

Mr. Somer, luxuriously sensible to the tan and beige fittings of his late model car, permitted himself a reflective smile as he thought of the way Jean finagled that biscuit account back into the fold. Getting her skinflint uncle to transfer that lump of cash to the business as window dressing was in itself a masterpiece of persuasion. Then recruiting that sales force! That, really, was nothing short of a miracle. Lining up those six experienced salesmen and giving them a pitch that surely should have become the definitive text of all sales managers. And on straight commission! Mr. Somer was filled with a genuine, if detached, admiration.

Where did it come from? Mr. Somer asked himself that

question for the thousandth time. No telling. The piece of earth that covers a rich vein of gold looks no different from the one that covers nothing but shale. When that big West Coast backer advertised in the trade paper for a New York broker, *he* would have as soon reached for that as present himself at the White House for a diplomatic post. Jean was on a plane early the next morning. Four days later she was back with a firm commitment and a contract to follow. That coup became the talk of the trade, and since then she'd had to beat off offers with a stick.

During these musings, Mr. Somer had dodged in and out of traffic, shot down Fourth Avenue, and was now at Fourteenth Street. It was when he passed that intersection that a change came over his features. An observer would have had to be with him from Fourteenth Street to his destination to witness the entire transformation. His eyes, particularly, would have borne watching, for their expression seemed to mirror an infinity of moods, all on a descending scale, until they arrived at a perfect nadir of inconsolable and unforgiving reproach. So did all his other features follow the cue of his eyes. His cheeks became even more gray and saggy, his nose looked pinched, and a subtle inner hand carved a line of spiritual pain around his mouth. The duodenal ulcer had become a serious kidney ailment.

He pulled up before that building on Hudson Street and looked at his watch. It was twenty-eight minutes after five. Precisely at five-thirty, a hatless woman wearing a sheared beaver coat came out of the building and walked to the car. She got in, passed her lips close to Mr. Somer's cheek in a kind of vague gesture, and then fell back against the seat and closed her eyes. Mr. Somer pulled away from the building, turned around, and began to drive uptown.

Mrs. Jean Somer had never been considered an attractive woman. At one time, it was fancied by her friends that she resembled a certain actress, but that actress was more noted for her talent than beauty. She and Mr. Somer had had an affair for almost a year before they married. In fact it was on the very evening that Mr. Somer planned to break it off that he proposed to her. One of those odd reversals of mind. There had been no question of his course until the very last instant, and then, losing nerve but still under the momentum of crisis, he changed direction and proposed to her instead. Once it was done, he felt neither regretful nor pious, but only philosophically bemused at the way things happened. Mrs. Somer, of course, knew nothing of that.

Now, reclining her head on the back rest, Mrs. Somer breathed deeply and deliberately, like one recovering from a shock. Her brown hair was neatly combed but dry and dead-looking. The face powder she had hastily applied before leaving the office flaked in the runnels alongside her nose. Her lips puckered grimly, like an infant refusing food. She looked exactly as a woman should who had worked too hard for nine hours.

Mr. Somer reached into his side pocket and extricated a cigarette from the pack he had there. He lit it and nudged his wife. Mrs. Somer opened her eyes (under each of which was a blue-tinted mouse of fatigue) and took the cigarette with a look of gratitude.

"Rough day," Mr. Somer stated. He *stated* rather than asked.

Mrs. Somer smiled with one corner of her mouth and took a long puff on the cigarette. "The *tel*ephone," she said, emitting the smoke with her words. "I just couldn't get off the telephone today. I never saw anything like it. It was . . . What did *you* do today?"

"Nothing," answered Mr. Somer.

"Did you take a walk?" asked Mrs. Somer.

"Yes, I had a nice walk."

Mrs. Somer sighed and pressed two fingers into the corners of her eyes.

"The salad dressing people were in today," she reported. "They're pleading with us to take the line. It's good. I had it laboratory tested. And the price is right. But I told them we wouldn't touch it unless they guaranteed five per cent brokerage on the basis of their last year's sales in this area. Which is fair, I think, since I know for a fact that they didn't do so hot here last year. I don't see why we should take all the risks . . ."

Mrs. Somer glanced at her husband again. He had listened to her recitation of the day's business with the same look he had so carefully brought into focus between Fourteenth and Hudson Streets. Saints in the last paroxysm of martyrdom might be expected to attain such suffering serenity.

"What do you think . . . ?" Mrs. Somer asked.

"What do *I* think?" Mr. Somer returned, scoring the "I" magnificently.

"Arnold . . ." she began, with tired supplication.

"No, no no!" he hastily assured her. "I'm not being sarcastic. I just think it's damned white of you to ask what *I* think. Frankly, I don't know. It's hard to judge these things when you get out of touch. It *sounds* like a good deal. That's about all I could say. I mean, a guaranteed five per cent for the year sounds terrific from what I remember of the business. I can't recall *my* ever having gotten it."

Mrs. Somer looked down at her hands, which lay limp, palms up, in her lap.

"There's no need for you to be out of touch," she said, quietly.

Mr. Somer smiled. Memory served him up scenes from that brief time when they worked together. Within days, literally days, the atmosphere had degenerated to that of a low palace intrigue. Everyone from the switchboard girl to the top salesman had, with the instinctive accuracy of people anxious about their jobs, sniffed out the true situation. Routine matters caused whispered conferences and pretty soon he was as fenced off from the real workings of the business as a soft-headed king might be from serious matters of state.

The crisis came — as crises do — over a little thing, over nothing at all. He had been out one afternoon seeing an account, and when he returned he noticed that the arrangement of desks in the office had been changed. He immediately saw that the new arrangement provided more light for both desks. Had the move been foolish or unnecessary, he probably would have said nothing about it, but it was the undeniable *rightness* of this insignificant matter which caused him to blaze up like a crumpled piece of paper. Quick, bright, furious — and then ashes. He put on his hat and coat and walked out.

He didn't go home that night, or the next. He came home on the third night and found Jean half-mad with guilt and terror. She wept, then, with more passion than he had ever seen her exhibit before. He ranted of pride, of being a man, and what she had done to both of them. Her self-abasement was complete. She was sorry, abysmally sorry. She had no intention of humiliating him, and she realized what an awful thing she had done. She simply wouldn't go near the office again. Not ever.

As luck would have it, he became sick immediately after.

Pleurisy. Jean was forced to continue at the office. During his illness and convalescence two things happened. The business prospered beyond all imaginable bounds, and he discovered the pleasures of an afternoon walk in Central Park. That was about two years ago, and since then both events had widened concentrically, like separate circles in a pond. They touched each other at a point, but for the most part found different shores. Mr. Somer never came back to the office . . . but neither did he descend from that mountain peak of injured pride.

When they arrived home, Mrs. Somer took three aspirin and a hot bath. Mr. Somer mixed cocktails in the living room. After her bath, Mrs. Somer joined her husband. Her face had a waxen look, and by the way she contracted her brows Mr. Somer could tell that the aspirin had had no effect whatever.

"It's here," she said, running her fingers along the back of her neck. "And here," indicating a spot on her right temple.

"Think this might help?" Mr. Somer asked, offering a cocktail.

Mrs. Somer shook her head and held up a deprecating hand. She sank into an easy chair, head back, eyes closed, precisely as in the car. Clearly she was in no condition for the dinner Mr. Somer had been anticipating. (Steak Chateaubriand, George had recommended at one point during their conversation that afternoon — and gave him the name of a restaurant that made it something of a specialty.)

Mr. Somer continued to regard his wife appraisingly. She was exhausted, no question of that, and the reason for it plucked at his conscience. She needed help. Not just another secretary or office boy, but someone substantial. An executive. But it was this sort of thing she would never undertake on her own. Such an action would set a seal of permanency on their situation.

"This is ridiculous," he said. "You need help. I'm coming down to the office tomorrow."

Slowly Mrs. Somer opened her eyes. Despite their being plowed with weariness, they showed instant alarm.

"Things piled up today," she said. "Being on the phone so long. Of course, if you *want* to, Arnold . . ."

Here it was again, thought Mr. Somer: the opening gambit of that tiresome game. He must threaten to resume his place, and she must pretend to welcome it. This charade had been the main prop of their relationship ever since he had ceased to come to the office. Neither believed the other, but there was nothing to take its place. Not love, nor passion, nor even a firmly entrenched enmity. Just this fuzzy play-acting which they must perform because they had found no way of admitting their mutual need.

And they did need each other. Jean needed him, because, ironically, the business, the money, everything was legally his. He surely needed her. Without her, as though at the wave of a wand, it would all disappear. Wordlessly and without gesture, they had been inching their way towards this recognition.

Mr. Somer swirled the olive at the bottom of his glass. There was a spirit of frankness in him, and he wondered how far it would go.

"Do you like it?" he asked. "I mean going downtown every day? Dealing with those cutthroats and thieves?"

Mrs. Somer looked at her husband cautiously. "I don't mind," she said.

"But do you *like* it?"

"Why do you ask?"

"I want to know."

"Yes," answered Mrs. Somer, catching his mood. "I like it very much. I love it. There is nothing else in life I would rather do. It was what I was made for. And I'm good at it, Arnold. You know that."

"I know," said Mr. Somer. "You're very good. You've got a business head. You'll make lots of money."

"We'll make lots of money," she corrected.

Mr. Somer set down his cocktail glass and went to the window. He clasped his hands behind his back and gazed out toward the city. Below was the park, dotted with yellow lamps. Off to the left, above the facade of Fifty-ninth Street, a steady respiration of light breathed against the evening fog. On, off . . . on, off. Mr. Somer was suddenly filled with an exquisite melancholy, a trembling joy. It was as if this city with its numberless restaurants, its theatres, its stores, its whole great weave of opulence had been constructed solely for him. He was on the threshold of his kingdom. It wanted only one step.

"But you need help," he said again, without turning around.

"Oh, I can get someone," he heard her say. "A young man who knows the business. Five, maybe six thousand a year."

Mr. Somer shrugged slightly. "If that's what you want," he said, and quickly continued. "Are we going to dinner?"

"Would you mind terribly if I didn't go with you tonight?" Mrs. Somer pleaded. "I really wouldn't enjoy myself, and I'm afraid I'd spoil it for you. Some scrambled eggs and bed is about all I want. Would you mind, dear?"

Mr. Somer found himself oddly thrilled at the sound of that "dear."

"Sure you won't mind if I go?" he asked in turn. "I hate to leave you alone."

"I won't mind at all," said Mrs. Somer. "Honest and truly. It would make me very unhappy if you didn't go."

"All right, then . . ." said Mr. Somer.

He got his hat and coat, tapped his pockets for wallet, handkerchief, keys.

"Well, good night," he said. "Make sure you get to bed early."

Mrs. Somer went with him to the door. There was a moment of embarrassment between them, a virginal tremor, but Mr. Somer stepped manfully into the breach and kissed his wife's pale, flaccid cheek.

"Take care of yourself," he said, with jocular severity.

Walking down the hallway to the elevator, Mr. Somer slipped on his gray suede gloves. A smile hovered on his lips, and as he rang for the elevator they formed a single word. "Chateaubriand," he murmured, merely because it made so rich and ample a sound, and because, for some reason, it described so perfectly the way he felt.

My Brother's Keeper

ALMOST the very instant Mr. Kent walked into the office, Miriam felt the irritation of his presence. Physically there was nothing disturbing about him. He was of medium height, slight in build, but the smile that hung on his lips had that angle of false ingratiation she particularly despised.

"Mr. Simon, please," he said.

"Do you have an appointment?" Miriam asked.

"No-o. I didn't know that was necessary."

"Mr. Simon usually sees by appointment," Miriam said, untruthfully. Mr. Simon saw, if at all, by whim. She took the card he extended between two fingers. It bore the name of Vincent Kent, and, in the lower left-hand corner, the name of the company. She didn't recognize it.

"Salesman?" she asked.

The smile became even more angular.

"If I could see Mr. Simon, I'd be better able to tell."

Miriam was used to every type of approach: coyness, bluster, charm. She preferred directness. The man who gave his card and announced the purpose of his call had, at least, the benefit of her neutrality.

"What sort of merchandise do you sell?" she asked.

"Well, no merchandise really. I represent a trade journal. This company's trade, I might add."

At that point, Mr. Kent raised his hand and rubbed the knuckle of his forefinger against the side of his nose. It was a violent gesture, done with such force that it left the contacted flesh red. It was obviously something he couldn't control. Miriam dropped her eyes.

"Just a moment," she said. "I'll find out if Mr. Simon can see you."

Mr. Simon, when he read the card, made a clucking noise of disapproval.

"Why do you bother me with such things? You know how busy I am. What is he selling?"

Miriam told him, and Mr. Simon closed his eyes in martyrdom. The world was a circle of time-consuming enemies, and it was precisely for such sorties that he depended upon Miriam.

"Since when . . ."

"All you have to do is say no." Miriam cut him off, a sharp edge in her own voice. She was, besides the receptionist, Mr. Simon's secretary and confidante — one of those work-horse factotums you find in most small businesses. Because of her value, Mr. Simon had come to recognize and respect the well-defined borders of her patience. Asked in a businesslike way (she did not even require the common amenities) there was no labor she would not perform, but Mr. Simon had to take his dramatics elsewhere. She simply wouldn't put up with them.

"O. K.," sighed Mr. Simon. "I'll see" — he picked up the card — "Mr. Kent in a few minutes. That's what I'm here for, I guess. To see salesmen. Tell him to wait."

Miriam walked back to the reception desk. She was more angry with herself than with Mr. Simon or the spastic stranger in the hall. She knew her job too well not to realize that she had been derelict. Dozens like Mr. Kent had been eased out of the place without Mr. Simon ever knowing of their call. If anything, it was that uncontrollable gesture that threw her off guard. It destroyed the man's poise in so sudden a flash that she could not help feeling sorry for him.

(Once she had turned away a salesman in a rather brusque way, and he had answered her rudeness with matching politeness. When he rang for the elevator, she noticed the shining mechanism that substituted for a hand. For days after, she inflicted a penance on herself. She left exposed her wound of remorse, denying it the relief of forgetfulness.)

Mr. Kent was standing where she had left him, hat in hand.

"Mr. Simon will see you in a few minutes," she said. "Please have a seat."

"Thank you."

He didn't move. Miriam glanced up at him. She judged his age to be in the mid-forties. He might have been good-looking once, but now his features were marked with that flabbiness which characterized a long illness or a too sudden loss of weight. Encased in their swollen pouches, his blue eyes retained an expression of pointless humor, such as people adopt when they have no self-assurance. Miriam had the uncomfortable feeling that he knew exactly what had gone on in Mr. Simon's office.

"Salesmen are a nuisance, aren't they?" he said, in a tone of deprecation. His hand flashed again, and the knuckle dug into the side of his nose. He tried to convert the spasm into something ordinary. He lowered his hand slightly and pretended to cough. "Still," he said, "we all have to make a living."

Miriam nodded curtly, not knowing how to react. She wished he would sit down and occupy himself with a magazine. She opened her book of shorthand notes as a cue, but it was lost on Mr. Kent.

"I haven't been selling terribly long," he went on. His lips pursed into a disagreeably coaxing smile. "I have the feeling that you guessed that, Miss . . ."

"Fisher," said Miriam. She began to type, deliberately leaving his question unanswered. A waist-high glass partition separated them and through it, in the upper part of her vision, she watched the blue material of his suit. She waited for it to move out of sight. When it did not, she looked up once again, prepared for cold finality.

He wasn't looking at her. His gaze inclined upward towards something his thoughts had projected, and his slack mouth and squinting eyes gave him the appearance of a man recalling a recent grief. From that angle, Miriam perceived for the first time the debased refinement of his features. Roughly she could sketch in the sort of college he had attended, the background that had lost its cohesion, the assumptions that had withered or fled beyond his grasp. He was no salesman — that was obvious. His presence here was probably one in a series of desperate little moves made in secrecy and killing embarrassment.

Aware of Miriam's appraising look, Mr. Kent blinked and assumed his artificial smile. His hand went once again to his face, but this time it fluttered nervously over mouth and chin and fell away to his side.

"What sort of man is Mr. Simon?" he asked.

"A businessman," Miriam answered, concentrating on the carriage of her machine.

"I see," said Mr. Kent, pleasantly. "I think I know what you mean. The no-nonsense type. Straight to the point. That's my difficulty. I digress. It's my one failing. Perhaps you can tell me how to stick to the point. You must see many salesmen."

Miriam shrugged slightly. The impending interview with Mr. Simon took on the proportions of disaster. She would have liked to take Mr. Kent by the arm and lead him to the elevator. "Take a tip from me," she would say. "Spare yourself the pain. You won't get an order anyway. Good-bye — and forget about being a salesman. Go back to your family in New Haven, or wherever you come from."

"I'm afraid I know very little about sales technique," she said.

Mr. Kent moved closer and rested an elbow on the glass partition. "I'll let you in on a secret," he said. "I'm not a salesman. Not really. When I took the job, I didn't think there'd be much to it. After all, selling is talking, and I do that fairly well. The trouble is that I talk about the wrong things. Or rather, I don't talk about the right things forcefully enough. No conviction, if you know what I mean."

"Then why sell?" Miriam asked.

"Well, I have to," he said. His voice lost its affability. A petulant note crept into it. "What else in the world is there for a man to do who hasn't a trade or profession? Nothing! Quite literally nothing! Believe me, I've tried. Of course, I have friends, but I wouldn't dream of imposing on them. Rather influential people, too. I think you'd recognize them, but I'd rather not mention names." Mr. Kent dropped his arm from the partition and dug that cruel knuckle into his flesh. "I have the reputation of being a drinker," he said. His easy manner returned, and he smiled in an aggravatingly superior way. "You can reform the habit but never the reputation. Which is a bit unfair, don't you agree, Miss . . . ?"

"Fisher," said Miriam. "Why don't you have a seat, Mr. Kent? Read a magazine."

Mr. Kent winked at her. "I'll do that," he said. But as he turned toward the chair, Mr. Simon came out of his office. He stood there, pot-bellied, sour, his sandy tufts stiff with truculence.

"Mr. Kent," he called, in a flat, uninviting voice.

Mr. Kent paled and fell into the posture of a brave man walking alone to the bullet-riddled wall. Some resource of nerve supported the smile that remained pinned to his lips as he passed Miriam on his way into Mr. Simon's office.

Miriam tried to work, but she could do nothing but wait for the unimaginable sound sure to be produced by so odd a contact. But nothing happened. Their voices seeped out to her with the alternate consistency of enamel and sandpaper, and at the end of ten minutes Mr. Kent emerged, zipping the top of his leather briefcase.

"Thank you, Mr. Simon," he said, shaking hands. "You've been *most* kind. Naturally I don't expect you to make up your mind immediately, but, if I may, I'd like to drop back in a few days."

Mr. Simon nodded with his head, his shoulders, his whole body. He seemed to be saying yes to everything, particularly to Mr. Kent's imminent departure. With one final nod, he ducked back into his office.

Mr. Kent paused at Miriam's desk. "Not bad," he said. "I may have a sale here." He rested his briefcase on the edge of the desk, and both hands on top of the briefcase. He leaned toward Miriam, bringing within range of her senses the spicy-sweet odor of shaving lotion. All his pale features sagged downward in an expression of weary anxiety. "What do you think?" he asked. "I mean, you know Mr. Simon. Is he the sort that says no outright if he means no?"

Miriam made a gesture with her hands and shrugged her

shoulders. The well-oiled mechanism of the routine lie was suddenly full of grit. "There's no telling," she said, with a frown.

Mr. Kent nodded, blinked, and again maltreated the side of his nose. An abstract look returned to his eyes.

"Be nice if it came through," he murmured. It was a fiberless wish, uttered without determination or real desire — rather as a child wishes for an impossible toy. He floated off to some mountain peak of vagueness and from that vast distance regarded Miriam.

"Yes," said Miriam, crisply. She felt an urge to snap her fingers before his face and shout, "Hey, wake up!"

Slowly, laboriously, Mr. Kent made his way back.

"Listen," he said, with a quick glance toward Mr. Simon's office, "I've *got* to get an order. I've *got to.* That silly ass of a sales manager will surely get me sacked if I don't come up with something pretty soon. He's already dropped a hint. See if you can't persuade your charming Mr. Simon to place an ad. The whole thing doesn't amount to a hill of beans, but it would mean a great deal to me." His voice dropped to an even lower register. It became almost a whisper. "Frankly," he said, "I'm at my last ditch. In the past year I've run through more jobs than you can shake a stick at. I just wouldn't have the strength to start again if I flubbed this one."

He backed away and concentrated a look of profound reliance on Miriam. They might have been childhood friends, long lovers come at last to the test of their affection. "You can believe this or not," he declared solemnly, "but I haven't had a drink since I took this job. If I get over this hurdle, I'll be all right. If I don't . . ." He made a tight-lipped grimace.

Stunned with this gratuitous load of confidence, Miriam stared at the man as he walked to the elevator and rang. The wildly unexpected can sometimes deprive one of speech, and Miriam sat there mouth agape, as if someone had dashed in and deposited an infant on her desk. The elevator came and with one foot inside Mr. Kent delivered a parting adjuration.

"I'm depending on you," he said, and disappeared.

With the sound of the closing elevator door, Mr. Simon thrust out of his office like a turtle out of its shell. He walked straight to Miriam's desk, his brow wrinkled with vindication and rebuke. He planted himself before Miriam and performed an alarmingly accurate parody of Mr. Kent's knuckle-to-nose reflex. Then, with upthrust arms and eyebrows, he silently called upon Heaven to witness his ordeal. Still wordless and shaking his head, he stumped back to his office.

Miriam flipped over the page of her notebook and stared at the squiggles blankly. A little blaze of fury started up within her, but it quickly subsided and she began to type.

Mr. Kent's first appearance was on a Tuesday. On Friday of that same week, Miriam came back from lunch to find him sitting in the outer office, thumbing through a magazine. His presence shocked her. She had not exactly dismissed him from her mind, but her intuitive thought was that she had seen the last of him. He was of that type that wanders in every so often, sets the office on its ear, accomplishes nothing, and is never heard from again. Persistence was the last thing she expected from Mr. Kent.

His smile was archly familiar. "I'm told Mr. Simon won't be back until late this afternoon," he said.

"That's right," said Miriam, walking to her desk. "You should have called first."

Mr. Kent got up and followed her to the partition. He performed his little act, and Miriam felt a strong desire to slap his hand.

"Did you get a chance to talk to him?" he asked.

"I?" Miriam stared at him with astonished eyes. "About what?"

"About what!" he echoed, looking instantly aggrieved. "About placing an ad in the trade journal I represent. Surely you remember . . . ?"

Miriam sat down at her desk and gathered the scattered clips into a little heap. She became suddenly conscious of the fact that her shoes hurt dreadfully. She had met her friend Sally for lunch, and they had walked miles looking for something suitable for tropical climates. Sally was to be married in a few weeks. She and her husband were going to Bermuda. The world was a catherine wheel throwing off lovely flames. One must forgive Sally everything these days — even a little thoughtlessness. Miriam had hoped to get back to the assuaging rattle of her typewriter and work off the poison of envy that had dripped into her system. Mr. Kent, with his weird antics and despairing eye, was her mood made flesh. If he vanished that instant, she would never question the benevolent miracle.

"You'd better make it next week sometime," she said.

"Next week!" He ran his hand over his thin, blond hair. "I take it then you didn't even speak to him."

Miriam noticed that a drawer was open. She slammed it shut.

"Where did you ever get the idea that I was supposed to speak to him?" she snapped. Her head was pounding idiotically. "Look here, Mr. Kent, I only work here. I'm not an officer of the company."

"Oh, for God's sake!" he almost whined. "I've been to this kind of office long enough to know the power you gals exert. All I asked you to do was to put in a good word for me. Is that so much? I mean, after all, what kind of world is this anyway where one person won't lift a finger to help another!"

"Well! . . . *Well!*"

Unreasoning rage poured into Miriam from a hundred hidden sluiceways. Everything was swept into the flood. Her shapeless body; her stringy hair; her mother's soft, galling solicitude; the nightly riot of argument and television; that hideous, *hideous* vase in the foyer she would one day smash; the loneliness that pinched at her heart with relentless fingers; the whole pointless mess of living.

"And who are you that I should help you?" Her voice skidded and careened like something headed for a wreck. "Who helps me, I'd like to know? Who do you think you are coming in here and demanding that people should help you? You've got some nerve, that all I've got to say! *Some damned . . . !*"

And madly, disgracefully, she was weeping. Two large drops fell on a typewritten page, glistened, and were absorbed. Miriam opened the bottom drawer of her desk and pulled out a tissue.

Mr. Kent withdrew deferentially. He examined the cuffs of his trousers; he rubbed his nose; he looked neither surprised nor contrite.

"I'll make it some other time," Miriam heard him say.

Fortunately her little reception room was separate from the rest of her office. The bookkeeper and the extra girl had not witnessed the scene. Miriam went to the washroom after Mr. Kent left and locked herself in for ten minutes. When she came out, she was wearing a little more powder and rouge than was her habit.

Mr. Simon returned to the office about four-thirty. As usual, his hat was on crooked and all his clothes looked dampened and crushed.

"Some letters," he threw at Miriam, in passing. "Five minutes."

She was used to it. Four-thirty to five, the easing-off period — it was anything but that for her. Mr. Simon's scattered senses came into focus at that hour. As he explained to her when she took the job twelve years ago, he didn't like a clock-watcher.

Straightening the things on her desk, Miriam realized with a drop of despair that she would speak about Mr. Kent. She couldn't say who she felt sorry for — herself, him. It was all one. They might inhabit different worlds, the histories of their grief might be written in foreign tongues, but for an instant each had given a cry of pain, and in that was a common shame. She chose the moment before Mr. Simon began his dictation.

"That salesman was in again," she said.

"What salesman?"

"The one who was in Tuesday. You know, the one who kept rubbing his nose."

Mr. Simon laced his fingers behind his head and cracked all his knuckles.

"That's nice," he said. "Did you throw him out?"

"You gave him permission to come back."

"*I* gave him permission! Are you crazy? What would I want that maniac around here for?"

Miriam shrugged. "I don't know. It's possible you were

thinking of placing an ad. They tell me it's worthwhile advertising in trade journals."

Mr. Simon looked at her suspiciously. "He isn't a cousin of yours or something, is he?" he asked.

"Does he look like my cousin?"

Mr. Simon gave a deep sigh. "Do you want to get home tonight?" he asked, matter-of-factly. "I've got at least a half a dozen letters to get out tonight. If you want to talk about that nut, I'll telephone for sandwiches and we'll spend a nice evening chatting."

Miriam stared down at the blank page of her book.

"I'm waiting," she said.

Mr. Kent's third and last appearance occurred exactly one week after his first. It was Tuesday, late in the afternoon. The door-latch of the elevator clicked before opening, and Miriam was seized with a sickly premonition. That Mr. Kent should walk out and remove his hat like a well-bred mendicant seemed a proper epilogue of the whole sorry little tale.

"How's Miss Fisher?" he greeted her. The blue, pin-stripe suit he wore was probably the only presentable one he had. He had worn it all three times.

"I spoke to Mr. Simon," she said quickly. "He doesn't feel that we can devote any money to advertising at this time. I'm sorry."

"Ah," said Mr. Kent. His mouth hung open. "Oh."

He returned his hat to his head, settled it neatly, and turned toward the elevators. Midway there he halted and looked toward Miriam. "You and I, Miss Fisher . . ." he began, shaking his head. But he didn't complete his thought. He left it for Miriam to finish in the thousand different ways that conscience might suggest.

The elevator took an eternity to come. Waiting for the sound of the door, it was as though a weight pressed down on her, keeping her head bowed over her machine. And when the elevator did come, and the door opened and shut, Miriam still sat so, with lowered head, as though to look up and see the emptiness in the hall was more than she could bear.

Sunday

HE dreamt that he was lying in a rowboat, and that the rowboat was fixed on the surface of a bay. The sun wrapped him in warmth. Extraordinary comfort! He couldn't have chosen a better situation. Directly below him (and the remarkable thing was that he could see *down* through the boards of the boat while staring up at the sky) four small fish came together, conferred for a moment, then darted off with the utmost urgency. Their decision, evidently, was that the boat should move, for that is what it did, nosing into the rushes, which parted with a dry sound.

It was at that point that the sun departed, leaving behind its warmth, and in the paradox of warmth and shadow he began to feel that terrible anxiety. He knew that when the boat pushed out on the other side, he would be on the open sea. Who could he tell? He must tell someone. The regret of all that he must leave was too much to bear. Yes, and here was the open sea — gray and choppy and endless — and now he must say good-bye. But to whom? Quickly, the boat is drifting out! Good-bye, oh, good-bye . . .

Ralph opened his eyes and stared across the room at the partially open drapes. As he stared, a vertical shaft of light sliced through the thin opening, covered his left eye with a golden patch, then quickly disappeared. Even in his frightened torpor, he marveled at how a passage of light could fabricate so complete and awful a dream. But where was it that he had been going? Where is it that one goes in such solitude?

Ralph lingered over the question for only an instant, and then he hurriedly began to pull in the strands of his life. There was the dresser, this was his house, today was Sunday, and (turning around and propping himself up on his elbow) here was Jean.

Jean . . . Ridiculously simple label for that brown-haired complexity hugging warmth and sleep. It was a pity he would forget the dream before telling it to her. He was almost certain he would. Perhaps if he could keep the key features in mind: rowboat, fishes, warmth . . . Come to think of it, it was suspiciously warm in the room. Ralph listened attentively, and, sure enough, he made out the steady hum of the heating unit in the cellar. She forgot to turn down the thermostat again! And after he had so carefully reminded her. Leaning over, Ralph investigated the mapless whorls of hair and approximated the position of his wife's ear.

"You forgot the heat," he whispered at the spot. There was an anguished stirring, a sound that struggled up through layers of fluffed wool. "You forgot the heat," he repeated punishingly.

Jean groaned and clutched her pillow. "Go away!" she implored.

Ralph got out of bed and put on his bathrobe and slippers. He went into the living room and looked at the thermostat. The indicator pointed cruelly at 70. This month the bill would be a pure disaster. Nothing less.

Yawning, he went to the large front window of the living

room and pulled open the drapes. There it was — Sunday in all its paralyzed glory. Mr. Venuto pushing the same baby carriage with the latest baby; the O'Donnell's sad little spaniel sniffing the ground, seemingly crushed by its own canine *Weltschmerz*. Ralph had one of those feelings of identical repetition. This scene, *exactly* this, had occurred before, countless times, possibly ushering in all the Sundays of his life. In a logical way, he knew this couldn't be true, since he and Jean had lived here for only two years (which took in all of their married life except those few months they had lived with Jean's mother); but, in another way, it was perfectly true. The scene fitted into every corner and crevice of a mood he could only describe as Sunday — and *that* particular mood had remained identical as far back as he could remember.

But why, he asked himself, going into the kitchen to put up the coffee, why did Sunday have to be so drained of vitality? Because the next day was Monday? Or could it be because the previous day was Saturday? Neither of these answers satisfied. The true answer lay in the path of his thoughts like a rock in a stream, and, with fluid caution, he swept by it, leaving little eddies of turbulence to mark the passage.

Since his marriage, particularly since Jean's pregnancy, a situation of some four months' standing, he had tried to keep his bouts of morbidity under control, and to a degree he had succeeded. Today, however, he could feel a fine stir of recrudescence. That dream hadn't helped any. Curious. It had none of the usual warped malignities. The sun had been so warm and bright, the slipping into melancholy so swift and abysmal. Even now Ralph could feel traces of the wrenching sob that wakefulness had stifled. What was it again? — boat, bay, fishes . . . There was something else — the ocean, yes — but something else. Incredible the way a dream evaporates.

By the time the coffee was ready and the pan sizzling with butter, Jean poked her dazed morning face into the kitchen.

"You reminded me *before* I had my bath," she said. "*You* were in bed already. You didn't say a word after I came out."

A little over two years had trained him in the way of such time lags.

"I naturally assumed you would turn it down," he said. "Are you trying to blame it on me?"

"You could have reminded me again," she said, grimacing at the eggs he had just cracked into the pan.

Ralph gave her a close look. "Do you feel sticky this morning?" he asked.

"No. I feel fine. I feel hungry. Did you squeeze the oranges?"

Ralph pointed to the brimming glasses.

During breakfast Ralph asked if there was anything they had especially planned for the day.

"Not that I know of," Jean replied.

"I would like to do something today," he said, making it sound as though it were a fresh inspiration rather than a calculated escape. "Maybe we'll go to the museum. How does that strike you?"

"Strikes me fine," she said.

Ralph caught the inflection. He smiled to himself. Like hell it does, he thought. It doesn't strike you fine at all. You're thinking I should do any one of the dozen things I promised to do around the house. Fix the garage door, start on the bookcases, straighten out the cellar. Of course I should. I know I should, but I can't . . . not today.

"There's something about Sunday activity," he said aloud.

"Sunday activity?"

"You know, doing useful things, reading the paper, it . . . it . . ." He shrugged, not knowing how to explain it. He was surprised that he should even have to try. "Do you know what I mean?" he asked.

"Not exactly," Jean answered.

Ralph remained silent, pressing his thumbs into the toast crumbs. He thought of that Sunday many years ago when he had been sick — not terribly sick; grippe, or something like that — and he had been confined to his room while his family practiced a solicitous inactivity in the living room. Even the radio was silent on the chance that he might want to sleep. Never had he felt such desolation. The silence expanded, until it seemed that the house must burst with it. In that oppressiveness all life became so enfeebled that total extinction seemed only a hairsbreadth away. No wonder, then, that Death should have introduced itself with a dark flourish that day. Alone in his room, he experienced for the first time in his life the overwhelming knowledge that his mother, his father, little Marilyn — all must die. Why hadn't anyone warned him of this horrible human condition? He had always regarded all talk of it as just another stricture to exact good behavior, but in that moment of revelation his bones shared in the certainty that it must come to pass. He would never forgive them — his parents, God — for their respective parts in this criminal futility. So he swore, and the treachery of it set its mark on the brow of all quiet Sundays.

"I wish," Jean was saying, swaying trance-like over the cup of coffee she held with both hands — "I wish I could avoid eating altogether. I get so *sleepy!*" She opened her eyes with great effort and looked at Ralph. "There's a Rembrandt exhibit at the Metropolitan," she said.

"Oh good . . . I know I should get started on the bookcases."

"Next week."

Ralph leaned toward her and kissed her below the ear. "Did you hear me make any noise this morning?" he asked.

"When?"

"Just before I woke up."

"I was asleep."

"I know, but I thought I might have made one of my weird noises. I had a dream . . ."

Jean set down her coffee cup. "Darling," she said, "I think I shall have to lie down for a little while."

"Nausea?"

"No . . . well, perhaps a bit. More fatigue. I feel absolutely drained. Don't forget about the dream, though. I want to hear about it. You'll tell me later."

Ralph went with her to the bedroom. "Fifteen minutes," Jean said, climbing into bed. "No more. If I fall asleep, I want you to wake me up. Promise?"

"I promise."

"Don't do the dishes until I get up."

"O.K."

Jean breathed a long sigh and settled into the pillow. Ralph stood there regarding her. She looked pale. Two brown smudges stained the area beneath her eyes. What a vicious thing life was. You could hardly touch a pleasure without drawing away a nettle of pain.

Ralph went into the kitchen and began doing the dishes. Glancing out the window, he could see Mr. Venuto engaged in conversation with Mr. Jensen. Mr. Venuto was making motions with his hand. He was probably explaining how he had discovered what was wrong with his car and how he had fixed it all by himself. Ralph envied Mr. Venuto. The man was steeped to the eyebrows in practical little affairs. That was the way to live — right up to the eyebrows in practical little affairs. No morbid philosophizing. Let the dead bury the dead.

Almost persuaded by his own monologue, Ralph's thoughts switched to the bookcases he'd been planning to build for the past few months. He would need a plane. You couldn't possibly square the edges without a plane. And he would countersink the holes, using wood-putty to level off. There was no question about the fact that once he got started on the bookcases he would do a nice job of it. In fact this whole Sunday business was nonsense, and he would absolutely get started today . . . The thought of staying at home had only to cross his mind, and his fear of Sunday pressed within him like a cold stone. No, he really had to get out of the house today. It was a matter of necessity, not choice.

Jean slept for about an hour and woke up feeling much improved.

"You let me sleep," she said, accusingly. "I guess I needed it. I'll get dressed right now. You still want to go to the city, don't you?"

"Only if you feel like it."

"I feel wonderful now," she said. "I really do."

"O.K., then," Ralph said. "Let's."

Jean dressed quickly, while Ralph warmed up the car in the garage. It was a cold, clear day; a nice day for walking along Fifth Avenue and stopping in somewhere for a hot chocolate.

The drive into the city was pleasant. Going over Queensboro Bridge, Ralph felt his mood sloughing off, and by the time they had found parking space for the car he was almost gay. They went to the museum and peered over shoulders at the canvases.

"Have you ever noticed how people must say something when they look at a painting?" Ralph whispered to Jean. He mimicked an imaginary dilettante. " 'Observe the chiaroscuro. Rembrandt invented it, my dear. I assure you. And the Noble Slav! Took a bum right in off the street, set a turban on his head, and painted him!' . . . Which only goes to prove that you can't tell a bum by his turban."

"Oh, you say things too," Jean said, reprovingly.

"What do I say?" Ralph demanded.

"Well, you said that if you stood in front of that painting of the old lady cutting her nails long enough, you got the feeling of respiration."

"Oh, that."

"If you heard someone else say it, it would sound foolish."

"Nonsense," Ralph said, trying to conceal his wounded vanity. "A perfectly innocent statement. I was talking about myself, not the painting."

"Isn't that what everyone else does?"

"You're being very detached and superior," Ralph said, vexedly, "but you know precisely what I mean."

Jean took his hand and looked up at him with soothing exclusiveness. "I know precisely what you mean," she said.

They went on through the rooms, condemned to silence by Ralph's satire on comment.

"I still didn't tell you my dream," he mentioned, casually.

"Your dream?"

"The one I had this morning — just before I woke up."

"Oh, yes. Tell me."

"Well, I dreamt that I was in a rowboat on a bay. It was a beautiful, sunny day . . ."

"An American Tragedy," Jean said.

"Not exactly. You weren't there."

"Naturally."

"Anyway, the boat began to move. It went through a growth of tall stalks, and then there was the ocean . . ."

"Yes?" said Jean.

"And that's about all," he said.

"Not very conclusive."

"No. Come to think of it, it was a pretty puny dream."

Jean looked at him, but Ralph just shrugged, pretending that the point of his story was its sheer pointlessness. He hooked his arm through hers, feeling the warmth of her body and the swelling that still gave him a faint feeling of queasiness.

He could have told her more. He could have gone on to describe the heart breaking sorrow he felt at being alone on a vast, gray ocean, knowing that he was leaving everything forever, but it flashed through his mind that to do so would surely revive the mood he had driven them out of the house to escape. Not that he had really escaped it. It was there, of course, its back turned momentarily, and Ralph was strained with the caution of avoiding the word, the unpredictable gesture, that would have it facing him again.

"I wonder how he must have felt," Jean said.

"Who?"

"Rembrandt. I mean doing his own portrait." They were standing before a self-portrait. "A little like Dorian Gray, I should imagine," she reflected, her head cocked to one side as she stared up at the canvas. "In reverse, of course. The picture stays young — middle-aged, at any rate — the artist gets old. It's sad. Darling, don't ever let me have my portrait painted. I couldn't stand it."

"How about photographs?" Ralph mentioned, pushing at her elbow.

"Photographs are different. They get yellow, unreal . . . Ralph, what *are* you trying to do?"

"Nothing. You're going to wear out that picture looking at it so long."

"But what's the hurry? We came here to look at pictures, didn't we?"

"Yes, we came here to look at pictures," he replied, "but it makes me nervous to stand in front of one so long." He forced her to continue on.

Well, he might have known it, he thought, trying hard to look thoroughly absorbed in the next canvas. Things of this sort have a fatal pull toward coincidence. Or was it coincidence? No, it damn well wasn't. It was contagion, pure and virulent, transmitted by God knows what shade of tone or maundering telepathy.

"I don't think you're enjoying this any longer," Jean said, looking depressed herself.

"It isn't a question of enjoyment," Ralph explained. "After a certain point, I lose all sense of discrimination. I might as well be looking at a subway poster."

"Then should we go?"

"I guess so."

They left the museum and walked east, stopping in at a drugstore for the hot chocolate they had promised themselves. The weather had turned leaden and raw, and the hours of the afternoon stood before them like so many soiled dishes in a sinkful of cold water. They decided to go to a movie.

After the movie, they hunted around for some new place to eat. Some *intime* place, Ralph suggested. He tried to recall the nice little Italian place someone in the office had once suggested, and after much mental racking it came back to him. They looked it up in the telephone directory, went there, and were caught in a swirl of hungry Sunday-nighters. Far from *intime,* but by that time Jean was too exhausted to move another step.

Since the museum, Jean had maintained a thoughtful reserve, refusing to enter fully into seriousness or levity. Several times Ralph was on the point of questioning her, but each time a nervous prudence prevented him.

"We'll dash home as soon as we're finished," he said. "You look bushed. Are you very tired?"

"Just normally."

Ralph reached over and took her hand. "Hey, face," he said, gently. "Do you love me?"

Jean nodded, avoiding his eyes. She reached for a roll, and with her hand poised over the bread basket suddenly froze in an attitude of wide-eyed wonderment.

"What is it?" Ralph asked, alarmed.

"The beast kicked me," she said.

"The *baby?"*

"He kicked me." She slumped in her chair and held her hand over her mouth. Ralph thought she was going to be sick, but in another instant he realized that she was laughing.

"What did it feel like?" he asked.

Jean shook her head, capping her mild hysteria with her hand. She finally composed herself and looked at Ralph. "A windshield wiper," she said, describing an arc in the air. "Zoop — like that."

"Isn't this an occasion," Ralph wanted to know. "We ought to celebrate. How about wine? I'll order a bottle of wine."

"Don't be ridiculous," Jean said. "I'm not supposed to drink wine."

"One glass can't possibly hurt." He ordered two glasses of sauterne.

They toasted the first kick. "To windshield wipers," Ralph said. "The symbolism is obvious," he expounded, setting down his glass. "Windshield wipers mean clarity of vision. He will be a prophet . . . Did it hurt?"

"Of course not. It felt funny."

They finished their dinner in an atmosphere of subdued hilarity. Neither could have said what was so funny, but conjecture on their child's semicircular thrust at life went on and on, skirting lunacy. When the waiter came with the bill, Ralph left him a large tip, saying that he had never gotten such a kick out of a meal. Jean rolled her eyes in horror. The waiter, chunky and sweating, earnestly suggested that they come again.

In the car, they both fell silent. Ralph switched on the radio, and they listened to music. Now that the kidding was done, they quietly contemplated the third presence. The insensible tumescence had assumed personality. As a sort of salute, Ralph pressed the button on the dashboard, and the wipers slid back and forth. "Junior," he said, with mock pride, and Jean smiled, leaning her head against his shoulder.

When they arrived home, the snow that had been threatening since the afternoon began to fall. Jean waited for Ralph on the walk as he jockeyed the car into the garage. She held out her gloved hand, palm up, and a few white flakes settled there. "Lovely," she whispered to no one in particular. Ralph came out of the garage and hustled her up the steps, searching for the key which he swore moved from one pocket to another at will.

In the house, they began to straighten up the usual Sunday disorder while still in their overcoats. It took about twenty minutes for the rooms to warm. Ralph showered first, getting the bathroom nice and steamy for Jean. By the time she had finished hers, he was half asleep. Jean sat down at the dresser and began removing her makeup. Their eyes met in the mirror. Ralph winked.

"Nice day?" Jean asked.

"Mm-hm."

"It ought to be registered that the first kick occurred on — what's today's date?"

"February the something," he said. "The thirteenth or fourteenth, I'm not sure which."

"Sunday, February the something." She rubbed the cold cream off with a tissue. She wasn't looking at Ralph's reflection now; she was looking into her own eyes, seeing something there that made her face turn wistful, then sad, then touched with fear. "And tomorrow's Monday," she said. "And so on, and so on . . ."

"What's that mean?" Ralph asked, looking at her.

"Nothing." Jean turned around and looked at him. All the premonitory signs of tears were there. "Oh, Ralph! . . . Ralph!" She ran to him and buried her face.

"What's the matter?" he asked, very quietly.

"I'm scared."

"Of what?"

She shook her head. "I don't know," she said, clinging to him. "Just scared."

"But of what?" he asked again, feeling as one who conducts a bitter catechism. "You can't be scared without knowing why. It is the baby? Birth?"

"No, no, no," she moaned, softly. "It's just, well, what's the use of happiness, love, children, if . . ."

"If what?"

"If you have to die," Jean said.

"Oh, that," he whispered, stroking her hair. "Oh, that." He took her by the shoulders, held her off, kissed her. "Come on," he said, "finish up and get into bed."

Jean dried her eyes, put on some more cold cream, fixed her hair, and crawled into bed. She shivered miserably. Ralph reached over and switched off the light. After a few moments, he got up and went into the living room, groping for the thermostat.

"I forgot it again," Jean whimpered.

"You did," he said.

Jean said she was sorry — sorry about the thermostat, sorry about being such a ninny. It was her condition. Pregnant women were known to get morbid. Ralph held her reassuringly.

She fell asleep long before he did. Ralph listened to her regular breathing. He hadn't dared to speak while she was still awake, fearing some catch in his voice would betray him, but now a torrent of comforting words came to him. The compassion he felt for her bore no resemblance to his own blotched self-pity. It was something else entirely, something which called for more than the old, helpless despair. What, exactly, it did call for occupied his mind so thoroughly that he could think of nothing else until he fell asleep. Not even death.

A Penny for Charity

MAX KELLER didn't feel well that morning. The muscles in his arms and across his back ached. His eyes were heavy. He tried to recall whether he had done anything the previous day that might account for this condition — lifting cartons, pushing furniture — but there had been nothing of the sort. A usual day, yesterday. In the evening, he had watched television.

After breakfast, Max stood in the kitchen and flexed his arms. Dora, his wife, looked at him.

"It hurts me, here," he said, crossing his beefy arms and trying to touch himself on the back. Then he flexed his arms again and heaved his shoulders. He looked as if he were making a ponderous effort to fly.

"You catching cold?" Dora asked.

"I'll let you know," Max answered.

"Dress warm," she said.

Max nodded. He looked at his watch. "The princess is still sleeping?" he said, referring to Selma, his daughter. "I hope for her sake she marries a man with a nervous stomach. Breakfast he'll never have."

"Don't worry," said Dora.

Max shrugged. "Who's worried?" He wasn't worried. He

was a little miffed. He liked to see his daughter in the morning. When she was younger, she delighted in taking breakfast with him. They knew, father and daughter, how to joke. Dora, God bless her, a wonderful woman, had a sense of humor like a fish. But that was an old story. From Dora you got good meals and worry by the yard. She liked to worry. What could you do?

"So — " said Max.

"Take some aspirin," Dora suggested. "Maybe you're catching cold."

Max sighed. He said, "Who knows? Maybe. I'm a lucky man."

He went to the hall closet and donned his winter outfit: cardigan sweater, jacket, muffler, overcoat, hat, and gloves. Then he kissed Dora on her soft, worried cheek and left for work.

Max was a grocer. In an era of supermarkets, it was a miracle that an individual owner could stay in business at all, but Max was several cuts above the average. When the "factories" (so Max dubbed the supermarkets) began to push him out of his long-established Brooklyn store, Max sized up the situation and took a risky plunge. He found a partner and located himself in the heart of Manhattan. From a housewife-type operation, he changed over to a fancy grocery, carrying imported cheeses, smoked meats, all kinds of frozen food, and hothouse fruits as costly as diamonds. For six months, he held his breath, and then he knew he had it made. After a lifetime of wrangling with penny-conscious women, he now had a trade that regarded prices as the grocer's business, not theirs. A lovely, clean enterprise.

Aside from the financial success, Max found himself in touch with an atmosphere which, far from being strange and unfriendly, proved to be a spiritual home. And *there* was a strangeness. Max, in appearance, was *the* platonic grocer, the archetype. Short, thick, tonsured like a friar, he looked as if he might have been born with an apron over his nakedness and a pencil on his ear. Who could have imagined that he was capable of romantic flights of the heart?

Max adored his surroundings. All about him were classy hotels and ultra-fashionable shops. Two blocks away was the park. His transient trade was inexhaustible. They came in often in pairs — two women, two men, a man and a woman. They chatted of the theatre, business, private affairs. Many of them were astonishingly beautiful women and grievously handsome men. Inadvertently Max would sometimes find out who they were and what they did, but for the most part their lives were hidden behind an iridescent veil. Max didn't want to know. He preferred his own speculations.

And then there were the young girls, the ones who flew into the store like spindrift blown from a wave. Excitement thrummed beneath their skin. Electric. These were the art students, the stage hopefuls, the lovers. They ordered cans of spaghetti and Italian bread. Cheap things, mostly, except the one or two items they bought to garnish their hopes and please their loves.

Max liked them. He liked almost all the people who came into the store. He was very content with his business.

He arrived at the store promptly at eight-thirty. Harry Williams, his partner, was already there. Harry was always there first. He was a bachelor who lived within ten minutes walking distance from the store. Max came all the way from Brooklyn.

"Good morning," said Max.

"Good morning," Harry returned. "What's the matter? You look lousy."

"Thank you," Max said, walking to the stock room at the

back of the store and taking off his outer clothes. He put on a freshly laundered linen coat and looked at himself in the ridiculously small mirror they had hanging on the wall. It was so small that Max had to inspect himself in segments. First his mouth and chin, then one cheek at a time, then his bald crown. It was difficult to tell, but Max thought he detected a flush on his face. "By God," he murmured, "I bet I got a fever." He walked into the store.

"How do you feel?" he asked Harry.

"I feel fine," said Harry. "*You* don't look so good."

"I heard you."

"You look like you might be running a little fever," Harry said.

Max remembered his partner's hypochondria. "Fever," he scoffed. "What d'ye call fever? A hundred and one? Two? That's not fever."

Harry backed off a pace and looked at Max as if a green patch had suddenly appeared on his skull.

"You take your temperature?" he asked.

"This morning," said Max.

"Is that what you had?"

"What's normal?" Max asked.

"Did you shake the thermometer down?"

Max wagged his head. "Harry . . . Harry," he lamented.

"It's no joke," Harry complained. "You could be walking around with something contagious."

Max felt a slight roll of nausea in his stomach. His jocularity dimmed.

"Don't be such an old woman," he growled.

Curious man, Harry. Hard to understand. Tall, good-looking, with graying hair at the temples, he looked like an actor or high-class con man. Anything but a grocer. It was a mystery to Max how such a man ever got into the grocery line. But when he advertised for a partner, there was Harry with the cash and a thorough knowledge of the business. All Max knew of Harry was that he had once been married, had no children he confessed to, and now lived in relentless solitude. In their five-year association, Max had invited Harry to his home twice for dinner. The man was as boring as he was handsome. Perhaps it was just because of the disparity in their dispositions that they got along so well. Harry took care of all the niggling details of business beautifully, and Max, of all people, charmed the customers.

The early morning hours were taken up with unpacking merchandise and stocking the shelves and refrigerating units. Max and Harry began to work in the automatic way of men who know what they're doing.

"I didn't feel so good when I got up this morning," Max confessed.

"You should have taken aspirin right away," Harry said.

Max, bending over a carton of canned peas he had just opened, grimaced at the geometric pattern of silver tops. What a hen, he thought . . . Cluck, cluck, cluck . . . *Take aspirin* . . . *Take your temperature* . . . Max straightened up. "*Aaah!*" he groaned, and then, "*Oooh!*" That wasn't so good. His head ballooned ceilingwards. The store tilted. Max gripped the edge of the counter and remained perfectly still. Things gradually righted themselves. No question about it. He was sick.

". . . grippe or twenty-four-hour virus," Harry was saying. "There's a lot of that going around."

"Do you have any aspirin in that medicine cabinet of yours?" Max asked him.

Harry kept a white metal box under the counter. It contained a specific for most of the minor ailments of life. He opened it, took out a bottle, and shook two pellets into Max's hand. Max swallowed the aspirin with some water.

"A shot of something wouldn't hurt," Harry recommended.

"Why, you got something?"

Harry submerged again and came up with a pint bottle of rock-and-rye. The seal was still unbroken. He poured Max a generous shot.

"Did you always have that bottle under there?" Max asked.

"Doesn't hurt to be prepared," Harry said.

Max marveled. The man was a fortress. Guns bristling from every hole. What the hell was he protecting? Inside the fortress was nothing. An empty yard.

"It's a pleasure not to feel well with you around," Max said. "All right. I'm one hundred per cent now. Let's get busy."

But Max was not one hundred per cent. He felt considerably more or considerably less than one hundred per cent. There was an increasing ache in all his muscles, an ache which probed deep, into his bones. He was light-headed. His eyes felt weak and watery. All of that added up to the grippe or flu. But concurrent with that was something else. Between the layers of his various discomforts flowed something thermal and alleviating. It eased the bite of pain. It imparted a dull radiance to everything and rounded all the sharp angles of contact.

Max tried to recall the last time he had been sick. It was difficult. His body was as blessed with health as it was deprived of grace. Yes. There was the time he got shingles, in the Brooklyn store. And then, years and years ago, in Vilna, when he lived with his parents, his brothers and sisters . . . They were all dead now. All. He was the youngest. And because he was the youngest, his mother always made a fuss. She nursed him in a room at the top of the house, a tiny room with two windows. Memory illuminated a corner of his mind, and Max could see the room in startlingly vivid detail. He remembered the bed, the apex formed over the window by the gable. Through that window, at a certain hour of the day, the sun would pour in like a golden flood. Max recalled the motes that floated in the sunlight. Goodness! How could he have forgotten! For so many years the memory of those serene, weightless specks conjured the sweetness of a bright, safe place. Time had pushed it out of his mind. Max sighed nostalgically.

At twelve-thirty, Max took off his linen coat and bundled up to depart. He had by this time consumed two more aspirin and two more shots of rock-and-rye. A ball of drowsiness and warmth rolled around inside of him. The surface was all chill and ache. Harry had muttered remedies like incantations all morning. Max would have liked to finish the day as a point of pride, but after the flurry of activity between ten and twelve, he felt his legs going rubbery.

"If you don't get a delivery by two, you better call up Joe Wasley and tell him to shake his tail," Max said. "We got practically no roast beef left."

"Don't worry," said Harry. "I'll take care of everything. And you take my advice . . . One lemon, sliced, in a pot with two cups of water; boil it until you got one cup left, then drink it as hot as you can."

"Yes, dearie," Max mumbled. "I'll see you in the morning."

"You're crazy!" Harry exclaimed. "You better not get out of bed for the next two, three days. I mean, what do you want, *pneumonia!* I'll get what's-his-name, the guy we had help us during Thanksgiving — Sidney. I'll call him . . ."

"Don't call anyone," Max said. "Wait till you hear from me. I'll call you up tonight and let you know if I'm coming in tomorrow."

Harry waved both hands at him. Max grunted and walked out of the store.

It was cold. The cold seized him with its fangs and shook him. His teeth chattered comically. He walked east toward the subway. He came out of the side street into the Plaza, and the winter sun glinting off metal and stone hurt his eyes.

At the corner, Max waited for the traffic light to change. He lifted his head, which he had kept retracted turtle-fashion in his coat collar. Buildings soared up all around him. This city! Everywhere he looked was a store crammed full of things he couldn't touch in a million years. Not that he wanted them. Max didn't envy the rich. Every day he passed Tiffany and glanced into the windows to see what impossible artifact of luxury was displayed. He felt almost a proprietary interest in the precious stones and delicate silver. But he didn't really want them. Just to know that they were there added a foolish luster to his life.

The light changed. Max was about to cross over to the other side of Fifth Avenue. He looked north, toward the park, and an idiotic longing came over him. He was sick, for God's sake! He could see Dora's face if she knew. He could see her clasp her hands together and implore Heaven to witness the lunatic behavior of her husband. Well, he would! Sick as he was! He would take a little stroll over there, just because he was sick, and just because it was a crazy thing to do. Maybe, when he was old, clutching at straws, he would remember this.

Max walked over to the park. He passed a man in a derby hat holding two hairless, shivering little dogs on a leash. A car backfired, causing a wild rustle of pigeons. The flock assembled over the skeleton trees, swept northward, swerved, fluttered down, and began to strut after food and love.

He would walk through the zoo and around to that side exit. That's all. Then he would go home. He felt terrible, all right. His face burned like flame in the icy air. His eyes kept closing against the hard brightness of the day. But he would persist. His heart beat with a heavy, erratic agitation, as if he were going to his first woman, as if the next few moments might reveal the purpose of Max Keller's passage on earth.

Dimly Max was conscious of laughter behind him. It had nothing to do with him. One shrill burst flew up, like the pigeons. Then he felt something at his elbow. Max turned and beheld a fantastic sight.

She was dressed in blue overalls such as janitors wear. Round her throat, like a knitted blue python, was wrapped an enormous scarf. On her head, a French sailor's hat with a white pom-pom. Her mouth and cheeks were rouged like a doll's. And she was beautiful! So beautiful that Max recoiled like a frightened hound.

"What?" he asked.

He did not pause to consider her costume. He did not see the other girls a little distance away, clustered like filings in a magnetic field of laughter.

"Will you give me a penny for charity?" the girl asked.

People, smiling, had stopped to watch. Max stood oafishly, caught between perplexity and enchantment. He stared wordlessly at the girl. Her hand, palm upward, stretched toward him.

"Can you spare a penny for charity?" she pleaded.

Then Max understood. It had something to do with schools. His own Selma had once tricked herself out in ridiculous clothes. She was at the time about the same age as this girl. But not so beautiful. This one looked ageless in these clothes and her painted face. Ageless as a clown. And she had put on these clothes and painted her face so grotesquely because she knew her beauty was beyond mock or diminution.

Max took off one glove and began to fumble in the coin pocket of his coat. It came over him all at once: a terrible rage. She had singled him out, the little bitch, because he was so perfect a foil for the joke! Yes she had! Short and waddling, he was hand-picked for the harlequinade. Scowling, Max turned and began to walk. The girl followed, plucked at his sleeve.

"Oh, can't you please spare a penny for charity!"

A whole life of being undersized and unhandsome and caring very much wheeled in fury and flung out an arm.

"Leave me alone!" he shouted . . . "I'm a sick man," he whined.

"A-a-a-h!" came from the onlookers. Mean wretch!

The girl looked at him with large, astonished eyes. Then she shrugged him out of existence and ran back to her friends.

Max walked as rapidly as he could through the zoo. The aspirin and the rock-and-rye had worn off. Now he was just sick. His bones felt bruised and nausea churned his guts. The subway was at the other end of the world, and he would have to get there on his hands and knees.

When Max got into the subway, he almost fell into a corner seat. He took off his hat and leaned his head against the cool steel plate beside him. His brain was a beehive. It droned and droned. Max closed his eyes, and in an instant he was asleep. Fitfully, he dreamed.

He dreamed he was in the store. People came in and helped themselves to stock from the shelves. They smiled at him wistfully, as if pitying his helplessness, and walked out with their arms loaded. His mother came out from the back room, swaying from side to side in her ancient grief. She poured whiskey in a glass until it sloshed over the counter. He could feel the trickle of it run down his neck, over the folds of his stomach. Harry, gorgeously dressed in woman's clothes, came through the front door. He wore a scarf. Smiling lewdly, he approached. He leaned over the counter, his scarlet mouth pursed for a kiss. "Liar!" Max tried to scream. "Prostitute!" Harry held out one hand, palm upward. In it were two aspirin.

Max awoke as the doors of the train were opening at his station. He was drenched in sweat. He scrambled to his feet, his hat rolling on the floor. Max retrieved his hat and staggered out of the train.

Dora had only to take one look. She became a machine of grim efficiency. She put her hand to his brow and nodded with exactitude, as if she knew to a fraction the degree of his fever. Max allowed himself to be led to the bedroom, murmuring, "All right, all right. Take it easy." Dora paid no heed. She helped him off with his clothes, put his flannel pajamas on the bed.

"Quick," she ordered. "Into bed. I'll put up tea."

Laboriously Max fumbled into his nightclothes, bemused and shivering. The bed felt cool and friendly. He could hear Dora rattling in the kitchen, making a telephone call, muttering deprecations. She bustled into the bedroom with a bottle of aspirin in one hand and a glass of water in the other.

"Take this!"

Max raised himself and swallowed two more pills. Sleep tugged at him. He fervently wished Dora would pull down the shades and leave him alone. He closed his eyes. No sooner had he done so than Dora was back with a scalding cup of tea, which she forced, spoonful by spoonful, between his lips.

He wanted to protest. "Go away, woman!" he would have commanded, if he could. The words boomed cavernously in his head, falling spent and unuttered. Things were becoming hopelessly confused. The delicate network of wires connecting the terminals of his life had fused in the heat of fever. The signals were weak and jumbled. Identities faded . . .

And then in one brilliant instant, Max perceived that it was all a mistake! He had picked up the wrong baggage somehow. He had only to present his check at the proper window, and this body he had worn like a borrowed overcoat, a gross jest, would be exchanged for his rightful form — and, ah, what that would be! Something tall, and princely, and shining . . .

Hands fussed with the pillow beneath his head. He didn't care. He was whirling down in delicious coils of darkness. Max surrendered to it gladly, like a child who knows he must pass through sleep to receive the gift he has been promised.